BLUEWATER ENIGMA

THE 13TH NOVEL IN THE CARIBBEAN MYSTERY AND ADVENTURE SERIES

CHARLES L.R. DOUGHERTY

Fort-de-France

Martinique

Ste. Anne

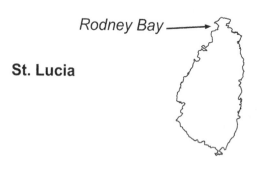

Rodney Bay ———➤

St. Lucia

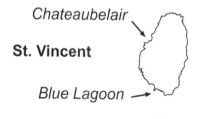

Chateaubelair

St. Vincent

Blue Lagoon ———➤

Bequia

Tobago Cays

1

"I don't see her," Dani Berger said, fumbling as she rushed to enter the gate code into the keypad. "She's gone."

"Get a grip," Liz Chirac said, nudging her out of the way and entering the code. "She's here somewhere."

Liz swung the gate open and held it, stepping back out of Dani's way. Irritated by their flight's delayed arrival into Miami, they were impatient to be back aboard *Vengeance*. Liz watched her friend charge down the dock. The duffle bag slung over Dani's shoulder was bumping against her hip, bouncing as she hustled to the slip where they had left *Vengeance*.

By the time Liz closed the gate and caught up with her, Dani was standing on the floating finger dock on the east side of the vacant slip. She stared at the empty expanse of water, thunderclouds forming on her brow. Liz dropped her own duffle bag on the main dock next to Dani's and stepped out onto the float. She put a hand on Dani's shoulder, feeling the tension in her wiry frame.

"They must have moved her for some reason," Liz said.

Dani whipped her head around, glaring at her. "Or some asshole stole her," she snapped.

"Slow down, Dani. Who would steal a 60-foot sailboat with all these million-dollar, 100-mile-an-hour testosterone rockets next door?"

Dani shrugged Liz's hand from her shoulder, scrambling back onto the main dock. She climbed the nearest piling like a monkey going up a coconut palm. Balancing atop it as she scanned the marina, she said, "Not here, not in any of the slips." She jumped down, landing like a cat. "She's gone."

"But nobody steals a boat like *Vengeance*," Liz said. "What would they do with her? She's too slow to run with and too big to hide. They can't even sell her. She's too easily recognized."

"It happens, Liz. She's gone." Dani looked at her watch. "The marina office closed an hour ago. Let's go find a security guard." She picked up her bag and slung it over her shoulder, fidgeting while Liz retrieved her own duffle bag.

"Let's walk up to the office," Liz said. "If we don't run into the guard, maybe there's an after-hours emergency number on the door."

Dani nodded. "Yeah, okay."

"There's some explanation, Dani. You know how rare this kind of theft is. Boats like *Vengeance* don't appeal to joyriders. It would take a skilled crew, and how could they avoid being spotted with her?"

"They could have had as much as two weeks to get her out of sight," Dani said. "Drug runners used to steal boats like *Vengeance* all the time; she'd haul a lot of illicit cargo without attracting attention. Dope, guns, cash, whatever. Make a run or two and then ditch her before the authorities catch on. That's the way they used to do it."

"But that was eons ago," Liz said. "Smugglers are more sophisticated now."

"They do what works. When the law gets wise to one scheme, they try something else. Maybe they've gone full circle -- back to the old ways. Miami was always a hub for that kind of thing," Dani said, as they walked up the dock.

They stopped, and Dani rattled the office door, rapping on the glass with her knuckles.

"There's nobody here," Liz said. She pointed at the card taped in the lower left corner of the window. "Let's call."

〜

U.S. Representative Horatio Velasquez opened the car door for his wife, helping her into her seat as the photographers' flashes blinded him. He ignored the reporters' shouted questions, smiling and nodding as he walked around to the driver's door and got in.

"I'm not that fragile, you know," his wife, Miranda, said. "I'm only six months. Or was that for the press?"

"Everything's for the press, at this point," he said. "I've got a lot of ground to cover to catch up with O'Toole before the primary."

"Before the primary? You're a shoo-in for re-election. What's O'Toole got to do with it?"

"Think about it," Velasquez said.

"I don't understand," Miranda said. "O'Toole's in the Senate."

"This isn't about my seat in the House, Miranda."

"But I thought he was going to run for President. Are you going after his Senate seat or something?"

"Or something," Velasquez said. "I've always been aiming higher than the Senate; you know that."

"You're thinking about running against him for the nomination?" Miranda's eyebrows rose. "For President?"

Velasquez grinned at her. "I've got a shot; I'm a Cuban-American and this is Florida. I'm popular with all the key factions."

"But there's more to it than Florida, Horatio, right?"

"Of course, there is. Don't act so dim-witted. If I can beat him on his home turf, what do you think's going to happen with the nomination?"

She frowned. "He's marrying that Montalba woman, right? So he's got an in with the Hispanic community, just like you."

"Not just like me. Marrying into it's not the same as being born into it. You should have learned that by now. You'll never be anything but my Anglo wife. Besides, she's from Argentina."

"So?"

"So, that's not the same as having Cuban or Mexican heritage. Not in the U.S. And she's filthy rich, besides. So's O'Toole."

"I see your point about Argentina, but what's being rich got to do with anything? Isn't that a plus?"

"It could be, under the right circumstances, but we've already tried having a billionaire for President. I don't think we're ready for another one, yet. All that money can be made to work against him."

"Why haven't you talked to me about this?"

"I'm talking to you about it now."

"But Diego's about to turn one, and this one will be a babe in arms on the campaign trail."

"I know," Velasquez said. "It's perfect. I'll be the up and coming father of young children, positioned against an old, rich, white-haired Anglo bastard." He glanced at her, taking in the set of her jaw and the creases on her forehead. "Right?" he asked.

"It's all about you, isn't it?" she said, biting off the words as she blinked back tears.

"Think of it, Miranda. You'll be the first lady; our children will grow up in the White House. How can you say it's all about me? I'm doing this for you and our children. Not to mention for our great country and all the generations to come. Somebody has to straighten this all out. Don't you see that?"

"And you, Horry? You're the one to straighten out 'our great country.' Is that it?"

"Better me than a scumbag like O'Toole. Think of what it will mean for Diego and his little sister."

"I *am*. That's what *bothers* me. But I don't get a vote, do I? Except in the polling place, and you can bet I won't cast it for you."

BEVERLY LENNOX STUDIED her dinner companion as he prepared to taste the wine the waiter poured for him. He was breathtaking. The dim lighting threw his dark eyes into shadow. She couldn't tell if they were dark brown or dark blue, but she'd like to find out. This was the first time she'd met him; their other contacts had been by phone.

She hadn't expected him to be so handsome. His voice on the phone had been smooth, and his manner, respectful, polite. She wasn't used to that. He wasn't at all the type who required her services. Most of the men Manny had sent her to had been repulsive.

Horatio Velasquez was the exception, and she'd been pleased when

Manny had ordered her to become Velasquez's full-time mistress. It was an easy job. Velasquez was self-centered and arrogant, but he wasn't abusive. Besides, he kept up the pretense of being a family man, so his demands on her time were limited. She'd never had such a sweet situation before.

She'd been distressed when Manny had told her to expect a call from this man, Berto -- no last name. She hid her reaction from Manny; she was skilled at that. It was part of her job. Still, she couldn't keep from asking if this meant she was no longer Velasquez's, exclusively.

Manny had laughed at her. "You do what Berto says," he'd ordered. "He is the boss. If he wants you, then you are his. You don't get to choose, you stupid *puta*. I need to teach you this again?"

Then he'd given her that special smile of his. Even now, the thought of that smile sent a chill down her spine.

When the waiter filled her glass, she realized that Berto must have tasted the wine and approved it. She'd been watching him, charmed by his style, as he'd sniffed at the little bit of wine the waiter had poured for him to taste.

When he'd closed his eyes and taken a sip, holding it in his mouth, her thoughts had wandered. Now, Berto was watching her, smiling as he held his glass out toward her.

She smiled back and lifted her glass, hoping she hadn't spaced out for too long. She was clean. She didn't do drugs, and she didn't want Berto to think she did.

"To your relationship with the Honorable Horatio Velasquez," he said. "May it be a long and pleasant one for you both." He smiled and looked her in the eye as he touched his glass to hers.

"Thank you," she said, raising the glass to her lips and tipping it slightly, but not taking any of the wine. She needed her wits about her.

"I wanted to meet you before I made my final decision," Berto said. "Manny is good at what he does, but some things are outside his experience. He's lacking in certain social graces." He paused.

When she didn't try to fil the silence, he smiled and nodded. "You're perfect. I envy Velasquez, in a way. Do you have any concerns about continuing with him?"

"No," she said. "He's easy enough to be with, and I think he's comfortable with me."

"I'm sure he is," Berto said, reaching inside his dinner jacket and withdrawing an envelope. He passed it to her and nodded his approval when she slipped it into her evening bag without looking at it.

"There are credit cards in your name. Don't concern yourself with limits on the cards; there aren't any. If you need cash, get an advance on one of them. Okay so far?"

She nodded.

He smiled and said, "There's also a passport for Velasquez, in a different name, of course. Follow the instructions in the memo that's in the envelope. You understand?"

"Yes," she said.

"Good. There's a number in there where you can reach me. If you have any questions or problems, call me directly. You will never hear from Manny again. He wishes you well, I'm sure. Are you all right with that?"

"With never hearing from Manny again?" she asked, in a neutral tone.

He smiled and nodded.

"Yes," she said.

"I thought you would be. And now, enough business. Let's enjoy our dinner."

2

———

"I thought you were going to jump through the phone and rip that marina manager's head off last night," Liz said, as the waitress poured fresh coffee for each of them. She and Dani were having breakfast in a pancake house around the corner from the hotel where they had spent the night.

"Just as well for him I got it out of my system while we were on the phone," Dani said. "I still can't believe the brass of those people."

"The marina management?"

"No," Dani said. "Whoever it was that marched in their office pretending to be a delivery crew." She shook her head and took a sip of coffee. "I guess I can't really blame the marina."

"He told you they had a letter with your signature on it?" Liz asked.

"That's what he said. He remembered it because of the timing. He said he wondered why we didn't just tell him about it when we brought the boat in, instead of sending the delivery crew in cold the day after we left."

"That timing is odd," Liz said. "Whoever it was must have known, don't you think?"

"You mean about us? Our travel plans?"

"Yes," Liz said.

"It almost sounds like they were watching us, doesn't it?" Dani asked.

"Yes, and showing up to take *Vengeance* while we were on the flight to New York, too."

"I'm missing something," Dani said. "What does our flight have to do with it?"

"If the manager had tried to call us to verify things, we couldn't have been reached."

"I didn't think of that. You have a criminal mind, Liz."

"You taught me well. He was going to call the police for us?"

"Yes. He offered. There's somebody they work with regularly, he said."

"Really?" Liz asked. "So this isn't such an unusual thing?"

"Yes, it is. He said they'd had a few go-fast boats stolen over the years, but never a big sailboat. But there's a fair amount of petty theft. People leave stuff out in the open on deck and then get upset when somebody takes it, from what he said. Anyway, they have a detective that they work with on a regular basis."

"What about our insurance?"

"He suggested we hold off until we talk to the police and get copies of everything from the files in the office."

"That makes sense. Do they have the letter that you supposedly signed?"

"He said he put it in our file himself."

"This seems a little too well put together," Liz said.

"Which part?"

"The fake delivery crew showing up the day after we put her in the slip, while we were en route," Liz said. "I keep going back to that. Some-body targeted us, specifically."

"Or *Vengeance*," Dani said.

"You mean like a theft to order?" Liz asked.

"It's not unheard of."

"I'm having trouble with that idea, Dani. How many *Bounty* replicas do you suppose there are?"

"I don't know. More than a few, I guess. The original was built in 1934. Connie and Paul didn't have a big problem finding *Diamantista II* when they decided they wanted one."

"But they're still not common," Liz said, "and each one was built to order, so no two are quite the same. It's not like a Beneteau 58 or something. If you put two of those side by side, nobody could tell one from the other."

"No, you're right about that. *Vengeance* is distinctive. You or I could pick her out of a crowd, even a crowd of her sister ships."

"That's my point," Liz said. "That's why I don't think it's a theft to order. Something else is going on here."

"Somebody could put her in a boatyard for a week and change enough stuff so we wouldn't recognize her, Liz. At least, not at a glance."

"But why do that?" Liz asked.

"Somebody wanted a Herreshoff *Bounty*," Dani said.

"Why not buy one, then? There are several of them listed; I checked on the web last night."

Dani sat back, frowning, as the waitress put their breakfast on the table. After the woman freshened their coffee and left, Dani asked, "What are you trying to say, Liz? That somebody wanted *Vengeance* because it was *our* boat?"

"That's the only thing that makes sense to me."

"Unless they stole her to make a drug run or two," Dani said, cutting a piece of fried egg and dredging it through the runny yolk.

"Then they would have just stolen her," Liz said. "Why go to the trouble of a forged letter from you authorizing a delivery crew to take her?"

Dani chewed the piece of egg, her brow wrinkled. She swallowed and said, "I guess that could have been a ploy to buy time, but I see your point. It does appear that they wanted *Vengeance*, but why?"

"I don't know," Liz said, "but I think there's more to this."

"Did you look closely at any of those listings online?" Dani asked.

"No," Liz said. "Why?"

"I was just thinking. We could settle with the insurance company and replace her, if any of them look attractive."

"I couldn't do that, Dani. She's not just another boat to me; she's home, my first love, all those trite, sentimental things. We're going to get her back. Just you watch."

❧

"YOU'RE ASTONISHING," Horatio Velasquez said, staring at Beverly Lennox's cleavage as she leaned over to put his breakfast on the table.

"I'm so glad you think so," she said, a shy smile on her glistening, dark red lips. "I have a surprise for you," she said, standing up straight, one knee flexed slightly, turning to the side to show off her figure.

Velasquez grinned, feasting his eyes, watching every ripple of movement as she untied the belt that held the diaphanous robe closed. She gave a theatrical shrug, letting the silk slide from her shoulders as she stepped in close, her pelvis inches from his face.

"What's this?" he said, reaching for the thick, creamy envelope, one corner of which was tucked behind the wispy triangle of her thong panties. He put the envelope beside his forgotten breakfast and hooked a finger in the thong, leaning toward her, his lips brushing her lower belly.

"Open it and find out," she purred, leaning over to kiss him on the cheek. "I'll wait."

He picked up the envelope, catching a whiff of the musky scent that drove him to distraction. Folding back the unsealed flap, he took out a passport and an airline ticket.

"Surprise!" she said, watching as he opened the ticket.

"St. Lucia," he said. "But I already have a passport." He frowned as he opened it.

"Not like that one," she said.

"Jeffrey Harold Starnes," he read. "He looks a lot like me."

"There is a remarkable resemblance," she said, leaning against him to look over his shoulder, her left breast grazing his cheek. " But it's been altered enough so that it won't be matched to you by a scanner. He answers to Harry, by the way, so if I mess up and call him Horry, nobody will notice."

He turned, kissing the side of her breast, and looked up in disappointment as she backed away a little. "It looks like the real thing, but it's too risky."

"You worry too much," she said, pouting. "It's real, issued by the State Department, just like yours."

"How?" he asked. "Your mysterious *friend*?"

She smiled. "Let a girl have some secrets."

"Is he CIA or what?"

"If I told you, he'd have to kill us both. Just roll with it, okay? I knew you shouldn't use your own -- talk about risky."

"Okay. Where are we staying? Somewhere private, I hope."

"We have a classic sailing yacht all to ourselves for the week," she said. "It'll be very private."

"But we don't know how to sail," he said.

"There's crew. A captain and a gourmet chef."

"Aw, damn," he said, frowning. "You'll have to wear clothes. Bummer."

"They're both attractive young women -- one's French, and the other's Belgian. I'm sure they won't care what *I* wear -- or don't wear. But you, on the other hand ... just don't get any ideas about messing with the help, hot stuff."

He grinned. "Like I said, you're astonishing. I thought you were kidding about arranging a getaway for us."

"Your schedule's still clear, right?" she asked.

"Absolutely, and I'm keeping it that way. No way I'm missing this."

"Good boy. Are you going to eat your breakfast before you go to the office?"

"It's cold," he said.

"I'm not." She slipped the thong from her hips and turned, striding toward the bedroom in nothing but her red spike heels.

GUILLERMO MONTALBA WAS SIPPING his second cup of coffee when the encrypted cellphone on his desk chimed.

"Yes?" he answered.

"Everything is set. The installation's done; it's all tested. Works great; you'll have Hollywood-quality video recordings. Did you give her the proximity key?"

"Yes, she has it. She knows to keep it with her credit cards. How close does it have to be to the sensor?"

"It's not that critical. If it's anywhere within a few yards, it'll wake the system."

"How do you avoid recording hours of garbage, then?" Montalba asked.

"The proximity device wakes the system. It doesn't start recording unless there's sound or motion in the immediate vicinity."

"Do I need to give her specific instructions about it? Like keep it in the room, or anything?"

"No, sir. It can even be left outdoors. It'll be fine, I assure you."

"What about retrieving the data?"

"There's ample storage for hundreds of hours. The preferred method is physical retrieval."

"I thought there was Wi-Fi." Montalba said.

"The system supports that for remote retrieval, but it's not well suited to this application. Unless we have a receiver in range for real-time streaming, the download speed's too slow. We'd have to shadow them within maybe 20 or 30 yards all the time to do that."

"How will you retrieve the data, then?"

"Swap out the disk drive. It only takes seconds."

"But that means you have to wait until nobody's around, doesn't it?"

"That's correct, but we can handle that. You said that retrieving it at the end of their stay would be satisfactory."

"Yes, that's right, but what if there's a failure?" Montalba asked. "How will you know?"

"The system is 100 percent redundant, and we can pass close enough periodically to stream a few seconds and make sure everything's working. We just can't sit next door and stream it all the time, okay?"

"Yes. What about the other stuff?"

"It's in place. Hidden, like where somebody would hide their stash. It's out of sight, but easy enough to find if you know what to look for."

"And you've got the fix in with the authorities? I don't want anybody going to jail."

"It's taken care of. They'll confiscate it and give them a lecture and a written warning, just as you ordered. Of course, they'll expect a bribe. Does the woman know where they need to be on that first day?"

"Yes," Montalba said. "She has written instructions. If there is a scheduling problem, she will let me know and I'll call you. About the bribe, though ... "

"Don't worry. They'll drop enough hints for even Velasquez to figure it out."

"Are they flexible on the amount?" Montalba asked.

"Yes. It's mostly for show. They're being well paid by our people."

"Excellent," Montalba said.

"Anything else?"

"About the equipment," Montalba said. "Can you leave it in place after this mission?"

"If you wish."

"And once it's awake, how long will it continue to function?"

"Indefinitely. It's powered from the ship's batteries, so as long as their electricity is on, it will record."

"What about the storage? What happens when it's full?"

"It loops back and overwrites the oldest recording, but remember, there's hundreds of hours' worth of storage, and it only records when there's sound or motion."

"If I have her leave the proximity key, can I eavesdrop on the crew after she's come back to the states?"

"Yes, sir. You'll have to let us know when to retrieve the storage, but that's it. Actually, it would be better not to rely on the proximity key, in that case. I'll just have them reprogram the system for continuous recording when they retrieve that data at the end of next week's exercise."

"Speaking of that, are your people set for her arrival?"

"Yes, sir. Still next week, is that correct?"

"That's correct."

"Please let us know if it changes. I'm going to give the team a little break until then, unless you object."

"No, that's fine," Montalba said. "Thank you. I'll be in touch."

3

"Well, that was frustrating," Dani said, stirring hot sauce into the bowl of black bean soup she'd ordered for lunch. She and Liz were sitting at a sidewalk table outside a hole-in-the-wall Cuban restaurant off Lincoln Road Mall in Miami Beach.

"I guess it went about the way I thought it would," Liz said. "The detective didn't offer much hope, did he?"

"No," Dani said, raising a spoonful of the soup to her lips, testing its temperature before she tasted it.

"But maybe they'll get fingerprints from that letter. Whoever it was did a good job of forging your signature."

"Yes, thanks to scanner apps for cellphones, no doubt. But I'm not holding my breath on the fingerprints."

"Why is that?" Liz asked.

"Anybody sharp enough to do that would have been sharp enough not to leave prints on the paper." Dani tasted her soup and added more of the pepper sauce.

"But the manager said the man took the letter out of an envelope and handed it to him. How could someone handle paper like that without leaving fingerprints?"

"Silicone's the way I'd have done it," Dani said.

"Silicone?" Liz asked, picking through her bowl of lobster salad. "How does that work? You mean like the grease?"

Dani shook her head. "The sealant. You spread a thin film over the pads of your fingers and let it cure. If you use the clear stuff, it's not noticeable. It fills the grooves, so the most you leave is a smudge, if there's even that."

"Where do you come up with that kind of thing? After all this time, you still surprise me."

Dani shrugged. "My misspent youth. How's the salad?"

"Good. Is your soup okay?"

"Okay, but not as good as what you make."

Liz smiled. "Thanks. It's the pork belly; that's my secret."

"Isn't fat just fat?" Dani asked.

"And silicone's just for flat-chested women, right?" Liz teased. "It's all in what you do with it."

"On a serious note, partner, what are we going to do now? We're missing the boat."

Liz looked at Dani's poker face until Dani lost it, choking on her mouthful of soup as she fought not to laugh.

"How long have you been waiting to spring that one on me?"

"It just came to me," Dani said, dabbing at her lips with her napkin. "Honest, it did."

"Uh-huh," Liz said, giggling and shaking her head. "Anyway, thanks. I needed that. I'm still in shock."

"I know. Come on back, Pollyanna. I miss you. It's just a boat," Dani said.

"I'm trying; I know you're right, and I feel silly for being so sentimental about her. But still ... "

"I feel the same way, Liz, but you just have to suck it up and move on. 'Illegitimi non carborundum,' as Phillip used to tell me when I was a sappy teenager trudging through the Central American jungle with him."

"What? That almost sounds like Latin."

"Almost," Dani said, spooning up more soup.

"But it's not, is it?"

"I don't know; fake Latin, I think. It means, 'Don't let the bastards grind you down.'"

Liz laughed. "I like that. That's a good thought to hold onto when we call the insurance people."

"It's going to be okay, Liz."

"You don't think they'll give us a hard time?"

"No. The agent's done business with Papa for longer than I can remember. They're not cheap when it comes to premiums, and they're not cheap when it comes to claims, either. You get what you pay for, and they know us. That counts for more than most people think."

"So what do you think they'll do? Are they going to mount some kind of search?"

"Yes. No doubt about that."

"How long?"

"You mean until they settle with us?"

Liz nodded, chewing a mouthful of salad.

"That's going to be up to us, most likely. They'll search for her, though. They'll want a recovery if they can manage it, but they'll pay us off quickly, if that's what we want. We've got a business to run; they understand that."

"I'd like to give it as much time as we can, Dani. Is that okay with you?"

"We'll take it a day at a time, how about? We don't have to set any deadlines just yet. It's not like we have a charter on the books right away."

"Good," Liz said. "Thanks. I'll work my way through this. *Non me dedam nisi pugnavero.*"

"What?" Dani asked. "You'll have to help me. Latin was a long time ago, for me."

"'I won't quit fighting,' roughly. I'm not letting the bastards grind me down. Not without a struggle, anyway."

"Atta girl!" Dani said. "Let's kick ass and take names."

~

MIRANDA VELASQUEZ MAINTAINED her composure until she got off the phone with her husband. Then she closed the bedroom door and shrieked like one of the banshees her Irish grandmother told her about when she was little. Hoarse after a few minutes, she opened the door and crept down the hall to the nursery, looking in on little Diego, hoping she hadn't awakened him.

Happy that he still slept, she went into the kitchen and poured herself a drink. Six months into her second pregnancy, she knew she shouldn't indulge in alcohol, but she was sure the craving she felt was in her genetic makeup. All the clichés about the Irish and strong drink had their roots in fact; she was certain of it. Her entire family sought solace in the nectar of the gods, as her father had called it. There wasn't a sober one among them.

She took the glass with three fingers of good Irish whiskey out onto the patio and sat in the shade. Holding the glass up to the soft light filtering through the moss-laden oaks, she contemplated the golden liquid. When Horry had first brought her here, before they bought the property, she'd thought the outsized house would be their castle. Now it was her prison, and he was the warden, the Cuban son of a bitch.

Her mother had warned her about the "spic devils," as she had called the Cubans. "Don't marry him, Miranda. They spend all their money on shotguns and mistresses, just like the 'Eyetalians,'" Mary Rose McGuire had said. Miranda had dismissed her mother's bigotry at the time.

Even now, confronted with Horry's philandering, she was put off by her mother's racism. But, as with the clichés about the Irish and alcohol, her mother's bias had some foundation. Her husband was a perfect example of the macho Hispanic stereotype.

She raised the glass to her lips, inhaling the eye-watering fumes from the 90-proof whiskey. She shuddered and kept her lips tightly closed as her nostrils burned. She set the whiskey on the table. She wouldn't do it. Not now, not today, not when there was a child in her womb. Even if the child's father was Horatio Velasquez.

She couldn't do anything about her disaster of a marriage, but she could still be a good mother. She picked up the glass again and poured the whiskey onto the ground.

If her father, "Big Mike" McGuire, were still alive, he'd thrash her slime-ball husband within an inch of his life. Of course, she wouldn't have told her father how Horry treated her, but she wouldn't have had to.

The irony was that her father was responsible for her husband's political career. If Horry hadn't tasted such power, maybe he wouldn't have strayed so often. Miranda laughed at herself despite the tears running down her cheeks. She shook her head. Still making excuses for him. Still in love with him, she admitted to herself, even after all this.

She knew he had a woman somewhere in the area. He barely even made an effort to hide it, and that was only because of his public image. He didn't see anything wrong with it, she was sure. He felt entitled to some comfort in exchange for his many sacrifices. He'd told her as much, and she, the "brood sow," as he referred to her, wasn't able to cater to his needs.

She'd show him. She wasn't sure how, but once this child was born and she was back on her feet, she'd deal with the bastard. One week retreat with the "movers and shakers of the party," his ass. She wasn't fooled for a minute. He was off on some junket with his latest floozy, probably funded by his constituents' contributions. She'd nail his sorry ass, but good. Brood sow, was she?

"You were right about the insurance claim," Liz said. "Now we just need to figure out what we want to do -- wait to see if they find her, or start looking for a replacement."

"I think I know how you feel about that," Dani said. "I understand; I feel the same way, in spite of my comments about her being just a boat."

"Should we set some kind of deadline for ourselves?" Liz asked.

"Probably," Dani said, "but we don't need to do it today. The claims adjuster said it would be a few days before they got through their process. I think we should give it a little time; we've had a rough day. How about a nice long walk before dinner?"

"That sounds good," Liz said. "I could use the exercise. Have you checked -- "

The ringing of Dani's cellphone interrupted her.

"It's Elaine," Dani said, looking at the phone's screen. She accepted the call and switched the phone to speaker mode. "Hi, Elaine. We're both here. We've got a problem."

"What's that, ladies?" the charter broker asked.

"While we were off gallivanting around New York, somebody took *Vengeance*," Liz said.

"Took? You mean like they stole her?"

"Yes. We spent the morning with the marina management and the Miami Beach police. We just got off the phone with the insurance company," Dani said. "Don't tell me you've got a charter for us."

"Okay."

"What do you mean, okay?" Liz asked.

"You said not to tell you I had a charter for you, so I won't."

"You do?" Liz asked.

"Yes," Elaine said. "In one week, with a pickup in Rodney Bay, St. Lucia."

"Can you shift it to Connie and Paul?" Dani asked. "There's no way we can deal with that now. Not that I can see."

"I could try, but the woman specifically asked for you two. Maybe I can get you a bareboat lined up to use. Your insurance company might pick up part of that. You could ask, anyway."

"Who is it?" Liz asked. "Somebody we've had before?"

"No, her name is ... let me look ... Beverly Lennox. And her companion is named Jeffrey Starnes. She's surprising him with the trip."

"How did she find us?" Liz asked. "Does she know one of our clients?"

"I don't know. She said she'd looked at your web page. I warned her that there might be a timing problem because you were on vacation. She was insistent, so I said I'd try to track you down and see if we could make it work. I knew you'd be back last night, but I was worried about whether you could make the pickup, with *Vengeance* in Miami."

"It would have been tight," Dani said, "but I guess it doesn't matter now. That's odd, though, that she'd be so insistent."

"Yes. I thought maybe you'd recognize the names, or something," Elaine said. "Should I check on chartering a bareboat for you?"

Dani and Liz locked eyes. Dani shrugged and raised her eyebrows.

"You might as well," Liz said. "It'll keep us from sitting here, fretting about what to do."

Dani nodded. "We've got a business to run. See what you can do, and keep us posted. Think you can sell her on a substitute boat?"

"Let me see what I can find, first. I'll get back to you before I discuss it with her," Elaine said. "I can't believe somebody would steal a boat like *Vengeance*. A plain vanilla boat, maybe, but not something as distinctive as *Vengeance*."

"That's where we come out, too," Liz said. "But we've gotten through the denial phase, now. I'm still struggling with acceptance, but as Dani says, we have to suck it up and move on."

"Right," Elaine said. "Let me see about a boat for you to use. I'll get back to you as soon as I can."

"Thanks, Elaine," Dani said, disconnecting. She pocketed her phone and stood up. "Ready for that walk?"

Liz nodded. "Let's check email first, though. I forgot all about it after last night."

"Okay," Dani said, as Liz opened their laptop and logged on to the hotel's wireless network. She moved to look over Liz's shoulder. "Looks like the normal junk," Dani said. "You know, I miss the ones offering to enlarge my penis. At least they were funny."

"Uh-huh," Liz said, scrolling through their inbox. "Wait a second. Look at this, from the marina in Rodney Bay." She clicked on the email and read the subject line aloud. "Invoice for last week's dockage, Sailing Yacht *Vengeance*."

Dani hunched forward and they read the email together.

"Yay!" Liz yelped, surging to her feet, almost knocking Dani down. She jumped up and down, clapping her hands. "She's there, Dani! She's there! We found her!"

Dani grinned. "Hallelujah! It says *Vengeance* has been in their marina for a week."

"But how?" Liz asked, trembling, her fists clenched.

"The delivery crew," Dani said. "Whoever the hell they were. They say the delivery crew left her there and told them we'd be in touch. Bizarre! They want to know if they should charge the card they have on file for us."

"Shall we call them?" Liz asked.

"Too late in the day," Dani said. "They'll be closed. I think we should book flights to St. Lucia. We can call the marina in the morning. We'll need to call the insurance people, too."

"Should we let Elaine know?" Liz asked.

"I think we should let her look for a boat, for now," Dani said. "We don't know what we're going to find when we get there. We may need that bareboat option. She won't commit us to anything without talking to us first, anyway. We can call her once we book some flights, though, just to let her know we're on the move."

"That makes sense," Liz said. "Let's book flights, and then we'll take that walk."

4

G uillermo Montalba stirred a spoonful of sugar into his first coffee of the morning. He raised the cup to his lips as he studied the online credit card statement. The charges that Beverly Lennox had incurred on the credit card he'd given her made him smile.

She might look and act classy, but she had the instincts of a street hustler. Besides the preliminary hold for $15,000 from the charter broker, Lennox had helped herself to a $10,000 cash advance. She'd been shopping, too. Jewelry, designer clothing, a day spa.

Good for her, he thought. He understood her behavior; he'd have done the same if their positions were reversed. She was feathering her nest and testing him at the same time. That was fine; he wouldn't rein her in. The amount of money she could spend on the cards wasn't significant to him.

Besides, the more she spent, the more damning the evidence against Velasquez would be. The cards were ultimately paid for by a political action committee Montalba had organized to support Velasquez's presidential campaign.

Velasquez was not Senator O'Toole's only competitor for the nomination, but he was the most obvious and most immediate one. Hence, Montalba's efforts to compromise him.

O'Toole's success as a presidential candidate wasn't essential to

Montalba's interests, but it might be a problem if O'Toole failed to win the nomination. O'Toole was powerful; that was what drew Montalba to him. A loss would diminish O'Toole's value.

During his years as a Florida politician, O'Toole had built one of the largest drug smuggling operations in the U.S. As Montalba had proceeded with his plans to consolidate and monopolize the drug trade in the States, he had acquired O'Toole's organization.

O'Toole mistakenly thought that Montalba was working for him. That was Montalba's plan. O'Toole, like many politicians, was egotistical and narcissistic. He had a strong need to be in control. Montalba had taken over O'Toole's illegal operations by letting O'Toole maintain the illusion that he was still in charge. O'Toole's perception was that Montalba had simply taken the place of the man who had been running the drug operation for him. Montalba, by funneling ever larger profits to O'Toole, had lulled him into ceding complete control.

By relieving O'Toole of the burden of dealing with troublesome details, Montalba had encouraged the senator to increase his isolation from the illegal activity. This suited O'Toole well. Since he had his eye on the presidency, he could ill afford to be caught with his hand in the drug trade. O'Toole saw himself as a silent partner in the drug business now.

Montalba's sister, Graciella, was Montalba's true partner. She and Montalba had contrived for O'Toole to seduce her, and she was now publicly engaged to marry the senator.

While Graciella was recognized everywhere as a wealthy socialite from Argentina, no one knew about her brother Guillermo. He was an invisible man, his existence known only to his sister. He never appeared in public, only occasionally allowing someone like O'Toole to glimpse one of his faces.

In the drug trade, he was only a rumor, a creature of the shadows, with a hideously scarred face. In his other encounters, which he kept to a minimum, he was a handsome, anonymous man, a wealthy recluse without an identity.

When they were in their teens, Graciella had killed their mother. They had survived to adulthood by trading on Graciella's looks and his vicious nature. After a few years, the two of them had accumulated enough money to vanish from Argentina.

By the time Graciella made her appearance on the South Florida social scene, she and her brother had amassed a fortune. That allowed Guillermo to remain invisible while continuing to add to their wealth.

O'Toole was just another asset in their portfolio; his value to them was in his political potential. It would be useful to the Montalba siblings to control the White House for a few years.

O'Toole's drug business wasn't the only one Montalba had taken over. He was well on his way to monopolizing imports into the southern U.S., from California east to Florida, Georgia, and the Carolinas.

There was one problem that he had not yet solved. A shadowy cartel that continued to elude him was rumored to be moving product through the Caribbean into the southeastern U.S. A woman named Connie Barrera appeared to be running it.

In contrast to Montalba's methods, Barrera had an unusual approach to consolidating distribution channels. Montalba bought out his competition, often resorting to violent tactics to encourage his competitors to quit the field. Barrera, on the other hand, arranged for her competitors to be discovered by law enforcement. She'd been instrumental in shutting down several of the largest operations in the Caribbean basin.

As best Montalba could tell, she was the last of his competitors. His efforts to penetrate her security had failed, but he had new information. A few weeks ago, Barrera and a number of her associates had gathered in Miami for a meeting.

Barrera and her husband, a retired Miami cop, ran a luxury charter yacht in the islands. Montalba was certain that this was a cover that allowed her to move freely around the Caribbean. The authorities were accustomed to the erratic movements of charter yachts and did not suspect her.

During their gathering in Miami, Montalba had learned that there were two more women associated with her. They ran a similar yacht, also in the Caribbean, and they had close ties to law enforcement throughout the islands. Further, they had connections with some mercenaries in the French islands. They drew upon both sets of contacts to keep Barrera's operation running smoothly.

When the meeting ended, the two women had stored their yacht in Miami while they took a two-week holiday. Montalba had taken the opportunity to have the yacht fitted with concealed surveillance equipment. He'd further arranged for Beverly Lennox to book a week-long getaway on the yacht for herself and Velasquez.

Montalba was pleased at the notion that he would be able to test the equipment by recording compromising videos of Velasquez with Beverly Lennox. He could foresee using the yacht for similar activities should another candidate emerge as a threat to O'Toole. As a bonus, he would be able to spy on the two women who were the movers and shakers in Barrera's business.

"THEN YOU DID NOT HIRE the three men?" the marina manager in Rodney Bay asked, eyes wide.

"No," Dani said. "They showed the marina in Miami a forged letter authorizing them to take *Vengeance*. The people at the marina had never seen them before. The police had them go through mugshots of the thieves known to steal from around the waterfront, but they didn't recognize anyone."

"Can you describe any of the delivery crew?" Liz asked the man.

"I'm afraid not. I asked the staff after you called this morning, but no one saw them. They brought the yacht in late one evening and tied her up to the fuel dock. Someone called the next morning and talked with the receptionist. All they told her was that you would be arriving in a few days and would settle any charges with us. We post our accounts weekly; that's why accounting sent you the email yesterday. We moved her into a slip that morning after they called. They left the keys in a cockpit locker for us."

"We are quite relieved to find her," Liz said. "Thank you for taking care of her for us."

"Yes," Dani said. "Thank you."

"You are most welcome. You've been good customers for a long time.

We're happy to accommodate you. After your call this morning, I went down and opened her up to air her out. She looks to be in fine shape."

"Yes, thanks for that," Dani said. "We took a quick look at her before we came to see you."

He nodded. "One of the staff told me. Will you be staying with us for a while?"

"We haven't made plans yet," Dani said. "We want to do a thorough inspection first. If she's all right, we may take her over to Ste. Anne this evening. We have friends there."

"Ah, yes. Mr. Davis and his wife, right?"

"Yes," Liz said.

"Another old customer," the manager said. "Give him my regards."

"We will," Dani said. "If we find anything amiss, we'll want to stay here this evening."

He nodded. "Of course. That will not be a problem. Just let us know, either way. If we can help, that's why we're here."

"Thank you," Dani said, reaching across the desk to shake his hand. "Let's go get to work, Liz."

Liz shook hands with the manager and they walked out onto the dock. "Should we call Phillip?" she asked.

"Yes. Would you do that while I do a quick survey? I want to make sure they didn't leave any nasty surprises or sabotage her somehow. That shouldn't take me long. I doubt I'll find anything we can't deal with quickly. If she's seaworthy, we can be in Ste. Anne by four or five o'clock."

"All right," Liz said. "Are you ready for him to call Sandrine?"

Phillip Davis's wife, Sandrine, was a senior officer in French customs. Dani and Liz had come up with the idea of asking her to give *Vengeance* a thorough inspection for any concealed contraband.

"I think so. Don't you?"

"Yes, I do."

"Ask them to call us if Sandrine wants us to put *Vengeance* in the marina for her boarding party."

"Okay. I'll tell him that otherwise, we'll just anchor," Liz said.

They'd already had a preliminary conversation with Phillip while they were in the taxi from the airport to the marina. He had suggested that Sandrine could order a drug dog and an explosives dog, as well as a thorough customs inspection. Dani and Liz were worried that the thieves might have left behind some kind of illegal cargo, either by accident or to cause trouble.

"I'm so happy!" Liz said, as they stepped off the dock onto *Vengeance*. "It's so good to be home."

"It is," Dani agreed.

$\sim$

"THANKS FOR YOUR HELP, SANDRINE," Dani said, taking a sip of wine. They were sitting on Phillip and Sandrine's veranda, looking out over the anchorage off Ste. Anne, Martinique.

"You are welcome. I am glad we can help."

"You saved us some big problems," Liz said. "It's a good thing you and Phillip thought of the dogs."

"Yes, I think so," Sandrine said. "The drugs were not many, but still they would have caused you trouble if customs was finding them somewhere else, yes?"

"A quarter kilo of marijuana and a few ounces of cocaine sounds like 'many' to me," Dani said. "That's not some casual user's stash. It was odd the way it was hidden, too."

"Maybe it is the person who uses the guest cabin on the trip down here. Taping the bags under the drawers was perhaps to hide from the other crew," Sandrine said. "It is a lot of drugs for a person, but it is not much for the smuggling, I think. As you said when my men find, is very strange, this whole thing."

"Stealing the boat, planting drugs aboard, leaving the boat and telling the marina to expect you in a few days," Phillip said, shaking his head. "Nothing about it makes sense. You checked the machinery and electrical spaces thoroughly, you said?"

"Yes," Dani said. "There's nothing aboard that doesn't belong there, now that Sandrine's people have been through her. Just the stash of drugs."

"The dog found no sign of drugs anywhere else?" Phillip asked.

"Nothing," Sandrine said. "We were extra thorough, because of the small stash. We were thinking perhaps they had used her to carry some large shipment, but there was no trace. We check even in the holding tank. Was clean."

"They couldn't have stopped anywhere. Not for very long, anyway, not to get here last week. They had a fast trip, as it was," Liz said.

"And if they stopped anywhere, they did not clear with customs," Sandrine said. "I have checked. Only in St. Lucia, they clear. They send me the crew list at my office tomorrow, but surely these people, they are using false passports. Still, maybe we learn something."

"When's your charter?" Phillip asked.

"We've got a few days," Liz said "It's not until next week. Elaine's supposed to get their arrival info and email it to us in the next day or two."

"And where's the pickup?" Phillip asked.

"Rodney Bay," Dani said.

"*Quelle coincidence!*" Sandrine said.

"Yes, isn't it," Dani agreed.

"Then you can stay here for a day or two?" Phillip asked.

"We planned to," Dani said. "Why do you ask? If you have plans -- "

"No, no. Nothing like that," Phillip said. "We're going to be here. I was asking because I think we should get Clarence to have *Vengeance* swept. Maybe he can do it tomorrow morning."

"Swept for what?" Liz asked.

"Somebody went to a lot of trouble to steal her, sail her down here, and get her back to you in time for this charter," Phillip said. "And you said Elaine told you the woman was insistent that it had to be *Vengeance*, right? She wouldn't agree to chartering a substitute."

"When you put it like that, it does sound even more strange," Dani said. "What are you thinking?"

"I'm not drawing any conclusions," Phillip said, "but remember when Connie and Paul had the new fuel tank put in *Diamantista II* up in Maine, and then those people chartered her to go to New York?"

"To nuke Manhattan?" Liz said. "You think we've got a nuke hidden aboard?"

"I said I wasn't drawing conclusions, but this is the same sort of situation. It's nonsensical to us, but it made sense to somebody. They went to all that trouble, and we don't know why. I have to wonder if your charter may be part of the scheme."

"But there are no explosives," Sandrine said. "The dog would have found them."

"Maybe not, if they were in the fuel tank, or glassed in the hull. Why don't you plan to stay here with us for a couple of days, and let Clarence give her a thorough going over?"

"You sure he's got the people on short notice?" Dani asked.

"Yes. He just finished up an operation. Somebody contracted with him and your Papa to look for nukes somewhere in South America. I think Marie ran the operation, and I know she's back. Sandrine and I ran into her at the marina when we were having breakfast this morning."

"It's probably a good idea," Dani said. "I don't imagine there's a nuke in our fuel tank, but who knows what they were up to?"

"Good. Sandrine can drive you back to the marina to pick up your stuff while I call Clarence and ask him to see if someone tampered with *Vengeance*."

5

"Clarence called earlier this morning," Phillip said. "He caught me while I was on my way back from taking Sandrine to work."

He was sitting on the veranda with Dani and Liz, enjoying a pot of strong coffee. Dani and Liz had both slept later than usual, exhausted from the stress of the last couple of days.

"Did he find anything?" Dani asked.

"Not yet." Phillip chuckled. "He just wanted to let me know that he was sending Marie and a couple of technicians to check out *Vengeance*." He looked down at his wristwatch. "They're probably just getting started."

"You said they'd been down in South America," Liz said. "Where?"

"No idea," Phillip said. "Your father and Clarence had a contract, Dani. I'm guessing with NATO, but I don't know. Somebody in Europe had picked up a rumor about a stockpile of nuclear weapons somewhere down there. Supposedly, they came from one of the old eastern-bloc countries, but nobody knew how or why. That's all I know; I wasn't involved, other than a little technical consultation. Scary world we're living in."

"Sometimes I envy Marie," Dani said. "She gets to have all the fun."

"She probably feels the same about you. She's had a hard life; still does, for that matter."

"I don't know much about her background," Dani said. "Just little snippets I've picked up from her."

"That's all anybody knows. I was still active when Clarence recruited her."

"He must have checked her background, somehow," Liz said.

Phillip laughed. "He tried, but he didn't get far. They worked out a compromise. She offered to prove herself by tackling what Clarence thought was a suicide mission. She accomplished it and showed up in his kitchen one morning after she'd been reported missing and given up for dead. He quit asking questions and hired her on the spot."

"Fascinating woman," Dani said.

"Yes. On a different subject, what do you know about these people who are chartering with you next week?"

"Not much," Dani said. "Beverly Lennox and her boyfriend. She's surprising him with the charter, from what Elaine told us. His name is Jeffrey Starnes. You're thinking we should check them out, huh?"

"If there's a way you can find out more about them, I would," Phillip said. "They have to be tangled up in the theft, somehow. The coincidences are too strong to overlook."

"We can call Luke and ask him for a favor," Liz said. Luke Pantene was a friend of theirs in the Miami Police Department.

"Where would he start, though?" Phillip asked.

"Elaine always gets a scan of the first page of their passports," Dani said. "It's a quick way to make sure they're serious. She won't book without that and a deposit. She's probably got a credit card, or maybe a wire transfer from a bank. It's worth a try. Excuse me while I go call her and Luke; I'll get that started."

"Clarence told me about the drug stash that Sandrine's people found," Marie LaCroix said, stirring sugar into her espresso. She was sitting with Dani and Liz in the restaurant overlooking the marina. "So we didn't waste any time looking for drugs. Because of the theft, we did check for fingerprints, though. Whoever those people were, they were profession-

als. They left not one single smudge of a print. Not that we could find."
She shook her head.

"Are we clean, then?" Liz asked the diminutive blonde woman. She
knew Marie must be in her late thirties, at least, but she had the look of
a clean-cut teenager.

Marie took a sip of espresso before she answered. "There are no
explosives and no tracking devices aboard *Vengeance*," she said, putting
the cup down in its saucer with exaggerated care. "No weapons of any
kind, for that matter." She gazed off into the distance, avoiding eye
contact.

"What's the matter, Marie?" Dani asked.

Marie shifted in her seat and looked first at Dani, then at Liz. She
shook her head and glanced down at her espresso. Picking it up, she
looked back out at the boats.

"Marie?" Dani asked. "What are you not saying?"

"It is not my affair," she said, still avoiding eye contact with either
Dani or Liz.

"What are you talking about?" Liz asked.

"I am surprised. That is all. What you choose to do on your yacht,
that is your business, between you and your guests."

Dani frowned. "You found something that you didn't expect, I
take it."

Marie looked at her and nodded. "I never thought you would do
such a thing. I do not wish to embarrass you. I'm sure you have reasons."

"Marie, I don't know what you're talking about, damn it," Dani said.
"Never mind our fragile feelings. What did you find that you're not
telling us about?"

"Your honey trap."

"Our ... " Liz frowned and shook her head. "What?"

"A honey trap?" Dani asked. "You mean ... "

"For recording the private moments of your guests, I suppose," Marie
said. "I make no judgments, and I will tell no one. But I thought I knew
you both. I, of all people." She shook her head, a wry smile on her face.
She drank the last of her espresso. "I should know better."

"You found bugs of some kind?" Dani asked.

"It is a first-class installation," Marie said. "You must have hired the best. No one will ever spot it. We only found it by using metal detectors on the bulkheads."

"Whoever stole *Vengeance* installed bugs?" Liz said, frowning. Then, "But you think we put them there?"

"You are telling me you don't know about them?" Marie asked.

"That's correct," Dani said. "Why would you ever think we bugged our own boat?"

"I am relieved, Dani, Liz. I apologize for my mistake, but let me explain."

"Please do," Dani said. "What did you find?"

"The guest stateroom," Marie said. "It is wired for sound and video. This is an installation of the highest quality, completely hidden. Placing the equipment would have required someone to dismantle all that beautiful hand-fitted teak cabinetry and trim. It was not done in haste. I think it would take some days, maybe. The wood has been hollowed out to accommodate the lenses and the fiber optic cabling. It was beautifully done. Never have I seen such work."

"The guest stateroom," Liz said. "They didn't do it to record us, then?"

"Only the guest stateroom has cameras. The rest of the boat is wired for audio recording only. You see, because of the way it was done, I didn't think it was the thieves. I assumed that you had done this to blackmail ... never mind. I'm sorry I thought this of you, my friends. Probably it is because I am exhausted; I do not think clearly."

"How does it work, Marie?" Dani asked. "It's not recording all the time, or broadcasting, is it?"

"No. The technician said that someone would use a remote activator to wake up the system. Then it senses sound or motion. It stores the data on a large capacity solid-state drive which is concealed behind the wood staving that is behind the main electrical panel. There is also an arrangement for Wi-Fi, but he said that would not be of much use unless someone was close by to monitor in real time. It would be too slow to download the contents of the storage device over Wi-Fi. That is another reason I thought that you had installed this."

"I see," Dani said, exchanging glances with Liz. "Whoever did this is interested in our guests, then, and not in us."

"It seems so," Marie said. "They went to a great deal of trouble. You have some important people coming, maybe?"

"We don't know yet, but we're checking. Our next charter guests have raised our suspicions. If you have a minute, we'll tell you about it."

"Yes, please. Now I am curious."

Dani and Liz outlined what they knew. When they were finished, Marie said, "This is most strange, yes."

They were silent for a few beats, and then Marie asked, "Do you wish for me to remove this equipment? Or disable it, maybe?"

"I don't think so," Dani said.

"Why not?" Liz asked.

"Marie, if you remove it or disable it, would whoever installed it be able to tell? I mean, remotely?"

"That is possible, yes. The technician, he thinks this is the main purpose of the Wi-Fi, for remote testing. Someone needs to be only nearby to do this, you see."

"Would the technician be able to install a master cutoff switch?" Liz asked. "So that we could disable it ourselves if we needed to?"

"Yes. He said this. Also, he can install a small indicator light so that you can tell if the system is active. This, he can do very quickly. You wish for me to have him do so?"

"Yes, please," Dani said.

Liz nodded. "Thanks so much, Marie. Can we buy you a late lunch?"

"I am glad to help. I will have the technician do the work this afternoon, if that is all right. And thank you for the offer of lunch, but I hope you will understand that what I most wish to do now is sleep, maybe for some days." Marie smiled, her eyelids drooping. "But you must promise to tell me what happens, and maybe you take me sailing when this is over, yes? Clarence owes me some time off."

"You can count on it, Marie. Just let us know when. We'd love to take you on a sailing holiday, any time," Liz said.

"Any time at all," Dani agreed.

~

"You decided to leave it all in place?" Phillip asked, as he poured wine for everyone. Dani and Liz were joining him and Sandrine for dinner at their villa. "I would have thought your instinct would have been to have them rip it out."

"Me, too," Sandrine said.

"It's not active right now, and Marie's guy put a hidden switch in for us, so we can turn it off if we want to," Liz said. "We both had the same reaction when she told us."

"You mean to rip it out?" Phillip asked.

"No, to leave it," Dani said.

"Why?" Sandrine asked. "I do not understand this."

"Okay," Dani said. "First, it's a connection to whoever stole *Vengeance*. I'm pissed off; I want to catch them and teach them a lesson."

Phillip chuckled and Sandrine shook her head.

"Besides," Liz said, "they'd be able to tell if we removed it. As much trouble as they went to installing it, who knows what they might do if they knew we'd found it? And their target has to be the couple that's chartering next week."

"Anything new on that front?" Phillip asked.

"Yes, but not much. Luke called back while we were moving *Vengeance* late this afternoon." Dani gazed out at the anchorage, admiring *Vengeance*. She was silhouetted against the developing sunset, bobbing to her anchor in the small waves that rolled around Pointe Dunkerque.

"He got all the information that Elaine had on them and ran a records search. Beverly Lennox's address is a long-term-stay, business-suite place; it rents by the week or month," Liz said.

"He got that by matching her passport up with drivers' license records," Dani said, "but even though she has a license, she doesn't own a car, and never had any auto insurance. The credit card she used for the charter guarantee is in her name, but it's brand new and has no credit limit."

"That's an odd collection of information," Phillip said. "A false identity, maybe?"

"That's Luke's suspicion, yes," Liz said. "He's doing some more digging, but it will take him a while."

"And the guy," Dani said, "Jeffrey Harold Starnes, is even more sketchy. There's nothing on him at all besides the passport. He's sure to be somebody else. He's 42 years old, with no history? Give me a break. Whoever set that up is a rank amateur. At least with the woman, they made some effort to give her depth."

"What about the passports?" Sandrine asked. "Are they real?"

"Yes," Liz said. "Issued by the U.S. State Department. They're the real thing, but Luke said there are several ways that can be made to happen."

"Still," Phillip said, "rank amateurs wouldn't have genuine passports. My bet is they never intended to use them for anything but covering their tracks on this trip. They didn't plan to do anything that would cause anybody to check up on them."

"I don't quite see your point," Dani said.

"Well, the woman's information is better put together than the man's. She looks more suspect to me. The guy's having a passport in a false name is suspicious, but it sounds like maybe he just doesn't want anybody to know he's spending a week in the islands with the woman."

"Hmm," Dani said. "Marie used the phrase 'honey trap' when she told us about the recording system. She thought Liz and I were in the blackmail game. That was sort of funny, until we figured out what was bothering her. She could be right about the honey trap, though."

"This honey trap, it is meaning blackmail?" Sandrine asked.

"Yes," Dani said. "This could be a setup to trap the man, whoever he really is."

"That's far-fetched," Liz said.

"It is," Dani said, nodding, "but this whole mess is surreal. It only makes sense if this guy is somebody important. If that's what's happening, they've gone to a huge amount of trouble to set him up."

"And even if that's so," Liz said, "why us? Why *Vengeance*? It doesn't make sense."

"It doesn't make sense to us, given what we know," Dani said. "But it might make sense to somebody with a broader collection of facts. You're right, though, Liz. There has to be a tie-in to us somehow."

"Speaking about *Vengeance*," Sandrine said, "I received the crew lists from customs and immigration in St. Lucia. The passports the three men used were forged. Not like the ones you described, that were officially issued to a person with a false identity. These were stolen U.S.

passports that had been modified, we think. These can be purchased in many places. They will not stand up to close scrutiny, but to check in with customs in a tourist port like they did, the risk is small."

"Yet another wrinkle in the story," Phillip said. "So those passports were probably used once and tossed. There's no telling who the crewmen were. They could still be in St. Lucia."

"Or anywhere else," Sandrine said. "Come, Liz. Shall we go prepare the food?"

"When do you think we should go back to Rodney Bay?" Liz asked, pouring coffee for herself and Dani. They had just finished breakfast of fresh fruit and *croissants* in the cockpit.

Dani shrugged. "We don't have to be there until mid-day the day after tomorrow, right?"

"That's right," Liz said. "Unless you're in a hurry, I'd like to stay here at least for today. I need to do some heavy provisioning; the larder's bare, still, after our three-week layup."

"Speaking of that, I wonder what the bastards ate? They must have been living aboard for a week, at least, on the passage down here. Did you check the groceries?"

"Yes," Liz said. "I wondered the same thing, and after what Marie said about fingerprints, I went through everything in the galley looking for stuff that I didn't leave aboard. I thought maybe they left some food of some kind, but there was nothing."

"Oh," Dani said. "Well, it was worth a shot. Back to your question, I'm fine staying here for another day. You can go shopping, and I want to freshen up the varnish around the cockpit."

"I didn't -- " Liz was interrupted by Dani's cellphone.

"It's Luke," Dani said.

"Good morning, Luke," Dani said. "Liz is here with me."

"Morning, you two. I've about run the course on your charterers; I don't have anything to add to what I told you yesterday. I checked with the surrounding counties to see if anybody might recognize them, but that was a long shot at best. They'd have been in the system if they'd had any encounters with the law. I'm not sure what else I can do."

"What about that credit card?" Dani asked.

"I made an informal request, but I didn't expect it to go anywhere. They told me to get a warrant, which is exactly what they should have done. Never hurts to ask, though."

"Can you?" Liz asked.

"Can I get a warrant?"

"Right," Liz said.

"No. I don't have enough to convince a judge."

"Even with the drugs we found?"

"Even with the drugs. There's not enough of a connection to Lennox and Starnes. I agree, the whole thing looks suspicious, but that's not how it works. Their identities are probably false, but again, there's not enough substance there. If they had used the false identities to conceal a crime, or even if we had probable cause to think that's what they were up to ... well, you see my point. We don't even have a good way to figure out who they are."

"What about facial recognition software?" Dani said. "You've got the passport photos, and her driver's license."

"Not good enough, Dani. I wish the technology matched the expectations people have from movies, but it doesn't. Without more data to narrow the search, we'd get thousands of hits. Now, if we had fingerprints ... "

"Fingerprints?" Dani said. "They'll be here in a couple of days, but how could we get their fingerprints?"

"Where's here, again? You may have told me, but it slipped my mind."

"St. Lucia."

"St. Lucia!" Luke said. "I was just involved in a case that had a tie-in there. In fact, it was your pals, Connie and Paul, that got me into it. Paul helped catch a killer using fingerprints from a glass he picked up in a restaurant."

"Right," Dani said. "Sandrine and Phillip told us about that last night. We had dinner with them."

"In St. Lucia?"

"No. We're in Martinique right now. We'll pick up the guests in St. Lucia, but it's only a couple of hours' sailing to get to Rodney Bay from here."

"There's a guy," Luke said, "a friend of Phillip's. He's the Deputy Commissioner of Police in St. Lucia."

"Cedric Jones?" Dani and Liz asked, in chorus.

"You know him?"

"Yes," Dani said. "He's an old friend of my father's."

"And I've been out to dinner with his nephew a few times." Liz said. "He's a detective there."

"Great," Luke said. "I'll call Cedric and work it out with him, but if you can get something -- a glass works well, but it could be almost anything -- that will hold their prints and give it to Cedric Jones, he can have somebody lift the prints and send them to me. Then we might find out who these people really are."

"We can do that," Dani said.

"Okay," Luke said. "Leave it with me. I'll be in touch after I talk with Cedric. Sounds like we have a little time. When do your mystery guests arrive, again?"

"The day after tomorrow, in the afternoon," Dani said. "Thanks, Luke."

"My pleasure. I can't wait to find out who we're dealing with, here."

Miranda Velasquez was sitting at her kitchen table when her husband breezed in. She had a glass of orange juice in front of her; a carafe of coffee and two cups were on the table. He poured himself a cup of coffee and pulled out the chair opposite her. Watching a pair of hummingbirds at the feeder outside the bay window, she ignored him.

"Good morning," he said.

"You spent the night here for a change?" she asked.

"I love you too, Miss Piggy."

"What's the matter? Did your little slut have other plans last night?"

"None of your business."

"When are you leaving for this *retreat*, as you call it?"

"Day after tomorrow. I've got an early morning flight to St. Lucia."

"St. Lucia?" she said, her voice shrill. "Is that where you're meeting her?"

"I'm meeting a few potential contributors. Don't let your fucked-up hormones get you in over your head. You don't want to piss me off. You think just because you're pregnant as a hippo you can get away with bitching at me? I'll take my belt to you without a second thought, put some stripes on that big fat ass. Don't press your luck."

"Leave me a phone number, in case something goes wrong," she said.

"There's no phone number; we're meeting on a private yacht."

"So I can't reach you?"

"That's right. You're on your own. Have a blast. Maybe you can find some kinky bastard that likes to do pregnant women. Just be discreet; no compromising pictures in the tabloids, okay?" He laughed. "Now cook my breakfast, will you? I'm running late."

She glared at him for a moment and stood up, stretching her lower back, rubbing it with both hands. She went to the refrigerator and opened the door. "Two eggs, or three?"

"Three."

"Scrambled?"

"No. Fried. And don't overcook them this time."

"Yes, master." She took the three eggs from the refrigerator and moved to the stove, breaking them into the frying pan.

"That's more like it. I hate it when you make them rubbery. How damn many times have I told you, I like them runny, you stupid bitch."

She glanced over her shoulder, checking to see what he was doing. He still sat facing her empty chair, his back to her. She whirled, the frying pan in her hand, and poured the still-raw eggs over his head.

"You bitch!" he roared, standing up, knocking his chair over as he spun to face her, already drawing his right arm across to backhand her.

She anticipated his blow, stepping back and letting it pass inches in front of her face. She swung the empty frying pan, putting her considerable weight behind it. The flat bottom of the pan landed squarely on his face.

He screamed in surprise and pain, clapping both hands to his nose. She laughed when she saw the blood pouring from behind his hands. He dropped his right hand and took a step toward her, stopping when she raised the 10-inch chef's knife in her other hand. She made a threatening gesture toward his crotch.

"Don't call me a bitch, you spic bastard. Touch me and I promise you won't have anything left to entertain your sluts with. You've got little enough as it is. From now on, you can cook your own damn eggs, and do it somewhere else. Get out of my house, and don't come back until you can behave yourself. I'll cut you in a New York minute, and if you hurt me, don't forget my brothers. They don't like you much anyway. I wouldn't give 'em an excuse to get rough, you greasy piece of Cuban shit."

She held her threatening pose until he went out the door into the attached garage. She waited until she heard his car leave, and then put the knife and the pan on the counter and sat down at the table, a smile on her face.

"I only wish I hadn't sounded so much like my mother," she said, her voice echoing in the empty kitchen.

BEVERLY LENNOX WAS HAVING another candle-lit dinner with the man she knew as Berto. He had called her and invited her to join him, alluding to their "project," as he had called it on the phone. She was surprised to find herself excited at the prospect of seeing him again. He was an attractive man, and so far, he had treated her with respect. That was a novel experience for her.

She followed the *maître d'* to a table in the shadows, in a private corner of the elegant restaurant. Her smile when Berto stood to greet her was genuine.

She reached to take the hand he extended toward her, surprised when he grasped hers gently, like he might hold a live bird. He lifted it toward himself and bent from the waist to brush his lips against her fingers. Releasing her hand, he straightened up, smiling and nodding.

She felt herself blush, feeling foolish at her reaction. Then she realized that might be the only thing that no man had ever done to her before. She returned his smile, but she wondered about his hand. The insides of his fingers felt odd; they were dry and slick, like plastic, almost.

"You look exquisite," he said, waiting to take his own seat until the *maître d'* had seated her.

"Thank you," she said.

"The dress is beautiful on you."

"Thanks. I used one of the cards; I hope that's all right?"

"It is why you have the cards. Of course it is all right. You deserve the best, and in all honesty, it is a good investment. Things like that affect how you are perceived by other people. That is important, you understand?"

"Yes, thank you. I'm not sure Horry notices what I'm wearing, though."

"Perhaps not consciously, but be assured that he sees how other men react to you. This increases his estimation of your worth, whether he knows it or not. Appearance is everything, in some situations. It determines how you are treated by people who don't know you, and it shapes what they think of you. But you know this. Forgive me. I do not mean to patronize. I only want to assure you that I trust your judgment -- and your excellent taste. Don't worry about the money. There is plenty."

She smiled and nodded, avoiding looking him in the eye. She watched his hand as he picked up a piece of bread. Her guess was correct; his fingers didn't straighten completely. They were claw-like, and the inside of his hand was a mass of scar tissue. She shuddered to think how painful the injury that caused the scarring must have been.

"Something is on your mind," he said. "Tell me what is troubling you."

"It's silly," she said, tearing her eyes from his hand, hoping he had not noticed her staring at it. "I'm not troubled, really." She struggled to find an explanation for her distraction. "I'm stunned. This is like some Cinderella fantasy."

"Good," he said. "That is a healthy reaction. I'm pleased. I apologize that your Prince Charming may not be what he should be, but then you were with him before you both came to my attention."

"I thought you came to me *because* I was with him, that your interest in me was for the -- shall I say *leverage* -- that I could give you over him."

"That is well said," he said. He studied her for a few seconds, his dark eyes reflecting the flickering candlelight. "You are correct, of course. I didn't know anything about you at first, except that you were with him. That was sufficient for my initial purpose. After our first encounter, I wanted to know more about you. You were not at all what I expected. At the risk of offending you, I think you are out of his league; you could do much better. That was my immediate impression when we first met, and I have made some inquiries since then."

"About me?" she asked, shifting in her chair and stroking the knife beside her dinner plate with her right index finger. She caught herself avoiding eye contact. She froze her finger and lifted her gaze to his. "What did you learn?"

"Please don't be nervous or offended by that. I always find out as much as I can about my business partners. Nothing I learned about you worried me; to the contrary, I'm quite impressed."

"Thank you, but I didn't know you saw me as a business partner."

"Well, again, you are correct. I didn't, not at our first meeting."

"And now?" she asked.

"And now, I view you as a *potential* partner."

"Potential?"

"Yes."

"And what would you require of me to actually become your business partner? To realize the potential?"

"Two things. We must complete our little project with Velasquez, but I think that will happen with no difficulty."

"And the second?"

"I would need your commitment to work with me on future projects."

"What future projects?"

He held her gaze for several seconds before he answered. "You can guess why I want the recordings of Velasquez, I think."

"You want to be able to influence him in his official capacity, I suspect."

"Yes. And you are comfortable with that?"

"Yes."

"You know that we will have to let him know what we have done, do you not?" he asked.

"Yes, or there would be no leverage. He'll at least have to know that I have compromised him. He may not need to know about you, personally. Only that someone has power over him."

He smiled. "It's a pleasure to work with you. So you can see that he won't be favorably disposed toward you after this is done, yes?"

"I expect he'll be angry with me."

"And does that worry you?"

"Only because I'll have to find another way to make my living. I'm not fond of him."

"I hope you will continue to use the credit cards to build a bit of security against the day he learns what we've done. Take what you need to be comfortable."

"I live well," she said, "and I like to earn my living. A financial cushion to keep me afloat for a while is one thing. Running up bills indefinitely on those credit cards is something else."

"I understand. How do you feel about what we're doing to Velasquez?"

"He's getting what he deserves. He's a despicable pig; he has no respect for anyone but himself."

"Good. You and I think alike. You know the world is filled with men like Velasquez, don't you?"

"In my line of work, I've met more than a few," she said.

"I expect so. If you partner with me, we will pick the ones who deserve what we are doing to Velasquez. You and I will help them to become better members of society."

She thought about that for half a minute, then she broke the silence. "Will I have some input as to the demands that we make on Velasquez?"

His eyes flashed in surprise. "What do you have in mind?"

"One of the conditions we impose on him should be to honor his marriage going forward. You know he has a one-year-old son, and his wife is expecting? I'd like to neuter the son of a bitch, but I think it would hurt him more to be forced to make things right with his wife, and to live with her for the rest of his life. But she may feel differently, I guess. Still, we should make him take care of her if she wants a divorce."

He nodded, but didn't say anything. She watched him, worried that the expression on his face didn't change for several seconds. Had she gone too far?

Then he laughed, a deep, rumbling belly laugh. She was relieved, but puzzled that the lower part of his face seemed stiff, almost frozen.

When he recovered his composure, he said, "I like you, Ms. Lennox. And I agree that we should make him stand by his obligations to her and the children, however she wants to handle their marriage. This is going to be an enjoyable partnership, I think. Shall we celebrate with a little Champagne while we consider what to have for dinner?"

7

"I'm disappointed that the selection of fresh fruits and vegetables wasn't better," Liz said. She and Dani had made the rounds of the grocery stores in Le Marin after breakfast, and Liz was putting things away.

Dani, up to her elbows in the engine compartment, looked over her shoulder. "Do you want to borrow Phillip's Jeep and go into Fort-de-France?"

"Not really. Do you?"

"I'm all right with it, if you need to go."

"I'm still beat, and if we stay here, we'll probably have another late night; Sandrine's in party mode."

"They haven't had much company lately, Phillip said. I guess she's making up for lost time. What do you want to do?"

"I was thinking we could clear out and head for Rodney Bay. We can anchor out tonight and get a good night's sleep. In the morning, we'll move into the marina and go grocery shopping. If I can't find what I need at the stores around there, Timothy will be thrilled to round it all up for us and bring it by the boat."

"That gives us all day tomorrow plus a few hours the next morning," Dani said. "That sounds good to me. We should call Phillip and let him know."

"I'll do that while you finish up with the engine. Maybe we can buy him and Sandrine a farewell lunch at the marina restaurant, if she can get away from the customs office."

"Good," Dani said. "I'm done; while you call, I'm going to take a quick shower and rinse the grease off."

Forty-five minutes later, they wedged their dinghy into the pack tied up at the main dinghy dock in the marina. They walked up the gangway and found Phillip and Sandrine waiting in the shade.

"I'm glad you could make it on such short notice, Sandrine," Liz said.

"We are not so busy just now," Sandrine said. "I have your clearance." She handed Liz a few folded pages.

"Thank you," Dani said. "We didn't mean for you to do that; we were planning to go into the office after lunch."

"It is not the big deal," Sandrine said. "Is easy for me, easy for you."

They stepped into the nearly empty restaurant and took a table. Once they were seated and the waitress had brought menus and taken their drink orders, Phillip said, "Cedric called me a little while ago."

"Oh," Dani said. "Did you tell him about our conversation with Luke?"

Phillip chuckled. "He called because Luke told him you were staying with us. He was looking for you."

"Oh," Liz said. "Do we need to call him?"

"No, not really. You should probably give him a ring to say hello and thanks, but he and Luke worked out all the details for the fingerprint check on your guests. Cedric wants you to drop off whatever you use to collect the prints at the Port Authority office. He asked me to tell you, because he was going into a meeting and wouldn't be available the rest of today."

"That sounds easy enough," Liz said.

"Yes. He set it up for the morning after your guests arrive, figuring you'll be going in to get your outbound clearance then anyway. If that changes, give him a call. It's not a problem to change it, but they rotate the people, so he might have to brief somebody new if there's a delay. He suggested wrapping whatever objects you have in newsprint and putting them in a padded envelope. Ask for the senior police officer; she'll be expecting you."

"Thanks, Phillip," Liz said.

The waitress brought the bottle of wine that Liz had ordered. After everyone had been served, Sandrine said, "When you have done with these people, you must come back to see us. Phillip saw everybody a few weeks ago in Miami at Mario's party, but I was there only the one night. Connie and Paul have been here since then, but I have missed you two."

"We'll do that," Dani said.

"And you must stay for some days. We will do shopping for some nice clothes, yes?"

"You just spent two days doing that with Connie when she and Paul were here last week," Phillip said.

"*Oui*, but all the time we are looking for the sexy shoes for Connie, and the dress she say is 'slinking.' I do not understand this 'slinking,' but the dress has much beautiful draping to show off the curves, yes? I do not buy something like that for me, because I do not wish that Connie thinks I am stealing her idea. But I like it very much, this dress. I must find one for me. You also, Liz. You would like. But Dani, I don't think so much for you. Is not what is called your *thing*, yes?"

"Slinky?" Dani asked. "You're right, Sandrine. Not my thing."

Phillip shook his head, waving the waitress over to their table. "We need to order so Sandrine can get back to work. She needs to make some money for this dress she's going to buy."

THE LEAN, fit man with the buzz-cut hair sat in the shade of the open-air bar. He'd chosen a table overlooking the dinghy dock that served the marina in Rodney Bay. He was glad he had come in early: the bar was beginning to fill up with a happy-hour crowd. If he'd been any later, he wouldn't have gotten a table that afforded him such a good view of the docks.

He had a tall glass of cold fruit juice in front of him, minus a few sips. He didn't like fruit juice much, but it was the only non-alcoholic drink they served that looked like a cocktail. To get it, he'd had to argue with the waitress. As soon as he sat down, she had brought him rum punch without being asked.

"Welcome to St. Lucia," she had said, plopping a fruity-looking drink down in front of him. "First one's on me for happy hour." She'd given him a come-hither smile. "Let me know when you're ready for more. I'm Annie. You staying in the marina?"

He shook his head and raised the glass to his nose, sniffing it. His eyes watered from the vapor of high-proof rum. He put the glass down.

"Thanks, Annie, but I'm a friend of Bill's. Can you bring me some of that without any alcohol, please?"

"Bill who?" she'd asked.

"Never mind," he said. "I can't drink alcohol. I have a problem with it."

"Oh, I'm sorry," she said. "I can do that, but I'll have to charge you for it. Fruit punch costs twice as much as rum punch. It's because the rum's so inexpensive here, you see."

"I understand," he said. "Thanks."

She nodded and picked up the glass. "You still want the fruit punch?"

"You have soft drinks? Like for mixers, maybe?"

"Yes, but it's the same, and they're watery. Nothing in cans or bottles. Liquor's cheap. Everything else has this tax on it. What would you like?"

"Just bring me the fruit punch, then."

She nodded and walked away, returning in a few minutes with the drink. "We only charged you half," she said, "because the first rum punch would have been free. I told the boss you didn't drink alcohol; he's a Seventh Day Adventist. I thought he'd understand."

"Thank him for me," he said. "I'm surprised he runs a bar."

"Well, he won't touch the alcohol, not even to move the bottles around. But he says it is not for him to judge what other people do; that's the Lord's prerogative."

"Sounds like my kind of man," he said.

"He is a fine man," she said. "Let me know if you need anything else. I started a tab for you."

"Thanks, Annie. I will."

As he watched her saunter away, he decided that he would forbid his subordinates to set foot in the bar. Annie and cheap alcohol would get them in trouble, for sure.

The men who had crewed for him when he brought *Vengeance* down

from Miami had moved on to another assignment. The two replace-
ments were both army rejects, dishonorably discharged from the 82nd
Airborne Division for drug abuse.

They had already challenged his authority; he'd broken the larger
one's nose to rein him in. The smaller one was more submissive, but he
was sneaky. Both of them were making snide remarks about his background as a Naval officer.

They'd also made no secret of what they'd like to do to the women
who ran the yacht, given a chance. His order that their mission was
surveillance and didn't include contact had led to the larger man
physically attacking him. He'd been tempted to do worse than
breaking the oaf's nose, but he'd restrained himself. He was short-
handed already.

He lifted the fruit punch to take a sip and paused with it halfway to
his mouth when he saw the two women arriving in a rigid inflatable
dinghy. The one in the bow tied it to the dock and then threaded the
end of a piece of stainless steel chain through one of the cleats. She
snapped a padlock in place and the two of them climbed onto the
floating dock and walked up the gangway toward where he sat.

When they got closer, he had no trouble recognizing them from
their photographs. Both dressed in white polo shirts with some kind of
logo over the left breast, they looked enough alike to be sisters. The
mid-thigh khaki shorts they both wore showed off their well-muscled
legs as they came up the ramp from the dinghy dock.

One had short, wavy blonde hair. That would be Dani Berger, he
knew. Liz Chirac was the one with the reddish-blonde hair pulled back
into a bun.

That little shit with the airborne tattoos was right. They were definitely babes. It was too bad the mission precluded physical proximity.

His eyes hidden behind mirrored sunglasses, he watched as they
came almost within arm's distance before they turned to follow the sidewalk to the Port Authority office.

"Did you want to make a grocery run after we clear in?" Berger
asked.

"We've got all day tomorrow," Chirac said. "Let's chill out this afternoon. We'll bring *Vengeance* into the marina in the morning and go

shopping then. That will save hauling everything out to the anchorage in the dinghy."

He smiled, admiring the view from behind as they climbed the stairs to the office. Their plans suited him; he could have his men test the surveillance system one last time once they were in the marina. If they found a problem, they'd have a perfect opportunity to fix it while the women were grocery shopping.

Now that he knew what they were up to, he didn't have to post a watch, either. He could give those two fools a little time off tonight; let them blow off steam. He took a last sip of the fruit punch and left some bills under his glass, including an oversized tip for Annie. She might come in handy; it wouldn't hurt anything for her to remember him favorably.

8

"Are you about ready?" Dani called down the companionway to Liz. *Vengeance* was in a slip in the marina, and Liz was below in the galley, checking her grocery list. They had reserved the slip when they were ashore the previous afternoon, wanting to get an early start on the provisioning this morning. It would be hot later in the day, but they would be done by then, relaxing in the shade of their big cockpit awning.

"Yes," Liz said. "Almost."

A minute later, she came up the companionway ladder and sat down near Dani. "Check this over for me and see if I missed anything," she said, handing Dani an index card.

Dani took it, frowning, and said, "I wouldn't know."

"Humor me, please. I might have missed something."

Dani shrugged and looked down at the index card. "No," she said. "It looks good to me. Let's go; we can talk about it on the way. Are we walking or taking the dinghy?"

"Let's walk over to the place in Gros Islet. We can take the dinghy to the supermarket by the mall; that's too long a hike with groceries."

"I'm ready," Dani said. "Lock her up."

Liz closed and locked the companionway doors, and they stepped over the lifelines onto the dock. Once they reached the marina parking lot, Dani broke their silence.

"We should be okay here," she said. "The note was a clever idea. When did you notice that the surveillance system was active?"

"When I went into the head to put on fresh sunscreen."

Marie's technician had mounted a warning light and the switch to disable the system in the medicine cabinet in the head that Dani and Liz used when they had guests.

"I wonder how long it was on?" Dani asked. "I don't remember seeing it when I was in there."

"You put on sunscreen right after we tied up in the slip," Liz said.

"Right. I would have noticed it then, I'm sure."

"Did you open the cabinet again while I was going through the fridge?" Liz asked.

"No," Dani said. "So it could have been on for what? Thirty minutes, maybe?"

"That's about right," Liz said. "Did we say anything damning? Do you even remember what we talked about?"

"We couldn't have said much. I put on my sunscreen and took my coffee up to the cockpit. You were rummaging in the galley lockers. We might have said something in passing, but nothing important."

"That's right," Liz said. "I remember now. You complained that it was stuffy in the slip and wondered if we should put up the awnings before we left."

"Right. And you said you wanted to hurry and go, so we'd get back before it got any hotter. That's about it."

"Then they didn't get anything," Liz said. "But why do you suppose they were monitoring us? They must know Beverly and what's his name aren't here yet."

"I don't know," Dani said. "Did you happen to notice anybody nearby? On the dock, or one of the other boats?"

"No. Why?"

"I'm wondering how they activated it. Marie said there was a proximity key, remember?"

"Yes," Liz said. "Wi-Fi, maybe?"

"No, she said the Wi-Fi would only work if the system was already activated. It had to be somebody nearby with a proximity key, whatever that is. I wish I had asked more questions, now."

"Like how close they had to be?" Liz asked.

"Yes."

"Let's just call her and ask," Liz said.

"Sometimes I think you're a genius," Dani said, slipping her phone out of her pocket. She scrolled through her contacts and touched Marie LaCroix's number. In a few seconds, she shook her head. "Voicemail," she said.

"You could have left a message," Liz said.

"I'll send her a text. I should have thought of that to begin with." Dani's thumbs flew over the screen. "There. We'll probably get our answer more quickly, anyway."

"Good," Liz said, "let's hurry and get the shopping done. Now I'm curious to see if the system's still active when we get back."

"Me, too. I guess we'd better start assuming somebody's listening, unless we check that indicator light. Now I wish we'd had him put it somewhere easier to see."

"Too late to second-guess ourselves," Liz said. "It will be fine, once the guests are aboard. We'll be on guard anyway, with them around."

GUILLERMO MONTALBA WAS LOST in thought when the encrypted cell-phone rang. He picked it up from his desk and accepted the call.

"Yes?"

"Good morning. Our surveillance team is in place in St. Lucia. Berger and Chirac returned to the boat and took it out of the marina sometime in the last few days. When the team resumed their watch yesterday, the boat was anchored out in the bay. They brought the boat back in this morning, and they're getting ready for the arrival of Velasquez and the woman."

"Are your people ready?"

"Yes, sir. They tested the surveillance equipment this morning and were able to hear the women discussing going to the grocery store. Hardly exciting intelligence, but we know the system is working."

"Good," Montalba said.

"Are Velasquez and the woman still expected this afternoon?" the man on the phone asked.

"Yes. She's ready. I met with her last night and covered the last-minute things."

"She will have them leave St. Lucia for Bequia tomorrow morning, still?"

"Yes," Montalba said. "And she will request that they hug the shoreline as they pass St. Vincent, as you suggested."

"Berger and Chirac won't like that. The wind shadow of the island means they'll have to run the diesel for that whole stretch. I'm sure they'll try to convince the woman -- "

"Her name is Beverly Lennox," Montalba interrupted. "Stop calling her 'the woman.'"

"Sorry, sir. They'll no doubt try to talk Beverly Lennox into allowing them to pass well out to the west of the island -- probably ten miles or more. They would have a sailing wind out there, and the trip would be more pleasant."

"She's prepared for that; she's an amateur photographer, and she's taking her camera equipment. She wants to be close inshore so that she can photograph the hillsides. She's their paying customer. They'll accommodate her."

"As long as they're not more than three miles out, preferably closer. The patrol boat can't go farther than three miles to the west unless they're in hot pursuit. Plus, there's the endurance question."

"What endurance question?" Montalba asked.

"The ability of the boat to stay at sea. The people we've made our arrangement with only have access to smaller patrol boats. An intercept far out to the west would require one of their larger vessels, and our contacts don't have that authority."

"I see. They do understand what's expected of them, don't they?"

"Yes, sir. They'll carry out a routine boarding and search the vessel for contraband under the pretext of a safety inspection. That's a relatively common thing. Berger and Chirac should take it in stride, at least until they find the drugs."

"All right," Montalba said. "And do they know where to look?"

"Yes, sir. Our team provided them marked-up photographs of the concealed contraband. An idiot would be able to find it."

"Once they find it, what happens?"

"The boarding crew will confiscate the drugs and document the search and seizure using their normal report forms."

"But no official report will be filed, is that correct?"

"Yes, sir. They will have a private conversation with Velasquez -- rather, Jeffrey Starnes. They will believe that he's a wealthy person, since he's chartered this luxury yacht. They will offer to 'lose' the report in exchange for whatever amount of money they can negotiate with him. Of course, this will all be recorded by the surveillance system. Then we will have implicated him in the crime of bringing illegal drugs into the waters of St. Vincent, as well as bribing law enforcement. This is all in accordance with your wishes, still?"

"Yes. That's perfect. What will happen as far as paperwork is concerned?"

"The boarding party will fill out two reports. One will describe a routine boarding where nothing was found, and the other will cover the confiscation of the drugs. They will have Berger sign them both, as she is the captain. They'll be mixed together, and she'll have a number of things to sign. She won't realize there are two conflicting reports. The original and the carbon copy of the report listing the drugs will be given to our field manager, who will forward them to me. Berger will be provided a copy of the routine boarding report, and the boarding party will file the original of the routine report through their chain of command as they normally would."

"So I will have the only record of the seizure of the drugs, then?"

"Yes, sir, once I forward it to you. I'm sure that Berger and Chirac will keep their mouths shut. They'll probably find out about the bribe from Velasquez and Lennox, but they won't dare say anything to anybody. They'll be relieved that their boat wasn't confiscated."

"Good. Thank you for the explanation."

"You're welcome, sir. Anything else?"

"No."

"I'll call after the boarding has taken place, then."

"I will be waiting," Montalba said, disconnecting the call.

~

"WELCOME ABOARD *VENGEANCE*," Liz said, as she took Beverly Lennox's hand and helped her up from the marina's floating dock. "I'm Liz Chirac, and this is my partner Dani Berger. She's the captain of your yacht, and I'm the first mate."

"And a gourmet chef, from what the broker told me. I'm Beverly Lennox, and this is Harry Starnes."

Harry stepped aboard without Liz's help. Once on deck, he grasped her right hand in his, he covered it with his left and shook it with enthusiasm. With a wide grin, he said, "It's great to be here, Liz. Call me Harry."

"We're glad to have you with us, Harry." Liz said, glancing around to see Beverly shaking hands with Dani.

When Dani shook Harry's hand, she asked, "How was the taxi from the airport? Did Felix take good care of you?"

"He did," Beverly said. "He gave us a good bit of background on St. Lucia, too. I guess you know he's a tour guide; he's full of interesting information."

"Yes, he is," Dani said. "He's our first choice for tours here in St. Lucia."

"He'll bring your luggage down to us in a minute or two," Liz said. "Why don't we move back to the cockpit? It's nice and shady under the awning, and I have a little fruit and cheese platter set out."

She shepherded them to seats in the shade and asked, "What can I get you to drink? We have a good selection of wine, cold beer, and whatever else you'd like -- whiskey, rum, the usual."

"I read about this St. Lucia rum in the airline magazine," Harry said. "It got rave reviews, but I can't remember what it was called."

"Chairman's Reserve?" Liz asked.

"That's it!"

"We have a bottle. It's quite good, but Dani and I both prefer Saint James Reserve from over in Martinique. We keep it aboard, too. If you like rum, you'll want to try them both while you're with us."

"Where'd Dani go?" Beverly asked.

"She and Felix are putting your luggage in your stateroom. She'll be -
_ "

"Hi," Dani said, climbing up the companionway ladder and stepping into the cockpit. "I put your bags in the big locker by your berth. Felix said to tell you he enjoyed chatting with you on the drive."

"He's gone?" Harry asked. "But I didn't pay him."

"We take care of that," Dani said. "Don't worry."

"I'll get you that rum, Harry," Liz said. "The Chairman's Reserve?"

"Sure."

"If you don't mind a suggestion," Dani said, "it's nice on the rocks, with a twist of lime."

"Sounds great," Harry said.

"Good," Liz said. "One Chairman's Reserve, rocks and lime. Beverly, what can I get for you?"

"Do you have a dry white wine?"

"We do," Liz said, standing up. "Dani?"

"White wine's fine for me, thanks." Dani slid into the place where Liz had been sitting. "How were your flights?"

"They were flights," Beverly said. "On time, no problems. Crowded, but that's flying these days."

"I like traveling at seven or eight knots, myself," Dani said. "Liz and I both hate flying; we did more than enough in our former lives. The flying itself is okay, but the hassle at the airports is awful. It's gotten worse since we quit flying all the time."

"Your former lives? What did you do before?" Beverly asked.

"I worked in a family business in New York, and Liz worked for the E.U. in Brussels," Dani said.

Liz set the drinks tray on the table and sat down. "I brought these little welcome-aboard shots of a rum-based liqueur called 'Shrub,'" she said. "It's a tradition of ours, if it's okay with you."

"Sure," Beverly said.

Harry nodded, smiling.

Liz passed the shot glasses around the table.

"To traveling under sail," she said, lifting her glass. "We're pleased you chose to spend your holiday with us."

The other three touched the rims of their tiny glasses to Liz's.

"Cheers," Harry said, and slugged down the shot. "Oh, boy! That is good."

Liz smiled. "Every island has its rum drink, but this one's special. It's from Martinique; it's white rum with a secret mix of herbs, spices, and fruit. They age it in the sun, like sun-tea, but with a kick. A friend of ours made this batch. Everybody over there has their own recipe. Help yourselves to some fruit and cheese."

Dani took a sip of her wine and said, "I don't want to rush you, but if you want to leave St. Lucia tomorrow, I should hustle over to the Port Authority office in the next half hour and clear us out. Have you thought about where you'd like to go while you're with us?"

"Bequia was recommended by a friend," Beverly said. "Is it far?"

"It's a nice day's sail," Liz said, "and it's a magical place. It's one of our favorite spots. We'll want to get a reasonably early start, so we can get in before dark. It's a fabulous spot to watch the sunset."

"I'm sold," Beverly said. "Okay with you, Harry?"

"Sure," he said, spearing a melon cube wrapped in prosciutto and popping it in his mouth.

"Then if you'll let me have your passports," Dani said, "I'll go handle our departure clearance. I need to get our papers."

She gathered up the four shot glasses and took them below. In a minute, she returned with a canvas briefcase and collected Beverly's and Harry's passports.

"I'll be back shortly," she said.

9

"Too bad she wants to hug the coast," Dani said. They were motor sailing at nine knots, about a mile off St. Lucia's western shore. "It's a beautiful day; we'd be having a glorious sail if we were out there." She was looking at the western horizon.

"It's her money," Liz said. "And she'll probably get some nice shots of the shoreline."

Dani shrugged, tweaking the autopilot. Beverly was on the foredeck with her camera, happily snapping away. Harry sat on the forward end of the coachroof, chatting with her and sipping coffee from a mug. Their conversation wasn't audible over the soft rumble of the diesel, but every minute or two, Beverly would turn to Harry and say something, and he'd hand her the coffee mug so that she could take a sip.

"Isn't that sweet?" Liz asked. "At first, I was afraid he was going to be a jerk."

Dani glared at her and put her index finger across her lips, shaking her head.

"It's okay," Liz said. "I switched it off. There wasn't anything to record, and the engine noise below deck would drown out anything anyway. Besides, the light wasn't on."

"Oh, okay," Dani said. "We need to be careful, though. We mustn't get careless. Wonder why it wasn't on? Maybe that proximity thing has a manual switch on it."

"Maybe," Liz said. "That would make sense. Marie's text said most of them worked from several yards away, but it wasn't on. Either they can switch it on and off, or it's broken. Which one is the keeper of the key, do you suppose?"

Dani thought for a few seconds. "She is. She seems more on top of things than he does."

"You think she's setting him up, then?"

"That's my bet," Dani said. "Why did you say you thought he was a jerk at first?"

"Maybe jerk's not the right word. He seemed phony at first, starting with that two-handed handshake and the big grin. I noticed he didn't do that when he shook your hand. Wonder why?"

"He's got the hots for you," Dani said, an impish smile on her face.

Liz stared at her for a moment. "You're teasing me."

"Yes, but I still think he has the hots for you," Dani said. "I saw how he shook your hand; it made my skin crawl. I took defensive measures."

"What did you do?"

"You know my handshake trick."

"You didn't!" Liz said.

"I was careful; I didn't give him the full treatment. Just enough pressure to let him know there was more available."

Liz shook her head. "You're incorrigible." She chuckled. "Wish I had thought of it."

"I had the advantage of being second," Dani said. "That was a slimeball salesman's handshake he gave you. You didn't have any warning, but I did."

"You think he's a salesman?" Liz asked. "What kind?"

"Snake oil," Dani said. "He's some kind of con man."

"I do wonder who they are," Liz said. "How long do you think it will be before Luke gets something back on their fingerprints?"

"Well, he hasn't even had time to get them, yet. I left their shot glasses at the Port Authority office last night. The senior police officer was expecting them; she said she'd get them to Cedric first thing this morning. But remember, he has to get somebody to lift the prints and send them to Luke. My guess is we're looking at a day or two, at best."

They passed a few minutes in silence. "If he's the mark, do you think she's going to blackmail him herself?"

"There's no way for us to know," Dani said. "My biggest question is why we're involved. If she's on her own, how did she get *Vengeance* wired? Stealing her and sailing to the islands to set this up argues that there's a big organization behind it."

"I agree with that," Liz said.

"Then she's probably just a bit player -- the bait for the trap," Dani said. "We'll be in a better position to guess about what's going on when we find out who they are."

"What do you think about lunch?" Liz asked.

Dani shook her head and frowned. "What?" she asked, looking sideways at Liz.

Liz laughed. "Okay, so it was an abrupt shift. I'm trying to figure out whether to serve lunch before we cross the Saint Vincent Channel, or after."

Dani pushed a few buttons on the chart plotter above the helm. "That's either a little before noon, or a little after two," she said. "You think it's going to be too rough in the channel? It's not blowing that hard, and we'll cross under sail. The ride shouldn't be too bad."

"I don't know," Liz said. "I guess I should ask them, huh?"

"Probably. Don't forget to turn the surveillance system back on."

"Think I should do that now?"

"Whenever. I'm just trying to keep it in mind. I don't want to forget it's there if it's on, or tip our hand if it's left off. For all we know, she may be able to tell somehow."

"I hadn't thought of that," Liz said. "I just assumed it was somebody that we don't know about that was monitoring it."

"I was thinking the same thing, Dani said, "but it just dawned on me that if she's a key part of this, she might be able to tell."

"Good thought. I'll go switch it back on before I ask them about lunch. We shouldn't tamper with it unless it's necessary, I guess."

～

"WHY COULDN'T we get one of them speedboats?" the smaller member of the surveillance team asked, as he stowed his gear.

The leader looked at him and shook his head. "You just can't keep your mouth shut and do what you're told, can you?"

"I just wondered, makin' conversation, like. I didn't mean nothin' by it, sir. But I know how to run one of them go-fast boats. I ain't never been on no sailboat before, though. That's all I meant."

"Fair enough," the leader said. "We chartered this because it won't stand out among all the others where we're going."

"Bequia, right?" the little man asked.

"Right. Mostly sailboats there, except for the local fishermen, and they've got locally built, open boats. A plain white boat like this with blue canvas? There's gonna be so many of them we'll have trouble remembering which one's ours."

"Yes, sir. Reckon that makes sense when you put it like that. This here boat's pretty little, though. We gonna be okay, crossin' that open water out to Bequia?"

The leader chuckled. "We'll be fine. Thirty-two feet's on the small side, but I've sailed boats like this from North Carolina to Bermuda and back."

"No shit?" the larger of his two subordinates asked. "On purpose? Uh ... I mean 'cause you wanted to? Or was it some kind of Navy survival training?"

That got a belly laugh from the leader. "I just did it for the pure pleasure of it. I thought you airborne boys weren't scared of anything. You jump out of perfectly good airplanes and think it's fun, but you're afraid of a little water? Pussies, that's what you are."

His two subordinates traded looks, but neither said anything. After several seconds, the bigger one broke the silence. "Will they already be there, you reckon?" he asked.

"Not unless they left before daybreak," the leader said. "I figure that's not likely. A boat like that, though, they'll make the trip in maybe 10 hours. I expect they'll pull in around sunset."

"So if we leave here now, we'll get there way before they do, right, sir?" the smaller man said. "You said it was about three hours from here?"

"Yes. It's only about eight miles. We'll probably do it in less than three hours."

The three men had flown from St. Lucia to St. Vincent that morning and picked up the bareboat charter at Blue Lagoon, on St. Vincent's south coast. Bequia was visible on the southern horizon.

The leader pointed through the porthole over the galley stove. "That's where we're going."

"How we gonna know where to anchor, then, sir, if they ain't there yet?"

"We'll drop the hook just inside the northern point of the harbor mouth and wait for them," the leader said. "Once we see where they go, we'll move."

"They ain't gonna notice us doin' that?" the big man asked.

"Not likely. When they come in, they'll be focused on finding a spot in the crowd. There'll be a lot of boats there; they won't notice us on their way in. If they see us moving around after they anchor, they'll think we're just another late arrival. Even if they do make the connection, they won't think anything of it. People move around in anchorages like that all the time."

"Sir?" the smaller one asked.

"Yes?"

"Reckon when the Coast Guard's gonna board them? They was gonna call you, right?"

"Yes. Could be any time, now," he said, looking at his wristwatch. "They should be across the St. Vincent Channel by now, cruising down the west coast of St. Vincent. I don't know where they're planning to intercept them, but I'd guess it'll be up near the northern end of the island. There aren't as many people up there to notice, if anything goes wrong."

"Thank you for explainin' sir."

"You're welcome. Thanks for shaping up. Maybe you airborne guys aren't as bad as I thought." He grinned. Then he noticed the looks they traded. "That's a joke, boys. I have a lot of respect for the 82nd Airborne."

"Thank you, sir," the bigger man said. "Reckon we ain't quite used to naval officers yet."

"We're gonna be okay," the leader said. "Let's go sailing."

"THAT BOAT'S COMING FAST," Dani said, pointing at an orange speck against the shoreline to the east.

"It popped up out of nowhere," Liz said, reaching for the binoculars. She raised them to her eyes and studied the boat. "It looks like a Coast Guard patrol boat -- one of those big orange RIBs."

"Bet we're going to get boarded," Dani said.

"You think they were watching for us?"

"There wouldn't have been any point in that gift Sandrine found for us, unless we were going to show it to somebody," Dani said. "Know what I'm talking about?"

"Yes, I do. They're headed straight for us," Liz said. "You must be right. Looks like they came out of Chateaubelair."

"I don't think Beverly and Harry have noticed," Dani said. "I wonder how they're going to react. I hope this doesn't upset them."

Liz leaned close and put her lips to Dani's ear. "Okay, I got it. You handle the boat and I'll watch them. Now quit playing for the surveillance system and act normal."

The Coast Guard RIB came up fast on their port quarter. When it was a few yards away, there was a blast from the siren and the blue lights on the cabin top began to flash. A voice blared over a loudhailer.

"Shut down your engine, *Vengeance*. We're coming aboard."

Dani throttled back and shifted into neutral. She leaned over to reach the engine instrument panel and pressed the stop button. *Vengeance* began losing way. Dani had left the sails up after crossing the St. Vincent Channel. Although there wasn't much wind, the sails damped the rolling and made the ride more comfortable. Without the engine, the sails were filling with a light onshore breeze, moving *Vengeance* along at a couple of knots.

The RIB approached within a couple of feet of *Vengeance's* rail, and a burly man in uniform said, "Good afternoon, captain. St. Vincent Coast Guard. We're going to board for a routine safety inspection."

"Do you want me to heave to, or drop the sails?"

"No, ma'am. You're okay as you are. How many people on board?"

"Four of us," Dani said.

"Any weapons?"

"No, none."

"Where have you come from?"

"St. Lucia."

"And where are you going?"

"Bequia."

"Okay," he said, giving the man at the helm a hand signal.

The RIB came in closer, the pneumatic tubes pressing against *Vengeance*. The man who had spoken stepped aboard, followed by two armed men. The RIB fell back a few feet and held its position.

"Where are your ship's papers and passports, captain?" the man in charge asked.

"They're below, under the chart table."

"Bring them up for me, please. Your friend can take the helm for a moment."

Liz stepped behind the helm and Dani went below. She returned in less than a minute, a manila folder in her hand.

"What would you like first?" she asked.

"The vessel's document," he said.

She handed it to him and watched as he studied it and made a few notes on his clipboard. He gave the document back to her.

"Your outbound clearance papers from your last port in St. Lucia, please," he said.

She passed them to him, and he made more entries on the clipboard.

"Passports," he said, returning the clearance documents to her and taking the passports, which she had ready in her hand.

He studied the passports, taking a moment to match each with its owner. Dani looked up and saw that Beverly and Harry had come aft. They were standing on the side deck, watching. The two coast-guardsmen blocked their access to the cockpit.

"This is a charter yacht?" the man in charge of the boarding party asked.

"That's right," Dani said.

"And you and Ms. Chirac run her?"

"Correct."

"You are from the U.S., and Ms. Chirac is from Belgium."

"That's right."

"How long has Ms. Chirac been in your employ?"

"She and I are partners in Venture Charters, LLC, the corporation that owns the yacht. She's not an employee."

"I see. Then you have been working together since you started this business?"

"Yes."

"And the vessel is in charter to Mr. Starnes and Ms. Lennox at the moment?"

"Correct."

"When did the charter begin?"

"Yesterday, in St. Lucia."

He spent half a minute scribbling notes on his clipboard. When he looked up at Dani, he asked, "Is there any contraband aboard?"

"None," Dani said.

"Very well. You stay with me in the cockpit." He turned to face Liz. "Ms. Chirac, please escort your guests to the foredeck and stay there while my men carry out their inspection below deck. We won't be long."

The two men waited until Liz and the guests were on the foredeck and then they ducked below. From where Dani sat behind the helm, she could see them shifting the cushions on the settees and making a cursory inspection of the spaces behind and beneath them. One man disappeared into the aft stateroom that she and Liz shared, and the other went forward, toward the guests' stateroom.

Within three minutes, the man who had gone forward mounted the companionway ladder and motioned to the man in charge.

"Stay seated, please, captain," he said, and moved to the companionway.

The man on the ladder whispered something, and the man in charge nodded. The man on the ladder shook his head. The man in charge frowned and took a smartphone from his pocket. He fiddled with it for a few seconds, flipping through pictures.

When he found what he was looking for, he showed it to the man on the ladder and whispered something to him. The man frowned and shook his head, but he went back below. In a moment, he returned and shook his head again. The man in charge called something to the one who was still out of sight in the aft cabin.

When both his subordinates were at the companionway, the man in charge held a brief, whispered conference with them. He returned to his seat and made more notes on his clipboard. The two men came up on deck and stood, waiting, on the side deck.

"Thank you for your patience, captain. We are finished. Please apologize to your guests for me and wish them a pleasant holiday in St. Vincent and the Grenadines."

"I'll do that," Dani said, as he handed her the clipboard.

"Please sign by the 'X'. Press hard, there are three copies."

"Don't you want to see our safety equipment? Flares, PFDs?" Dani asked, examining the papers.

"That won't be necessary, captain. Your vessel is quite beautiful, and well maintained. I'm sure you have far more than the minimum required safety equipment."

He stood and took one of the forms from his clipboard. "This copy is for you. If you should happen to be boarded again in our waters, show it to the officer in charge. Perhaps it will save you from the inconvenience of another inspection."

"Thank you," Dani said.

He gave her a curt nod and waved the RIB over. Within seconds, the three men had dropped into the RIB, and it was racing away in the direction of Chateaubelair.

Dani waited until Liz and their guests were back in the cockpit, and then she leaned over and started the engine.

"What did they want?" Harry asked.

"Just a routine inspection," Dani said, watching Beverly's face. "It happens. Not often, but it's far from unusual. No big deal."

"Before they chased us away, I heard him ask about contraband," Beverly said. "What was that all about?"

"Oh, they always ask that," Dani said. "Like somebody would be dumb enough to say, 'Oh, yeah, I've got a few drugs -- just for recreational use.' Or a case of automatic weapons." She laughed at her own joke, noticing that Beverly wasn't amused.

"We've actually had some of them tell us that if we have contraband, we should throw it over the side while they look the other way," Liz said. "More than once."

"But we never carry anything illegal," Dani said. "It's not worth the risk; they could confiscate *Vengeance*."

"Really?" Beverly asked. "Even if it was your guests who brought it aboard?"

"Yes," Liz said. "We're careful about that. There are some places here where the local drug dealers tip the police when a tourist buys."

"Why would they do that?" Harry asked. "Sounds like that would be bad for business."

"The police shake down the tourists and split the proceeds with the dealer who turned them in. It's not like tourists are repeat customers. It's kind of a typical island deal. Nobody gets hurt too badly, and maybe the tourist learns a lesson."

"What do you do if your guests bring drugs on the boat?" Beverly asked.

"Given airport security, we assume they're bought locally," Liz said. "That means there's a chance the dealer is working a scam, like we just discussed. We explain that, then we give them a choice; they can toss the drugs, or we'll have to turn them in ourselves. It's only happened a couple of times, and the people got rid of them in a hurry. Nobody wants trouble with the police."

"What would have happened if they *had* found drugs in our luggage?" Beverly asked. "Assuming it wasn't a local dealer that turned us in, that is."

"That depends," Dani said. "Like anywhere else, most of the authorities are honest, but a few aren't. They might have arrested us, or they might have hustled us for a bribe. Or both. Marijuana is a huge cash crop in St. Vincent, so there's more corruption here than most of the islands."

"Well, that whole experience was unnerving," Harry said.

"It's behind us now," Dani said. "No harm, no foul. Forget it and enjoy the rest of the trip."

"Can I get anybody some refreshments?" Liz asked.

"No, thanks," Beverly said. "I'm okay for now. I'm going to take some more pictures."

"I feel a nap coming on," Harry said.

"Let me know if you change your minds," Liz said, sitting down behind the helm next to Dani.

10

Beverly sat on the forward end of the coachroof, her camera in hand. She was glad that Velasquez had opted for a nap; she needed time to think. Reflecting on her conversations with the man called Berto, she speculated on whether she had been too quick to trust him.

Why had he insisted that she have *Vengeance* hug the shoreline of St. Vincent? She wondered about that when she had first read the instructions in the memo he had included with the passports and credit cards. He had suggested that she purchase an expensive camera and take up photography to explain her request.

In the absence of those instructions, she would have let Dani and Liz choose their route. As it was, they had tried to persuade her that the trip would be better farther offshore. As carefully as Berto had arranged everything else, she was sure he had a reason for wanting them close to the St. Vincent shoreline on their way to Bequia, but back then, she couldn't think what it could be.

Could he have set up the boarding by the Coast Guard? He could have, but why would he have done that? She pondered what Dani and Liz had said about marijuana and corruption in St. Vincent. Could those men from the patrol boat have planted drugs? Were they part of some elaborate setup that Berto hadn't told her about? Were they going to be boarded again, and this time, would the Coast Guard find drugs?

She knew Berto had people watching them down here. He'd mentioned that he might send her a text and ask her to invite Dani and Liz to have dinner with her and Velasquez at some point. He told her that wasn't unusual on charters like this one, and that it would give his local people an opportunity to retrieve the recordings and replace the disk with a fresh one.

She wanted to trust Berto; he had treated her well, so far, unlike the other men she'd known. She'd been excited at the prospect of a business relationship with him. That was a flattering idea. It was a first for her -- a man who valued her for something besides sex. Was he playing her? She shook her head. She didn't want to think that.

He trusted her enough to be open about using her to blackmail Velasquez. Why wouldn't he trust her with the knowledge that the blackmail scheme included planting drugs, if that's what was happening? It hadn't occurred to her to question Berto's motive for wanting to frame Velasquez.

She was frustrated with herself; she knew she was smarter than most women in her line of work. Smarter than most of the men she encountered, too. She should have wondered about Berto before.

She had assumed that he wanted leverage over the congressman, perhaps to shape legislation, or secure influence in some other form. Now she wondered if he planned to throw Velasquez under the bus, get him locked up in some hellhole of a third-world prison. She knew her role was to be bait, but now she wondered if she was destined to be roadkill as well. Berto had no reason to sacrifice her, personally, but he might have no qualms about her being caught up in Velasquez's downfall.

She set her jaw. She hadn't survived all she'd been through just to end up like that. As soon as she got a few minutes alone in their stateroom, she'd search it to see if the Coast Guard men had left a surprise. If they had, she was sure it would be in the space that she and Velasquez shared. If her suspicions were correct, any contraband would be linked as closely as possible to Velasquez.

Then she began to wonder about Dani and Liz. Were they in on

Berto's scheme? She needed to get to know them before she could decide, but the surveillance equipment was a problem. She had to find a way to get them off the boat for a little while, so she could talk with them. Shopping, maybe? That could work, and Velasquez wouldn't have any interest in that. Was there shopping in Bequia? She could ask them about that now. It was a safe topic, even with the possibility of the recorder picking up the conversation. She raised the camera and snapped a few pictures.

Satisfied with her plan, she got up and went back to the cockpit.

"WHAT DID YOU SAY?" the leader of the surveillance team asked. He had been half asleep when his cellphone rang. His two subordinates were up in the cockpit with high powered binoculars, ogling women on passing boats.

"I said, there were no drugs on the yacht *Vengeance*."

"That's impossible. I put them there myself, taped to the underside of the drawers in the forward stateroom. Maybe 8 ounces of grass and a few ounces of coke. Your boarding party fucked up."

"I beg your pardon," the man said, his singsong island accent making him sound haughty rather than angry. "I led the boarding party myself. I showed the men the pictures you sent -- two different men checked. One of them held up one of the drawers for me to see. There were remnants of adhesive, but that is all."

"Shit," the leader said. "They must have found them, somehow."

"Perhaps so, but there is nothing that I can do, now."

"Can we arrange another boarding?"

"That would be quite unusual. Berger is a regular in the islands. The yacht is in our waters often."

"What does that have to do with anything? I paid you your asking price."

"And we delivered our end of the deal; I can't manufacture drugs out of thin air, and at this point I dare not plant them during a search."

"Why not?"

"As I said, Berger and Chirac are regulars in the islands. They know how things work. A second boarding by the same crew this soon would be enough to cause them to escalate the situation. They know this doesn't happen. Once? Okay, this is not remarkable. Twice within a few days? That is something quite different."

"Not if you found drugs. I'm sure you could take some with you. St. Vincent is famous for -- "

"Listen to me, sir. I know how these things work here; I've been in the Coast Guard for 15 years. The second boarding would raise eyebrows. If we attempted to plant drugs on the second boarding, it wouldn't be credible. We could have done it on the first boarding, but you chose to do it instead."

"We aren't talking about a case that would hold up in court, man. We want to set them up so that they'll bribe you, remember? I get all the reports."

"One phone call to a higher-up from Berger or Chirac, or one mention to the officer when they were clearing in, and it would be over. I am sorry, but I cannot help you."

"What if *I* plant more drugs?"

"There is still the matter of the second boarding. I cannot help you."

"Look. I paid you $20,000 E.C. So far, you've done nothing to earn it. Help me out here. I get what you're saying, but is there another way?"

"Perhaps. There is a man I know who is responsible for domestic drug enforcement. You understand the distinction between my job and his?"

"You're tasked with interdicting smugglers, and he's responsible for busting local dealers. Is that it?"

"Close enough. The yacht is bound for Bequia. Where are you now?"

"We're in Bequia, on a charter boat in Admiralty Bay."

"Is it possible that you could somehow plant more drugs on *Vengeance*?"

"Yes, I'm sure we could, if they leave her at anchor to go ashore, say for a meal. I think I can do that. What's your idea?"

"I will speak with the man who runs domestic drug enforcement. If he is interested, he could receive an anonymous tip which he could record. That would justify his raiding the yacht. You understand?"

"Yes, I think so. I could maybe pay you a little more."

The Coast Guard man chuckled. "For my assistance?"

"And for him."

"No, I don't think so. I will do this since our plan didn't work, but I do not wish to talk with you again. There is risk. If he is interested, he will call you soon, and you can work something out with him." With that, the man disconnected the call.

The leader of the surveillance team took a moment to organize his thoughts. As much as he didn't want to, he needed to report this problem to his supervisor. At least he had a backup plan to discuss.

VELASQUEZ WAS SPRAWLED on the queen-sized berth in the forward state-room, assessing his chances with Liz Chirac. She was a knockout; both of the women were, for that matter, but Dani Berger was a little too sure of herself. He put her down as probably a ball-buster, better left alone. Liz, though, she was sweet-natured, accommodating.

And besides she had that ginger hair. He was a sucker for gingers. From the texture of her hair, that was her natural color, too. That was important; real gingers didn't have much body hair, and that was a turn-on for him.

Beverly was starting to wear thin. Too much of a good thing, he guessed. She was like having another wife. Always there, willing to do whatever he wanted, predictable. Not as much of a pain in the ass as his wife, but still, she was becoming boring.

He wasn't ready to ditch her; she was the perfect mistress. He liked the setup they had; she wasn't even a financial burden like some of her predecessors had been. With her trust fund, or whatever, all he had to do was pick up the tab for a few gifts and meals.

And she was discreet. He definitely didn't want to screw that up, not with the party's increasing demands on his time. Maybe in the run-up to the primary, he'd have to cut her loose, but until then, he'd hang on to her.

Liz, though, she was something different. A little treat for all the hard work he'd done over the last few weeks. Like going off his diet every so often. He knew it couldn't last, didn't even want it to last, not really. A big part of it was the challenge, the thrill of the chase. She'd probably put up a little resistance; they all did, except the pros, and he avoided them. They were too risky for a career politician.

Speaking of his career, that might make Liz a little more of a challenge; she didn't know who he was. He liked that idea. If you were *somebody*, women would let you do anything you wanted. It was almost too easy, like with Beverly. But Liz didn't have any idea how powerful he was. He'd have to rely on his native charm with her. He chuckled. That made him feel younger; it was like turning back the clock to when he was just starting out, before he became *somebody*.

There were some tactical issues, though. First, there was timing. After today, he'd only have six days to score. Then there was Dani. She and Liz seemed to be pretty tight. He'd wondered for a moment when he'd first met them if they were partners in a broader sense, but after watching them, he didn't think so.

Dani projected a kind of tough-chick image, but not like that. She could be fun, too, probably. A girl like that could be a real kick, if you had the time to work with her, which he didn't. Besides, Liz was just more to his taste. A sweet girl, eager to please. He shook his head, hard, snapping his focus back to the task at hand. He couldn't let himself get distracted. He wanted to work through this while he had a little time alone to think.

"Let's see," he thought, making notes on a mental image of a chalkboard. "Timing -- six days. Berger -- get her out of the way," at least long enough to score. After the first time, Liz would no doubt help with that. And then there was good old Beverly. He had a fleeting thought of a threesome. That could work; he was pretty sure he could count on Beverly. Liz, though ... maybe, but he'd need to feel her out a little before he could broach that topic with her.

Then it hit him. He needed to figure out how to use Beverly to get Dani out of the way and leave him alone with Liz. He smiled. He'd work on that. Maybe he could plant a seed with Dani about taking Beverly snorkeling, or hiking. She liked both of those things, and Dani seemed like the type to do that. He'd watch for an opportunity, now that he had a plan.

11

"I see," Montalba said. He was livid, but he kept the anger out of his voice.

"These things happen, sometimes," the man on the phone said, "but our field manager has a backup plan."

"And what is that?"

"He will plant more drugs, and he has arranged for a raid by St. Vincent's drug enforcement squad. The plan is intact; it's just delayed by 24 hours."

"And how will he plant the drugs," Montalba asked, "with four people on the yacht?"

"I believe you said you could communicate with Beverly Lennox," the man on the phone said.

"I can send her a text message," Montalba said.

"You could have her take everyone to dinner this evening. There are some fine restaurants in Bequia. Our men will be watching the yacht. They'll plant more drugs while the people are ashore."

"Very well. I should send that text now. I'll be back in touch when I have confirmation from Ms. Lennox." Montalba disconnected the call and sent the text.

Checking the time, he decided it was too late for coffee and too early for wine. He swiveled his chair and put his feet on his desk. The drug bust wasn't essential; the recordings would be sufficient to control Velasquez. He wanted more, though. He wanted something to hold over Berger and Chirac.

They were close to Connie Barrera. Montalba didn't quite consider Barrera his nemesis yet, but she was a potential threat. Since his last run-in with Barrera, he had gathered a great deal of data. He now knew that Barrera and her husband shared a number of friends with the two women who owned *Vengeance*.

His latest information reinforced the rumor that Barrera ran a new cartel. She was working to control the movement of illegal drugs and other contraband through the Caribbean into the U.S. She had not yet caused him a problem, but he wanted to be prepared in case she did. Berger and Chirac were part of the same organization.

When he had discovered that their yacht was stored in Miami Beach while they were on holiday, he'd recognized an opportunity. He could compromise Velasquez and gain some intelligence about Berger and Chirac at the same time. As it developed, he would also have the ability to eavesdrop on them after he had finished with Velasquez.

Beverly was making her way back to the cockpit when she felt her phone vibrate. Her hands full between holding on to the boat and carrying the camera, she sat down on the side of the coachroof and slipped the phone from her pocket. She had a text from Berto, asking her to get everyone off the yacht this evening, and to let him know how long it would be unattended.

Putting the phone back in her pocket, she continued working her way to the cockpit. Dani and Liz scampered around the deck like there was nothing to it, but the slight movements of the boat disoriented her, causing her to stumble if she didn't hold on.

Berto had warned her in his instructions that her cell phone might not work at sea, but that it should function normally within a mile or two of shore. Maybe that was why he'd told her to have them hug the shoreline.

"Did you get some good shots?" Liz asked, as Beverly sat down in the cockpit.

"I hope so. It's amazing how green the hillsides are, and even from here, they smell lush and rich. I'm not sure photographs can do them justice."

"I know what you mean," Liz said. "I've been trying for years to capture that on canvas, and I haven't managed it yet."

"On canvas," Beverly said. "You're an artist?"

"It's a hobby," Liz said. "I try."

"She's being modest," Dani said. "She's quite good, actually."

"I'd love to see some of your work," Beverly said.

"Most of the paintings on the bulkheads below are hers," Dani said.

"Oh, I'm impressed! At first glance, I thought some of those were photographs with artistic filters. Except that one, the impressionist sunset. I like it, but it's so different from the others. You're really versatile."

Liz laughed. "Thanks, but I'm not that versatile. I didn't paint that one; a friend of ours did that."

"Well, she's talented, too," Beverly said.

She saw Dani and Liz trade looks, and Dani burst out laughing.

"Did I say something?" Beverly asked, frowning.

"No," Dani said. "It's just ... " She was overcome by another fit of laughter.

"Forgive her, Beverly," Liz said. "It's just that it was painted by a man. You'd have to see him to understand why she's so tickled."

"I take it he must not be a typical artist, whatever that is."

"That's for sure," Dani said. "Sorry, Beverly. Maybe we can find a picture of him. Then you'd understand."

"He's a Rasta man from Dominica," Liz said. "A literal giant, and very unassuming. He doesn't want anybody to know he paints; he's afraid his friends will think he's a sissy."

"How did you come to be friends? Through your art?"

"Not exactly," Liz said. "Dani has some deep roots in the islands. Her father's from Martinique, and she spent a lot of time down here as a child."

"Martinique? That's a French island, right?"

"Yes," Dani said. "It's actually part of France, what's known as a *département*."

"But I thought you were American."

"I am. My mother's from the U.S. I was born in New York, but I have dual citizenship."

"Do your parents live in New York?"

"My mother does. She and my father split up not long after I was born."

"I see. Does he live in Martinique, then? Is that why you're so familiar with the islands?"

"He used to," Dani said. "But he lives in Paris now. When I was growing up, he was doing a lot of business down here, and my mother was too busy to raise a child, so I ended up getting shuffled around to different friends and relatives down here."

"That can be hard for a child," Beverly said. "I had that kind of child-hood myself. I never felt like I had a home, really. I didn't know any better when I was little, but as I got older, I began to see how other kids lived. I envied them. You probably know what I mean."

"I understand what you're saying," Dani said, "but it wasn't like that for me. Things are different down here, from a cultural standpoint. I felt like I was at home wherever I was; everyone made me welcome. I felt sorry for the girls I went to school with in New England. Their lives seemed boring to me."

"You went to school in New England?"

"For a while. A private girls' school; my mother insisted on that. But I spent all my summers and vacations down here."

"That must have been some contrast," Beverly said.

Dani smiled. "Yes."

"How did you and Harry meet?" Liz asked. She saw that Dani's smile was forced and sensed her irritation with all the questions.

"Through mutual friends," Beverly said.

"In Miami?" Liz asked.

"Right," Beverly said.

"I always enjoy visiting Miami," Liz said. "It's so different from the rest of the U.S."

"It is that," Beverly said.

"Are you from there originally?" Liz asked.

"No. We moved there when I was in my early teens."

"I'll bet it was a fun place to be a teenager."

"There were a lot of distractions," Beverly said.

"I can imagine," Liz said, grinning. "What do you do there, if you don't mind my asking."

"I'm in the entertainment business."

"How exciting!" Liz said. "Are you some kind of star? Should I recognize you?"

Beverly smiled. "I'm nobody special, nobody you've ever heard of. I'm one of those anonymous people who manages to eke out a living among the rich and famous by doing all the boring stuff they don't want to be bothered with. I'm an odd jobs kind of gal, freelancing. It's pretty much hand to mouth, but I survive. It beats having a real job, I guess."

"You must have had some interesting experiences," Liz said.

"I suppose, but to me it's just work, and I can't really talk about it too much, or I'll be out of business. Discretion is a big part of what I offer my clients."

Liz nodded. "I didn't mean to pry. I'm just always interested in our guests; everybody has a story."

"I'm sure," Beverly said. "Hey, I've read that there are some really fine restaurants in Bequia."

"There certainly are," Liz said.

"I'd like it if you ladies could join us for dinner ashore tonight, my treat."

"That's very nice of you," Liz said. "What do you think, Dani? Are we going to get there early enough?"

Dani studied the screen of the chart plotter above the steering pedestal, tapping two of the buttons. She frowned and shook her head. "It's going to be too late to clear in. That little interruption by the Coast Guard cost us over an hour on our ETA."

"It only seemed like a few minutes," Beverly said.

"The problem is that the tide turned while they were aboard," Dani said. "We were at a sort of critical spot. We're going to carry a foul current the rest of the way to Bequia, as best I can tell."

"Wow. There's more to this than I thought," Beverly said.

"Tidal currents can be tricky," Dani said. "Especially close inshore on the leeward side of one of these big islands. There are some funny eddy currents that vary from day to day depending on the wind."

"But there's hardly any wind," Beverly said.

"In here behind the island, there's not," Liz said. "But it's blowing at 15 to 20 knots in the open water. It's from an easterly direction, and that creates a wind-driven current that wraps around both ends of the island. It can add to or subtract from the tidal current. It can make a big difference in boat speed. What are you seeing, Dani?"

"Speed through the water's nine and a half knots, but our speed over the ground's down in the sevens."

"That means there's about a two-knot current holding us back," Liz said. "Thanks for the invitation, but I guess we'll be stuck with my cooking again this evening."

"I'd hardly call it being 'stuck,' Liz," Beverly said. "I can't imagine we'd get a better meal ashore than what you can prepare. I was just enjoying talking with you, and I thought it would be fun. Maybe tomorrow night?"

"Sure," Liz said. "That will be great, but does that mean you want to stay in Bequia for a while?"

"Oh, I think so. From reading that cruising guide in our cabin, it sounds like there's plenty to do there for a couple of days."

"There is. There's a nice beach and a couple of great reefs to snorkel, if you're interested," Dani said.

"Good. Then that's what we'll do," Beverly said. "I'd better go wake up Harry, or he won't be able to sleep tonight."

"THERE'S a problem with your plan for tonight," the surveillance team leader's boss told him, when he answered his encrypted satellite phone.

"Shit! What's the problem? I busted my ass to put it together on short notice."

"Timing," his boss said. "The client heard back from his inside source. Tonight won't work."

"Inside source? You mean that woman that's screwing the mark?"

"Spare me the smartass remarks. Your fuck-up with the wasted boarding delayed their arrival to the point where they'll get in too late to go ashore for dinner."

"Then what does the client want us to do? For all I know, they're going somewhere else tomorrow. I don't know when we'll get another shot like this. I got the local cops lined up to act on my 'anonymous' tip, see. It's tough to put shit like that together."

"You're in luck. They aren't going anywhere tomorrow. Their plan is sightseeing in Bequia, and dinner ashore tomorrow night. Make it happen."

"Okay, but it may cost us. The drug squad guy is greedy; he already hit me up for more than I paid the Coast Guard. He may up the ante even more if I reschedule."

"Quit bitching and get it done. The money doesn't matter; the client's paying for it, and he doesn't give a damn about the cost. It's pocket change to him. And don't mess it up; I hear he's plenty pissed off already."

"Yeah? Tough shit."

"You having a bad day? You don't usually piss and moan so much, man. Shit happens. Suck it up and move on."

"Yeah, I will. Next time though, I'm picking my own team."

"You got personnel problems?"

"You might say that. These two are dimwits."

"I don't know but I've been told; airborne is as good as gold," the boss chanted in a mocking voice. Then he laughed.

"Two things fall from the sky," the surveillance team leader said. "Rain, and birdshit. These two are definitely not rain."

"Whip 'em into shape then, swab jockey," his boss said.

"Semper Fi, asshole. Let me go. I gotta get ahold of this cop."

"Do it. Keep me posted if anything changes."

"Yeah, okay. Hey?"

"Hey, what?"

"Since we're going in anyway, should we swap out the disk drive?"

"Well, let's see. It's been what? One day? You think there's enough on it to make it worthwhile?"

"Hard to know. It'll be 48 hours, plus, by the time we pick it up.

There might be some action on there. Like I said, we're going in anyway, so it'll only take a minute. If the client's pissed, maybe giving him a little something extra could sweeten him up."

"You're pretty smart for a fuckin' sailor," his boss said.

"I'm surprised a jarhead knows what smart looks like."

"They sent me to a special school," his boss said. "Yeah, sure swap it out and let's see what we got. You're right; it might help make up for the screw-up on the boarding."

"Good. Gotta make that phone call. I'll let you know when it's all nailed down."

"Roger that," the boss said, disconnecting.

12

"It's a relief to be able to have a normal conversation," Liz said, as she and Dani left the customs and immigration office in Bequia.

"It certainly is," Dani said. "I'm glad she wanted to stay on the boat and relax instead of coming with us."

"I guess they aren't feeling time pressure," Liz said. "I'm happy enough that they wanted to stay here an extra day. This business of having to mind what we say to one another in our own cabin is stressful."

"Yes. We've got a little time to ourselves; let's walk and talk. I told them the snorkeling would be better in the late morning, and that you could have a light lunch ready for us when we got back. Are you okay with that?"

"Sure," Liz said. "Do you think we can delay going back long enough for the Rasta market to open? I could pick up a papaya and some limes to round out my seafood salad."

"Oh, I think so. They seemed to want time alone, anyway. Let's go have coffee with Mrs. Walker." Dani led them onto the pedestrian walkway along the waterfront, heading toward Mrs. Walker's restaurant. "It's been too long since I've seen her."

"After meeting your mother, I have a new appreciation for why you're so close to Mrs. Walker," Liz said. "I know she took care of you when your father was busy, but I always wondered about the bond you have with her. Now I think I understand."

"She was more of a mother than my mother was, that's for sure. While we've got some privacy, though, let's talk about Beverly and the boarding yesterday."

"You think she had something to do with that?" Liz asked. "Because she wanted to hug the coast?"

"Not just that," Dani said. "It was a setup. I've been going crazy because I couldn't tell you."

"Tell me what?"

"The man in charge had pictures of the stash in his cellphone. I caught a glimpse of them when he was showing them to one of his men."

Liz stopped in mid-stride, putting a hand on Dani's arm. "Are you sure?"

"Yes."

"How could you not tell me?"

"It wasn't easy, but I knew we were going to need to talk it over. There was no way we could do that aboard the boat with them and the surveillance system."

"That puts things in a different light," Liz said. "She almost surely knew about it, don't you think?"

"It seems that way to me," Dani said. "It explains her wanting us to hug the shoreline."

"You don't believe her photography was the reason?"

"I don't know," Dani said, "but as long as we're stopped, let's call Luke. He's had time to get those prints; maybe he'll know who these people are by now."

"Wasn't he going to call you?"

"I guess you missed that when we were with Phillip and Sandrine. After Cedric called Phillip, Phillip called Luke back and told him about the surveillance."

"I did miss that. Phillip must have told you that when Sandrine and I were in the kitchen, or something."

"I guess. I'm sorry I didn't mention it. This notion that *Vengeance* is bugged is taking a toll on me."

"Me, too," Liz said. "Phillip told Luke about it?"

"Yes. They thought it would be safer for us to call Luke, rather than the other way around."

"That's sensible," Liz said.

Dani sat down on a bench overlooking the anchorage and took her cellphone out of her pocket. Liz took the seat next to her as she placed the call.

"Luke?" Dani asked, when he answered. She held the phone between her head and Liz's, so that Liz could hear. She had the speaker on, but with the volume turned down for privacy.

"Yes. Dani?"

"And Liz," Dani added. "Good morning. We're where we can talk. Are you?"

"Sure, and I'm glad you called; I've been going nuts since I ran those prints."

"You found something?" Dani asked.

"Nothing on the woman; she's not in the system. But -- get this -- Starnes is none other than U.S. Representative Horatio Velasquez. Ring a bell?"

"Not for me," Dani said. "But I see why he's using a fake i.d., now. I'm guessing he's married?"

"Bingo," Luke said. "Married, with an infant son and a pregnant wife. And not just that. He's making noises like he wants to run for President next time."

"Do you think somebody's planning to stop him?" Liz said.

"Or hold this over him after he's elected," Luke said. "Or maybe they want to lock in his vote in Congress. I don't know. But we're just guessing. It explains why somebody set him up, though."

"I think this Beverly Lennox is part of it," Dani said.

"She might be, or she might just be inadvertently caught up in it," Luke said.

"I don't think so," Dani said. "Listen to this." She told him about Beverly's request to hug the St. Vincent shoreline, and the Coast Guard boarding.

"It's suspicious, but not conclusive," Luke said.

Dani frowned.

"Tell him about the pictures," Liz said. "You forgot that."

Dani repeated her story of seeing the pictures of the stash on the boarding officer's cellphone.

"Hmm," Luke said. "That confirms that somebody set this up, and it makes her look more suspicious, for sure. Lucky for you that Sandrine's people found the drugs. I'm going to dig a little deeper into this Lennox woman. I'll check out the long-term-stay place; see if she left any trail there. Stay in touch, and be careful."

"Okay, Luke. Thanks. Don't call us; we'll call you."

"Okay," Luke said, and disconnected.

"Let's go see Mrs. Walker," Dani said, standing up and putting the phone back in her pocket.

~

"HA!" Sharktooth said, when Dani and Liz entered Mrs. Walker's restaurant. "I tol' you they would show up." He sat at a table with the slender, elegant woman, a large plate of ham and eggs in front of him.

She smiled, the dark, smooth skin of her face crinkling with pleasure. "Come in, Dani, Liz. Will you have breakfast with Sharktooth?"

"No, thanks," Dani said, leaning over the table to hug the old lady. "We've already eaten. You don't look any different; how do you do it?"

"I decided years ago that I was old enough," Mrs. Walker said. "So, I just don't get older. There's not much to it, really."

"What are you doing here?" Liz asked Sharktooth. "We were just telling one of our guests about you yesterday."

"Huh? 'Bout me?" Sharktooth's brow wrinkled into a frown. "What about me?"

"She was admiring that painting of the sunset from Prince Rupert Bay," Liz said.

"Oh," Sharktooth said.

"Well?" Dani asked, looking him in the eye.

"Well, what?" he asked.

"What brings you to Bequia?"

"Business," he said. "I had to see a man in Kingstown 'bout some t'ings yesterday, so I come to visit. I hear you hidin' drugs on *Vengeance*."

"You've been talking to Phillip, or Sandrine," Liz said.

"Mm-hmm. Phillip call me jus' now. So we know you be here."

"Wait a second," Dani said. "Phillip knew we were here?"

"Mm-hmm." Sharktooth smiled, enjoying her confusion.

"Tell her, you big rascal," Mrs. Walker said. "You're being a bad boy."

"Yes'm," he said, looking contrite. "Luke Pantene called Phillip right after he talked to you. Phillip knew I was down here, so he thought maybe he'd catch me in time."

"In time for what?" Liz asked.

"For me to meet you at the customs office. He didn't know you'd already cleared in when you called Luke."

"So why are you here, eating breakfast, instead of waiting for us at the customs office?"

"Already, I am here to order breakfas', when Phillip calls. So I call the customs office an' my frien' there tell me you already been there. So, I t'ink I may as well eat my food. If you don' come here, then I go find you."

"Then you know we were boarded yesterday, and who the guests are, and everything?" Dani asked.

"Mm-hmm. Where your guests now?"

"On *Vengeance*," Dani said. "Why?"

"Curious, tha's all."

"Sit down, girls," Mrs. Walker said, rising from her chair. "I'll get you some coffee."

Dani and Liz pulled out chairs and joined Sharktooth at the table while Mrs. Walker went back to the kitchen.

"How long will you be here?" Dani asked.

He shrugged, chewing a mouthful of eggs. He swallowed and said, "No special plans. Why?"

"Are you on *Lightning Bolt*?" Dani asked.

"Mm-hmm." He loaded more of the eggs on his fork, pausing before he lifted it to his mouth. "Why you ask?"

"If it's not too inconvenient, we could use a little help," Dani said.

Liz frowned and started to speak, but stopped when Mrs. Walker returned with a carafe of coffee and two mugs. She poured for Dani and Liz, and refreshed Sharktooth's cup before she sat down.

"Did Phillip tell you that we think the woman is orchestrating whatever this is?" Dani asked.

"Yes," Sharktooth said, setting the forkful of eggs down on his plate and taking a sip of the fresh coffee. "He said you thought she wanted you to stay in close so the Coast Guard could board you yesterday. Tha's what you mean?"

"Yes," Dani said. "And did he tell you that the boarding officer had pictures of the drug stash in his cell phone?"

"Mm-hmm. Setup. No question 'bout it."

"After the boarding, I saw her sending a text on her phone," Dani said.

"I saw that," Liz said. "When she was coming back to the cockpit, while Harry was taking a nap, right?"

"Right," Dani said.

"I meant to mention it when we were talking a few minutes ago, and it slipped my mind. I was watching her when she was making her way along the side deck. I think she actually stopped and sat down on the coachroof because she got an incoming text. I saw her pause and put her hand over her pocket the way you do when your phone vibrates. Then she sat down and took the phone out of her pocket and fiddled with it for a few seconds before she came back and started talking with us."

"That's when she gave me the third degree," Dani said.

"That was hardly the third degree, Dani," Liz said, "but I could sense your irritation. That's why I changed the subject."

"I felt like I was being interrogated, anyway," Dani said.

"I know, so I asked her a few questions. I thought she was a little evasive."

"Yes. So did I. And then she invited us to dinner ashore."

"Last night?" Sharktooth asked. "I heard you got in after customs closed."

"We did," Liz said. "The dinner invitation is for tonight. And I saw her sending another text after we agreed."

"I knew it," Dani said. "That's almost got to be another setup. I was suspicious before you mentioned the texts, but now I'd bet on it."

"Where are you going with all this, Dani? You've lost me," Mrs. Walker said.

"Mm-hmm. Me, too," Sharktooth said.

"I think she and whoever she's working with wanted everybody off the boat," Dani said. "They either want to plant more drugs, or check on their surveillance equipment, or something."

"Ah!" Sharktooth said. "You want me to watch *Vengeance* while you all go to dinner."

"Will you?" Dani asked.

"Mm-hmm," Sharktooth said, lifting the forkful of eggs from his plate and shoveling them in his mouth. "My pleasure."

LIZ WAS STEAMING seafood for their lunch when Harry came down the companionway ladder.

"Feeling better?" she asked.

Harry had opted to stay aboard *Vengeance* rather than joining Dani and Beverly on their snorkeling expedition. He had complained of nausea, and had been sitting in the cockpit. He smiled at Liz and stepped into the cramped galley with her.

"I'm fine," he said. "I just didn't want to go snorkeling. I thought it might be more fun for us to get to know one another."

"Us?" Liz said.

"Yeah. You and me."

When she didn't respond, he put a hand on her shoulder and moved up close behind her.

"Don't," she said. "You'll make me burn myself."

"Sorry," he said, his hand sliding down her arm. He took a half-step back. "Hot work for a hot lady."

"I'm used to it," she said. "If the steam is making you uncomfortable, maybe you should go back up on deck."

"It's you," he said.

"Sorry?" she said, turning toward him and stepping out of the narrow galley. She backed away, putting more space between them. "What do you mean by that?"

"I mean you're hot. I couldn't help but noticing. And I've got this thing for redheads."

"I thought you had a *thing* for Beverly."

He grinned. "Yeah, well, what can I say? She wanted to come down here, and I didn't want to disappoint her, you know?"

"Then don't," Liz said, keeping her voice even.

"Aw, you don't have to be that way. She's open-minded."

"Is she?" Liz said. "You don't want to ruin her dream trip for her."

"She'll understand. I feel like that guy in the story, you know?"

"I'm afraid I don't," she said.

"Like I brought a ham sandwich to a steak dinner." He laughed.

"Look, Harry. I like Beverly; that's not a nice thing for you to say. It makes me feel uncomfortable."

"We could just give it a little try, Liz. See how it goes. If we get on all right, maybe she'd even join us. Would that make you feel better about it, knowing she was in on it?"

"No, Harry. I'm sorry. Beverly may be open to that kind of thing, but I'm not, okay?"

"Okay. That's cool, Liz. We'll just keep it between the two of us, if that suits you better."

"The two of you sounds better," she said. "Let's just pretend we didn't have this conversation, okay? No harm, no foul? Isn't that the saying you Americans use?"

"Don't pretend to misunderstand me. When I said between the two of us, you know I meant between you and me, Liz. Now come on. Dani and Beverly are gonna be gone for a while yet. He moved closer, putting a hand on her shoulder. "You know you want to, babe. Let's just do it. It'll be great, I promise. I won't do anything you don't like. You call the shots, okay, beautiful?"

"You really mean that?"

"Sure, I do. Try me."

"Take your hand off my shoulder; I don't like your touching me."

"Aw, you're just playing hard to get. Let yourself go."

"Harry, listen to me. It's not going to happen. You're a handsome man, but I find your behavior repulsive. Dani and I run a professional business here, not a floating brothel. If that won't suit you, we'll

refund your money and you can both leave as soon as Beverly
gets back."

She tried to back away, and he raised his other hand, now holding
both of her shoulders. She whipped her right arm up and across his left
forearm, gripping his right wrist in her right hand. She twisted from her
hips and drove her left hand into the back of his right arm, twisting his
wrist with her right hand.

He stumbled forward, trying to get away, and she increased the pressure on his arm until he cried out.

"You're hurting me," he said.

"It's not an accident," she said. "I told you I didn't like to be touched.
You believe me now?" She cranked his right arm up behind his back.

"Yeah, I get it."

"Good," she said. "I'm going to let you go, and you're going to resume
behaving like a gentleman."

"And if I don't?"

"Don't go there. Believe me, I don't want to hurt you or your wife."
She released her grip and shoved him away.

"Beverly's not my wife," he said.

"Somehow, I knew that. I wasn't talking about Beverly. She's here by
choice, maybe, but I'll bet your wife thinks you're somewhere else. If
you go home with a broken arm, it might be tough to explain, so behave
yourself."

"Okay, okay. Lighten up. You can't blame a fella for asking." He shook
his arm, rubbing the muscles she'd stretched.

"But I can blame a fellow who won't take no for an answer. Now, go
back up on deck and chill out. I need to finish our lunch before Beverly
and Dani come back."

13

"I'm glad they wanted to do an island tour," Dani said. She and Liz had dropped their guests off at the taxi stand near the dinghy dock and helped them arrange an excursion to see Bequia. "She's okay, except for asking a lot of questions, but there's something creepy about Harry. Or maybe it's just me."

"It's not just you," Liz said. "He's a creep, all right. He hit on me while you two were off snorkeling before lunch."

"He did?" Dani asked, eyebrows rising. "How did you deal with that?"

"I tried to talk my way out of it," Liz said, "but he wasn't taking no for an answer."

"What happened?"

"You would have been proud of me. When he wouldn't stop touching me, I put him in a bar hammerlock and offered to break his arm."

"Atta girl!" Dani said, grinning and raising her right hand, palm out. Liz chuckled and high-fived her.

"He really is a jerk, then," Dani said.

"But we already knew that," Liz said.

"Yes, but he's a worse jerk for ignoring your protests."

"I don't know," Liz said. "I thought he was as bad as they came, leaving a pregnant wife and a child to come play in the islands with a ...

well, whatever she is. I wasn't too surprised when he decided to try his luck with me."

Dani frowned. "It's strange, but I like her, even knowing she's up to no good. Why is that, do you suppose?"

"I feel the same way about her," Liz said. "I think it's because she doesn't present herself as being anything other than what she is."

"A hooker, you think?" Dani asked.

"That conjures up an image that's at odds with the way she behaves," Liz said. "Hooker, escort -- terms like that have some connotations that just don't fit her. She's reserved and pleasant, and she comes across as thoughtful and smart. I can't figure out what she sees in him. He's scuzzy. I was pretty sure he was going to make a play for one of us before the cruise was over."

"Better you than me," Dani said. "I wouldn't have had your restraint, I'm afraid. That would have been the end of the charter, right there."

"I offered that," Liz said, "before it got physical, but he had his mind on something else."

"She booked this, though. I wonder how she would have reacted if he'd taken you up on canceling?"

"I thought about that before I offered to refund their money and terminate the charter."

"And what did you decide?"

"That he wouldn't take me up on it. He was too determined to have me. But I had to make the offer."

"I'm glad he didn't," Dani said.

"Glad he didn't what?" Liz said. "Try to rape me?"

"No. We both know how that would have come out. I'm glad he didn't take you up on your offer to end the charter."

Liz scrunched her brow up and shook her head. "I don't understand."

"It would have set us back too far," Dani said.

"Set us back? " Liz asked. "We don't need the business that badly. A one-week charter's no big deal."

"Oh, it's not that," Dani said. "I want to get to the bottom of this, and I think we can learn something from playing out the rest of their week."

"Get to the bottom of what?"

"Whatever's going on here. Somebody stole our boat and wired it for sound and video."

"But we've got a pretty good idea that somebody's setting him up for blackmail," Liz said.

"Yes. No question," Dani said. "But that doesn't explain 'why *Vengeance*.' There's something else going on besides the blackmail plot."

Liz didn't respond for several seconds. "What could it be?" she asked.

Dani shrugged and shook her head.

"Do you think somehow we're a target, too? For surveillance?"

"That's all I can come up with so far," Dani said.

"But why us? What could anybody learn by eavesdropping on us?"

"If we knew that, it would go a long way toward letting us figure out who it is."

"But we already have a good idea why they want to blackmail Harry, or whatever his real name is," Liz said.

"We may be wrong," Dani said.

"Now I'm lost, Dani. What are you thinking?"

"We leapt to the conclusion that the charter guests were the target of the surveillance, and then we found out he was a congressman and it seemed even more likely, right?"

"Yes. And then she led us into that ambush by the St. Vincent Coast Guard; they knew about the drugs."

"Maybe," Dani said.

"Maybe? But you saw the pictures of the stash on his phone."

"Oh, the Coast Guard knew about the drugs, all right. My 'maybe' was about her leading us into it."

"Well, she did," Liz said. "We wouldn't have been there except for her."

"But they could have intercepted us farther offshore, Liz. I keep thinking that the drugs would have been overkill if all they wanted to do was blackmail the congressman. With the recordings, he's dead meat. They didn't need a drug bust."

"You think *we* were the target of that?" Liz asked.

"Maybe."

"But what about the idea that she asked us out to dinner so somebody could have access to the boat?" Liz asked.

"We'll know more after tonight," Dani said. "If somebody tries to sneak aboard, then we'll be pretty sure she's part of the setup. Plus, Sharktooth may be able to learn something from them."

"And if she is?" Liz asked.

"One step at a time," Dani said. "Maybe Luke will find out more about her."

"What should we do with the rest of the afternoon?" Liz asked, after a moment.

"I don't know, but I don't want to go back to the boat. I can't stand the idea that we can't talk openly in our own home."

"Me, either," Liz said. "Let's take a walk up to the old battery above the Devil's Table. I could use the exercise."

"THEY JUST PILED in their dinghy again and headed for town. They gotta be going to dinner, this late." The small man peered out a porthole on the little chartered sloop. "Want me to head over there and do it?"

"No," the team leader said. "That's the kind of thing I'm trained for. Besides, I need to figure out the best place to put the package."

He unzipped his duffle bag and took out a black Lycra dive skin. As he pulled it on over his tank suit, the larger of the two men rummaged in a locker and came out with a sealed plastic bag. He held it, waiting until his boss had zipped himself into the suit.

"Why you wearin' that?" he asked. "Scared you'll get bit by one of them jellyfish or somethin'?"

Taking the package and tucking it into his dive skin, the leader pulled the zipper all the way up. "No. Makes me harder to see. White skin catches the light."

"Huh," the big man said. "What about your face, then?"

The man in the Lycra suit grinned and reached in his duffle bag again, coming up with a stick of black grease-paint, which he began to smear on his exposed skin.

"I see," the big man said.

"You boys behave yourselves. I won't be long," the leader said, as he climbed up into the cockpit, keeping low to avoid silhouetting himself in the lights from town. His two minions watched as he slithered under the lower lifeline and lowered himself into the water without rippling the surface. He ducked his head underwater and disappeared.

When he judged that he'd covered about half the distance to *Vengeance*, he drifted up, letting his head break the surface. He pirouetted in the water, checking the horizon. Finding nothing to worry about, he took a deep breath and sunk into the water again.

He stayed under until he was beneath *Vengeance*. Putting one hand on the bottom of the boat, he worked his way to the boarding ladder that was hanging amidships. He surfaced with one hand on the lowest step and looked around for several seconds, listening, studying the play of light and shadow on the water's surface.

Satisfied that he was unobserved, he held on and pulled the zipper of his suit down far enough so that he could take the sealed bag out. Besides the drugs that he would plant, there was a super-absorbent microfiber towel in the bag. He would use that to dry himself off at the top of the ladder before he went aboard. It wouldn't do to leave a trail of wet footprints on the deck.

As he reached for the next higher step, he sensed motion in the water around his legs. Then there was an explosion of bright light in his head and he felt himself sliding back into the water.

SHARKTOOTH WRAPPED a big arm over the unconscious man's shoulder, grabbing him around his chest. He put a foot against *Vengeance's* underbody and pushed off, pulling his victim against the side of his chest, keeping the man's face out of the water. In less than two minutes, he rolled the still-unconscious man onto the swim platform of *Lightning Bolt*, the go-fast boat that he used for rapid travel between the islands.

Hoisting his bulk out of the water, he grabbed a handful of Lycra and dragged the man to the transom. With no apparent effort, he scooped the man up in his arms and stepped over the transom and into the cockpit of the 50-foot, heavily modified Cigarette boat.

He took a moment to tie the man's wrists and ankles before he started the engines. The three 600-horsepower engines were barely audible with the water-cooled exhaust system in use. When he valued speed over stealth, Sharktooth could open the exhausts and cruise at well over a hundred knots, but tonight, he wanted to attract as little attention as he could.

He retrieved the anchor and idled out of the harbor, heading west. Once he was out of earshot of the harbor, he pushed the throttles forward, running at an almost silent 60 knots until he was out of sight of land. He cut the power and let the unlighted boat drift.

Opening a locker, he took out a bucket and dunked it over the side, filling it with seawater. He turned and poured it over the man's face, watching as he gagged and coughed. He writhed on deck, trying to avoid the stream of water.

"You have a good nap?" Sharktooth asked, as the man blinked and shook his head.

"Who the fuck are you?"

"You be nice," Sharktooth said. "I'm the las' mon you ever gon' see. No need to be vexed."

"What do you want?"

"Tha's bettah. You jus' need to answer a few questions befo' you die in peace."

"WHERE THE HELL do you reckon he is?" the small man asked his companion. They were playing cards in the main cabin of the 32-foot charter boat, waiting for their leader to return from planting the drugs on *Vengeance*.

The big man shrugged. "Beats the hell outta me. I don't much give a shit, either. Maybe he drowned."

"He's a SEAL, man. He wouldn't drown swimmin' no farther than that. It ain't over a hunnerd yards. Shit, I could swim that with my hands tied behind me. Somethin's wrong. You think he done set us up or somethin'?"

"What the hell are you talkin' about? Set us up how?"

"I don't know, but he shoulda -- " he was interrupted by a loud thump from up on deck.

"I bet that's him," the little man said, mounting the companionway ladder.

He was back in thirty seconds, a bloody package in his hand.

"Whatcha got there," the big man asked.

"I don't know," the small one said, beginning to unwrap it. "This is a piece of that fuckin' wetsuit thing he was wearin', but it looks like he done bled all over it."

"That weren't no wetsuit. Wetsuits is made out of rubber, you dumb-ass. Lemme see that." The big man snatched the package and flicked open a folding combat knife. Slicing away the Lycra, he muttered, "I'll be a son of a bitch."

"What?" the little one asked, crowding in to get a look. "It's the damn drugs."

"You sure?" the larger man asked.

"Hell, yeah! I wrapped 'em in that there plastic my own self."

"What the hell could this mean? You think somebody took him out?"

"Wouldn't bother me none. He's a dickhead. But why would they throw the drugs on our boat?"

"Did you see anybody when you went up and got the package?" the big man asked.

"Uh-uh. Nobody, no boats moving around, nothin'."

"Somebody musta swam up and throwed it on the deck, then," the big man said. "I think maybe we better call in. What do you think?"

"Yeah, probably so. You gonna do it?"

"You got seniority," the big man said. "It's your job, asshole. Comes with the territory when you're second in command. What's the matter? You scared they'll fire your ass or somethin'?"

"Reckon that's about the worst could happen, ain't it."

"Yep. We ain't in the army no more. There ain't much they can do to us, is there?"

"Gimme the sat phone," the little one said. "May as well get it done." He scrolled through the directory and placed the call. It was no sooner answered than a siren blared outside their open porthole. He set the phone on the saloon table and stood up to look out, ignoring the man's voice that came from the phone.

As soon as the siren went silent, a voice blared over a loud hailer, "St.

Vincent Marine Police. Everybody aboard *Sosueme* on deck, now, with your hands in the air."

"*Sosueme*," the little one said. "That's us, ain't it?" He looked over his shoulder when the big man didn't answer and saw that he was already through the companionway, his hands raised. He picked up the phone and said, "Our leader's missing and we just been busted by the cops. Send help."

"Roger that," the voice on the phone said. "Can you tell me -- "

The little man dropped the phone and raised his hands as a man in body armor came down the companionway ladder, a pistol in his hand. A second man crouched in the companionway, an M4 automatic weapon pointed at him.

"Don' move," the man with the M4 said. "You are under arres'. Put both hands on the back of your head and turn around, slowly."

The little man complied, and the man who was already below snapped a handcuff on one wrist and pulled his hands down behind his back, cuffing the other wrist.

"Got him cuffed," the policeman said, turning the little man around and frog-marching him to the companionway. "Up the ladder, slowly," he ordered.

The little man climbed into the cockpit and saw that his companion was already in the patrol boat, face down in the bilge. "What's -- "

The policeman behind him swiped his pistol across the back of the little man's head. "Don't talk until I say to. Get in the boat and lie down next to your friend."

14

They were almost finished with their first course when Dani felt her phone vibrating against her thigh. She swallowed a sip of wine and returned the glass to the table. "Excuse me for a moment," she said. "I'll be right back."

She went into the ladies' room and entered a stall, closing the door and taking her phone out. She sat down and touched the home button, entering her access code. She read the brief text message from Sharktooth.

"Intercepted intruder. All good. Expect no further trouble tonight. Respond when you can for complete story."

She wanted to respond before she went back to the table. The prospect of waiting an hour or more to satisfy her curiosity was daunting. She forced herself to put the phone away and return to the dining room, where she found that the busboy had cleared the remains of their first course. "Sorry," she said, sliding into her chair.

"No problem," Harry said, cutting his eyes to the side to watch her as she sat down.

She felt herself blush; his look made her skin crawl. She was glad the dining room lights were dim.

"They're about to bring the main course. You're right on time," Beverly said, "but you missed the excitement."

"Excitement?" Dani asked. "What happened?"

"The waitress stopped by to tell us the latest hot gossip," Harry said. "The tour guide told us this afternoon that Bequia was like a small town; he wasn't kidding."

"What happened?" Dani asked.

"There was a drug bust in the harbor while we were eating our first course," Liz said. "Two men on a boat named *Sosueme* were arrested, and the police towed the boat out of the anchorage."

"*Sosueme*," Dani said. "I saw that boat. It was anchored close by. A little 32-footer from a no-name bareboat charter company. I figured this was their first stop out of Blue Lagoon. There were three men aboard. Some kind of guys' getaway, I guess. I was worried they'd get drunk and rowdy; I thought we were in for a noisy night in the neighborhood."

"Three men?" Liz said. "The waitress said they only arrested two; that's strange."

"Maybe the third one was just visiting," Harry said.

"Or he delivered the drugs and left," Beverly said. "It could have been one of those setups like you told me about yesterday, huh? If they bought the drugs from him and he turned them in?"

"It could be," Dani said. "And here we missed all the entertainment. If we had been on *Vengeance*, we would have had front-row seats."

"Well, that's all right with me," Liz said. "I'm happy to enjoy a fine dinner ashore, cooked by someone else. That's much nicer than staying home and watching the neighbors get arrested."

"I agree," Dani said.

"Excuse me," Liz said, getting up and walking in the direction of the ladies' room.

Dani watched Harry following her with his eyes, a hungry look on his face.

"She's very pretty, isn't she," Beverly said, looking at him across the table.

He flinched like a child caught stealing sugar. He looked at Beverly and smiled, shaking his head. "She's not my type. I always heard redheads were hot-tempered, anyway."

"But she's more of a strawberry blonde," Beverly said. "I wouldn't call her a redhead, would you, Dani?"

"No, but she has the temper, all right. She's slow to anger, but you don't want to see her when she's upset."

MONTALBA WAS SIPPING WINE, waiting impatiently for a report on the evening's activities in Bequia. When the encrypted phone rang, he answered it midway through the first ring. "Yes? Is it done?"

"We're trying to work out what happened," the man on the phone said. "What we know at the moment is that the leader of the surveillance team is missing, and the other two men have been arrested."

Montalba restrained himself. He took a deep breath and set the wineglass down on his credenza. In a calm voice, he asked, "What do you think *might* have happened?"

"The team leader was planning to board the target vessel as soon as the four people went ashore for dinner. As best we know, he did that; or at least he left the vessel he'd chartered, expecting to board the target. We got a call from his second in command, and he said, 'Our leader's missing and we've just been busted by the cops. Send help.' After that, we heard the police cuff him and take him away. Then we heard them searching the boat, talking to one another. They found a packet of drugs wrapped in a wet, bloody cloth. That's all that's on the transcript. Our people disconnected when the police found the phone. It will erase itself after three wrong passcodes."

"What transcript?" Montalba asked.

"We routinely record incoming calls from our field teams. The recording's been transcribed."

"What about the packet of drugs?" Montalba asked. "What were they doing with drugs?"

"They were going to plant them on the target vessel, on your orders."

"Then what were they doing on their boat, if the leader had already gone to plant them?"

"I don't have an answer for that, yet, sir."

"Are your people drug users?"

"No, sir. We're a government contractor, remember? We have a random drug-testing policy, but all our people are routinely tested, in addition to the random spot checks. That could have been a backup stash of drugs, or perhaps the ones that the Coast Guard should have recovered yesterday."

"Tell me about this missing team leader."

"A former naval officer, sir. A navy SEAL. He commanded numerous covert missions behind enemy lines. It's hard to imagine -- "

"How was he getting to the 'target vessel,' as you call it?"

"His plan was to swim; they were anchored no more than 100 yards away."

"It's unlikely that he didn't make it, then, isn't it?"

"Yes, sir. I agree."

"If he's missing, he must be on one of the boats or still in the water," Montalba said.

"That about covers it, sir, but by now, we would surely have heard from him, unless something happened to him."

"Could somebody have been waiting for him aboard the 'target vessel?'"

"Of course, that's possible, but extremely unlikely, since he and his team had the target under surveillance for several hours before he left. And before you ask, it's even more unlikely that anyone would have been able to overpower him. Needless to say, he's an expert in hand-to-hand combat."

"Can you check with whoever was going to conduct the law enforcement raid after he planted the drugs?"

"Yes, but we're holding back on that. The plan was that the team leader would plant the drugs and then wait until the people had returned from dinner. At that point, he was to call his contact in the police, and the raid would have followed."

"And are the people back aboard?"

"I can't confirm that, sir. All our assets in Bequia are out of action at the moment."

"What are you going to do to recover?"

"We're moving a backup team in. They'll be there around daybreak. We're also arranging for a local lawyer to deal with the two men who were arrested. The timing on that depends on the local authorities. We expect that the two men will know more about what could have happened to their leader, but right now, all we can do is wait."

"I see," Montalba said, through clenched teeth.

"I'll call as soon as we learn anything new, sir," the man said.

"Please do," Montalba said, disconnecting the call.

THEIR GUESTS RETIRED to their stateroom after they returned from dinner. Dani and Liz sat in the cockpit behind the helm, enjoying a cool onshore breeze. Dani leaned over and cupped a hand around Liz's ear.

"I got a text from Sharktooth during dinner," she whispered.

Liz took her phone out of her purse and showed it to Dani, tapping the messaging app to show her that she had heard from him, too. "Did you respond yet?" she whispered.

Dani shook her head. "You sleepy?" she asked, in a normal tone.

"No, I'm wired," Liz said. "How about you?"

"Me, too. Let's go for a moonlight dinghy ride."

"Great idea," Liz said.

They unlocked their RIB and climbed down into it, careful not to make noises that would disturb Beverly and Harry. Dani untied the painter and shoved the dinghy away from *Vengeance*, letting it drift a hundred yards before she started the engine.

"Where are we going?" Liz asked.

"I saw *Lightning Bolt* anchored on the north side of the harbor, not far from the ferry dock," Dani said. "I thought we could see what's on Sharktooth's mind, if he's home."

"It was all I could do not to send him a text as soon as I got his," Liz said. "I only managed to restrain myself because I thought you probably already answered him when you went to the ladies' room."

"I started to, but then I remembered he was planning to stay here tonight." She pointed at his brightly colored go-fast boat in the shadows near the commercial docks.

Throttling back as she approached *Lightning Bolt*, she killed the outboard and let the dinghy drift the last few yards. She stood and fended them off the side of Sharktooth's boat, not wanting to alarm him by bumping into it. She needn't have bothered, she realized, when his deep voice sounded from below.

"Come on aboard, ladies," he said, his tone soft.

Dani looked at Liz, taking in the surprise on her face. Dani smiled and shrugged. She tied their painter to a midship cleat and hoisted herself up onto the side deck. Liz was right behind her.

"How did you know it was us?" Liz asked, as Sharktooth appeared in the companionway, silhouetted in the light from the cabin.

"Jus' guessin'," he said. "Nobody else gon' come callin' this time of night."

"We decided to come over here so we could talk, instead of sending you a text and then having to whisper about it," Dani said.

"Mm-hmm, I thought mebbe you'd think of that. You want anything to drink? Tea, mebbe?"

"Tea would be nice, if it's not too much trouble," Liz said.

"Jus' made some fo' myself. Water's still hot. Come on below."

As he busied himself in the small galley, Dani said, "Okay, tell us what happened."

"Mon swim up to *Vengeance* from a little boat anchored close by. *Sosueme*," he said. "So I grab him an' -- "

"Where were you?" Liz asked.

"In the water. I hide in the shadow under the transom, watchin'. I think it won't be long, cause they mus' be watchin' for you to leave."

"So you grabbed him," Dani said. "Did he put up much of a fight?"

"No. I knock him out while he climb the boarding ladder. Swim back here with him, an' take him for a little ride, out where nobody hear him if he scream."

"And what did you learn from him?" Dani asked. "Who's behind this?"

"He didn't know. He worked for a company called SpecCorp. It claims to provide security and intelligence-gathering for businesses, but it's mostly a contractor to the U.S. government."

"What kind of contractor?" Liz asked.

"Black ops. They do stuff the government doesn't want to get blamed for. Illegal stuff," Sharktooth said. "They work for other people, too -- anybody who pays them."

"They're the ones that were shadowing Connie and Paul once," Dani said.

"Mm-hmm. Tha's right."

"Who are they working for?" Liz asked. "Surely the U.S. government's not behind planting drugs on *Vengeance*."

Sharktooth smiled and shook his head. "Keep believin' that, Liz."

"They were?" she asked, her voice rising in pitch.

"I don't know, but you give them way too much credit. He didn't know who was paying SpecCorp for this little bit of work. Their field people never do know who the client is. That's how they protect the client's identity if they get caught."

"What else?" Dani asked.

"He was one of the three who stole *Vengeance* and sailed her down from Miami. One of the men with him installed the surveillance system while they were on the way."

"Are those the same men who were on *Sosueme*?" Dani asked. "I saw three men aboard earlier."

"Not the same men. The two who sailed down with him went on to another job. The two with him on *Sosueme* were assigned to him after he got *Vengeance* down here."

"We heard they got arrested," Liz said.

"In a drug bust," Dani added.

"Mm-hmm. The mon I caught, he had drugs to plant on *Vengeance*. He paid off the mon who runs the drug enforcement squad in St. Vincent. He was goin' to call them once you were back aboard, and they were goin' to raid you and find the drugs."

"We suspected as much," Dani said, "but why us?"

"Not you," Sharktooth said. "The target was your male passenger. The police were going to solicit a bribe from him to keep the whole thing off the record. They don't know who he is, but somebody's planning to blackmail him. And the woman, she's part of it."

"You were right, Dani," Liz said.

Dani nodded. "But what about the drug bust on *Sosueme*?"

"Once I finished with the mon, I had no use for the drugs, so I thought the right thing to do was return them to their owners. I swam over and put them in their cockpit."

"And you tipped the police?" Dani asked.

"Mm-hmm. The Chief Superintendent here is a friend of mine and your father's. He's an honorable man. I was in touch with him earlier, after the business wit' the Coast Guard. After I learned the mon who run the drug squad is crooked, I called the Chief Super and told him what was happening, most of it, anyway. What he needed to know. He arranged for the arrest of the men on *Sosueme*. An' prob'ly have the crooked p'lice arrested, too."

"This SpecCorp thing bothers me," Dani said. "They've popped up before with Connie and Paul, and now they're after us. I don't like that we can't find out who they're working for."

"Mm-hmm. Phillip and I talked about that. He had an idea."

"What's that?" Dani asked.

"We call him up; it's easier if we can all talk." Sharktooth picked up his satellite phone and punched in Phillip's number.

"Sharktooth?"

"Yeah, Phillip. Dani and Liz wit' me. Let's talk about your idea on SpecCorp."

"Did you tell them about the video clips?" Phillip asked.

"Not yet," Sharktooth said. "I sent Phillip some short video clips of Rick Norris tellin' me what he knew 'bout SpecCorp's surveillance of *Vengeance*."

"Rick Norris?" Liz asked.

"The mon I caught tryin' to board *Vengeance*," Sharktooth said.

"He was a former Navy SEAL, a Lieutenant Commander," Phillip said, "or so he told Sharktooth."

"You must have had quite a conversation," Dani said. "Talkative, was he?"

Sharktooth grinned. "Mos' people talk a lot when they t'ink the longer they talk, the longer they live. I show you the video, if you like."

"Just tell us about the good parts," Liz said. "We need to get back, in case the guests wake up."

"Already tol' you mos' of the important stuff. Listen to what Phillip wants to do."

"Okay," Liz said, "tell us."

"Yes, please," Dani said.

"I'm thinking about sending them a little message," Phillip said.

"Them?" Dani asked. "You mean SpecCorp?"

"Yes," Phillip said. "Just to throw them off balance, give them something to think about. I've known some of their higher ups for a long time. They're bullies, not nice people, and they think they're hidden away where nobody can reach them."

"Okay," Dani said. "What are you going to do?"

"The CEO's a guy named Delaney. I went through Ranger School with him, a long time ago. He's scum. He lives in a heavily guarded compound in Northern Virginia. Guys in body armor with automatic weapons and dogs. Got the picture?"

"Yes. Go ahead," Dani said.

"I have some friends who live in his neighborhood. I'm thinking maybe they could drop off a memory stick with the video at his house. He's not stupid. He'll connect the dots."

"Sounds like fun," Dani said. "Sorry I can't deliver it personally."

"That's how I feel, too. I didn't want to do it without talking with you."

"I'm in," Dani said. "How about you, Liz?"

"Why not?" Liz asked.

"The only down side is the potential for escalation," Phillip said.

"That's all? Escalation's a downside? Not to me." Dani said. "How soon can you do it?"

"Probably sometime tomorrow. I've already talked to them; I just wanted your okay before we pulled the trigger."

"What do you think they'll do?" Liz asked.

"SpecCorp?" Phillip asked. "I think they'll relay the message to the people who hired them. Like I said, they're bullies. It's one thing when they're hiding behind a government client and picking on people who can't fight back. Delaney won't like being threatened on a personal level."

"Do it," Dani said. "By the way, Sharktooth, what happened to the man you grabbed, this Norris guy?" Dani asked.

"That thief?" Sharktooth asked. "He escaped. Stole a hundred dollars' worth of chain, too. But greed got him in the end."

"I don't understand," Liz said.

Sharktooth winked at Dani. "You tell her."

Dani nodded. "I'll bet he stole more chain than he could swim with."

"Why wouldn't he have just dropped it, then?" Liz asked.

"He didn't want to lose it, so he wrapped it all around his waist and fastened it with a shackle, would be my guess," Dani said. "Greedy, like Sharktooth said."

Sharktooth smiled and nodded. "Mm-hmm. Dani, she know how stuff happens. More tea, ladies?"

"We'd better get back to our guests," Dani said. "Thanks, Sharktooth, Phillip. We'll be in touch."

"My pleasure," Sharktooth said, standing up to see them to their dinghy.

15

"This is a follow-up to last night's report," the man on the secure phone told Montalba. "The situation is still fluid, but I wanted you to have the latest information."

"All right. What have you learned?"

"We have another surveillance team in place as of about an hour ago. The people on the target vessel had a late breakfast in the cockpit, and they're hanging out aboard the boat."

"Okay," Montalba said. "That's good. What else?"

"Before I continue, sir, do you know what their plans are?"

"No. Why do you ask?"

"The surveillance team is using a speedboat at the moment. They wanted to get to Bequia from St. Vincent as quickly as possible. That works all right as long as they stay in Bequia, but depending on where the target vessel goes, a sailboat would be less conspicuous."

"You should do what you need to do to follow them wherever they go. I'm not privy to their plans."

"I see, sir. We'll handle it, then. No problem. Now, the rest of what I have is from the two men who were arrested, via the lawyer we sent in."

"Do you trust him?"

"Yes, sir. We've used him before."

"Okay. What's he learned?"

"The team leader left to deliver the package to the target vessel at approximately seven p.m., when the people left to go ashore in the dinghy. He was well camouflaged; they lost sight of him once he was a few yards away," the man said. "They began to worry when he didn't come back after an hour. An hour and fifteen minutes after he left, they were in the main cabin of their boat debating whether one of them should go looking for him. They also discussed calling in for instructions. Before they agreed on the next step, they heard a thump from the back of the boat. When they went up to check, they found the unopened package of drugs that the team leader had been carrying. It was -- "

"Did they see who left it?" Montalba interrupted.

"No, sir, there were no boats moving in the vicinity, and no sign of life nearby. The package was wrapped in a blood-soaked piece of fabric that they identified as part of the camouflage dive skin their leader was wearing."

"Does that mean he didn't return with the package, then?"

"That's the implication, sir, but we don't know how the package got there, or why it was wrapped in the fabric. As soon as they opened it and saw that it contained the drugs, they called in for instructions, but the police boarded them before they had time to say anything. As I told you last night, the phone line was open during the arrest and part of the search. That's all we got from the two men."

"I see," Montalba said. "Not much, but it makes some sense, I guess. Did they know why the police chose to raid their boat instead of the target?"

"The lawyer made some inquiries. The police were acting on an anonymous tip."

"Were these the same cops who were supposed to bust the target?"

"No, sir, and that's where this gets strange. The man in charge of the local narcotics squad has been arrested by their equivalent of internal affairs."

Montalba thought for a moment. "It sounds as if your man in charge didn't do his homework."

"We don't know, yet, sir. The Coast Guard officer who carried out the boarding the day before yesterday was arrested early this morning, as well. As I said, the situation is still fluid."

"I think your target turned the tables on you," Montalba said. "Maybe they had better connections with the police than you did."

"Our working theory is that somebody captured the team leader and interrogated him, sir. He was the one who made the arrangements with the local authorities."

"Somebody?" Montalba asked. "I want some background on who that somebody could be, do you understand me? I want to know everything there is to know about those two women who run that charter yacht, and I want it fast. Your organization's performance has been poor. If I don't have some answers before the day is out, I'll be calling your CEO. Got it?"

"Yes, sir. Loud and clear. I'll handle it, sir. Rest assured that we will --"

Montalba disconnected the call while the man was talking. While he'd been on the secure phone with SpecCorp, he'd received a text message on the prepaid cellphone that he reserved for Beverly Lennox. He opened the text.

"Dinner last night uneventful," he read. "Further instructions?"

He frowned. Had she expected something to happen at dinner? The woman was smart; he had to give her that. Too bad the SpecCorp people weren't as bright as she was. He poured a cup of coffee and sat back, pondering what to tell her.

∾

BEVERLY WAS in the head putting on sunscreen when her cellphone chimed. She picked it up and read the text from Berto. "Make the most of your time in the islands. No further instructions; just get good video."

She'd left Harry up in the cockpit with Liz and Dani. They were drinking coffee and relaxing in the shade of the big cockpit awning. They had finished a late breakfast, all having slept in after their big night ashore.

Dani had asked what they wanted to do today, and Beverly had stalled, hoping to hear from Berto. She had asked Dani about possible destinations, and Dani and Liz had both suggested the Tobago Cays, since Beverly enjoyed snorkeling. Harry was indifferent; he was content to sip rum drinks and ogle the women on nearby boats.

Beverly pulled her hair back, putting it in a ponytail. She slipped on a thin, white linen bathing suit cover-up over her orange thong bikini. The sun was too hot for bare skin, even in the shade. The reflected rays had burned her over the last two days in spite of her liberal applications of sunscreen.

She studied her reflection in the mirror and decided she looked too frumpy. She'd noticed the hungry looks that Harry was giving their hostesses when he thought no one was watching. She smirked at her reflection and shook her head, untying the cover-up and letting it hang open.

That was better, but she still worried that if he made a play for Liz or Dani, it would ruin things. She needed to keep his attention, as much as she didn't want to. Getting kicked off the yacht wasn't part of Berto's plan for them.

She reached back and untied the top of her bikini and let it fall, shrugging her shoulders to settle the translucent cover-up in place. She retied the cover-up, but loosely, showing plenty of cleavage.

She turned, looking back over her shoulder at her reflection. The cover-up stopped about halfway down her hips, the bright white linen contrasting with the orange straps of the skimpy bottoms. She pouted and winked at herself in the mirror.

Dressed for work, she gave her makeup a last check and turned off her phone, putting it on the shelf by their bed as she made her way back up to the cockpit. Harry greeted her with a wolf whistle when she came up the ladder, and she acted embarrassed. That always pleased him.

"What do you think, Harry?" she asked, as she sat down across from him and leaned forward to pour herself a mug of coffee from the carafe.

"Humma-humma," he said, leering at her as the cover-up fell farther open.

"No, silly boy. I meant about going to the Tobago Cays."

"Oh," he said, licking his lips. "Sure, why not."

"Are you ready?" Dani asked.

"Any time you are, babe. Old Harry's always ready."

Dani locked eyes with him, her icy blue gaze burning into his skull. When he looked away, she shook her head and got to her feet. "Let's get the awnings down," she said.

"Go ahead and get started," Liz said. "Let me secure the galley. I'll be with you in no time."

Five minutes later, they had the awnings rolled up and lashed on the coachroof. Liz went forward and picked up the control for the anchor windlass while Dani started the engine. When Liz gave her a thumbs-up, Dani engaged the transmission briefly and *Vengeance* crept forward as Liz took in the anchor chain.

By the time Liz had the anchor lashed in its chocks, Dani had raised the mizzen sail and uncovered the main. Liz hoisted the main while Dani held the bow into the breeze. When Liz cleated the halyard and scrambled back to the mainsheet winch, Dani cranked the helm to the starboard and shut down the engine.

As the bow came around, Liz payed out the mainsheet, keeping the mainsail full. By the time the bow pointed out to the open water, they were making eight knots almost dead downwind, with the main out against the starboard shrouds and the mizzen all the way out to the port.

Liz moved back to sit beside Dani at the helm, and Beverly said, "It's magic."

"It is indeed," Dani said. "Pure magic."

"What about the other sails?" Beverly asked.

"We couldn't keep them full on this course," Liz said. "They'd be blanketed by the main. Once we round the point up ahead, we'll turn south and put the wind on our beam. Then we'll roll out the staysail and the Yankee."

"I see," Beverly said. "Is it okay if we go up on the bow deck now? We won't be in the way?"

"Not at all," Dani said. "Go up there and enjoy the ride. If you're lucky, you may have a porpoise or two for company once we're out there."

"I want to freshen up my sunscreen," Liz said, winking at Dani. "You okay for a few minutes? I won't be long."

"Sure," Dani said.

MONTALBA WAS THINKING about Beverly Lennox as he sat in his dimly lit office, his feet on his desk. He stroked the scar on his cheek, his thoughts wandering. She was physically attractive, but all women in her line of work were physically attractive.

He was struck by her self-possessed manner. Not that she wasn't willing to follow his instructions, but he got the sense that for all that, she was her own woman. There was a hint that there were some things she wouldn't do, some line she wouldn't cross. He wondered where that line was drawn.

She didn't do drugs; he'd made sure of that before he recruited her. He knew better than anyone the perils of employing dopers. That was another thing that made her a bit unusual in her line of work. He wondered if there could be something in her background that would account for that.

He'd held back telling her about his plan to frame Velasquez with planted drugs. She didn't need to know about that, and he had thought she'd be more convincing during the drug bust if she didn't have to conceal that knowledge.

Still, her recent text made him wonder how much she suspected. "Dinner last night uneventful." He wondered again what she could have meant by that. She must have sensed that he had planned for something to happen during their dinner ashore. Why did she think that? And what had she expected?

She was smarter and more intuitive than he had anticipated. She might be dangerous. Once this was over, he'd keep her close until he learned more about her. The ringing of the SpecCorp-provided encrypted phone broke his concentration.

Swinging his feet to the floor, he swiveled his chair and picked up the phone from his credenza.

"Yes?"

"Who is this?" the caller asked.

"I beg your pardon?" Montalba asked. The caller's voice wasn't familiar. "Whom were you calling?

"This is Delaney. I needed enough speech to match your voice."

"Good afternoon, Mr. Delaney." Montalba wasn't too surprised to get a call from SpecCorp's CEO. Apparently, his dissatisfaction had been passed up the chain of command. "I've been thinking I needed to call you."

"Yeah, well, the feeling's mutual. When you called me on O'Toole's recommendation a while back, I thought we had a good understanding."

"That was on a different matter," Montalba said. "Perhaps I should have called you personally about this job, but the man you had assigned to handle the last one assured me that it wasn't necessary."

"Look, uh ... I don't like not knowing who the hell you are. You got a name?"

"We discussed that. You were happy enough with my investment in your business. Must I remind you that it was not small, Mr. Delaney?"

"Things are different now," Delaney said.

"Yes, they are. I'm beginning to realize the shortcomings of your operation. That makes me even more glad to be anonymous."

"I don't think we can continue to do business, then," Delaney said.

"Are you resigning?" Montalba asked, his tone bland.

"Fuck, no, I'm not resigning. This is my company; I built it from nothing."

"Ashes to ashes, dust to dust," Montalba said.

"What?" Delany asked. "What the hell's that supposed to mean?"

"Look, Mr. Delaney, I'm a businessman. Through my companies, I own a majority interest in SpecCorp now. If you don't like that, you can leave, and start again with nothing, so long as you don't violate the anti-competitive clause in our agreement. Or I might allow you to buy me out, depending on the offer."

"No court will enforce that anticompete clause," Delaney said.

"I wouldn't rely on the courts to enforce it; that's not my way of operating."

"Is that a threat?" Delaney asked.

"I suppose that depends on you, Mr. Delaney."

"I could go to O'Toole," Delany said.

"You could, but I assure you, he can't help you. This is between us. Troubling O'Toole could result in an unpleasant outcome for you."

"Look," Delaney said, "we've gotten off on the wrong foot, here."

"I think so. Perhaps we could start over," Montalba said. "Is there a problem?"

"Yeah, there is. This was presented as routine surveillance, a honey trap for a congressman who may become a nuisance to our mutual friend, O'Toole."

"Yes," Montalba said.

"You misled us. Got us into the middle of a Class-A goat fuck," Delaney said.

"You're still angry."

"No shit! I'll try to stay cool, but I'm fuckin' furious. I've been played."

"I'm sorry, Mr. Delaney, but I assure you, *I* didn't *play* you. Can I ask what's happened?"

"You said you were thinking of calling me," Delaney said, tension still in his voice. "Why? To warn me?"

"To warn you? No, I was displeased with the way your people were handling the job. Can you start at the beginning, please? I do not know why you are angry, but I think we both want to see O'Toole get the nomination when the time comes."

Montalba heard Delaney take a deep breath and exhale. "Yeah," he said. "Yeah, we do. I've had a bad day, and it's because of this *job*, as you put it."

"I see," Montalba said. "I'm sure your people have informed you by now of what's happened down in the islands, but I sense there's something they haven't shared with me."

"They don't know," Delaney said. "Most of them don't know any more about me than I know about you. That's by design. I keep a low profile; plenty of people around would like to do me in."

"I understand what it is to live that way," Montalba said.

"Yeah, I can tell you do. Anyway, here goes. I live in a 25-acre compound in Northern Virginia, heavily guarded. Nobody gets in or out without my knowing. My wife was having a brunch for her bridge club today, so I had extra security in place. Ten men instead of five. They penned the dogs for the guests' arrival, and then released them once everybody was in the house. You got the picture so far?"

"Yes. Go ahead."

"The ladies were eating their pastries when this scruffy guy waltzed into the dining room and went straight to my wife. She jumped out of her chair and asked who the hell he thought he was. He said, 'Now don't be that way, Eva.' He gave her a big hug and a kiss. When he stepped back, she tried to slap him."

"Tried?"

"Yeah. He grabbed her arm and planted a memory stick in her hand. 'Give that to your husband, sweetheart,' he said, 'And tell him to mind his ways, or I'll come back to see both of you.' Then he walked out like he owned the place, whistling the *Colonel Bogey March*."

"What about the guards and the dogs?" Montalba asked.

"My wife went looking for them. She found them locked in the kennel, all in one big pile. Tranquilizer darts stuck in their necks. Men and dogs all mixed up together."

"And you think my *job*, as you called it, had something to do with that?"

"The memory stick was loaded with several video clips. They showed parts of the interrogation of the man who was in charge of our team in Bequia," Delaney said. "He told them everything he knew, but that was limited to the details of the operation and his personal background. Nothing for you to worry about."

"He told them he worked for you?" Montalba asked.

"Negative. He told them he worked for SpecCorp. He didn't know anything about me. I'm invisible unless I choose to reveal myself, like in your case."

"So how did they connect him to you?" Montalba asked.

"I don't know. You know who these people are? The women?"

"On the boat?" Montalba asked.

"Yeah."

"Danielle Berger and Liesbet Chirac," Montalba said.

"Uh-huh. You asked my people to get background on them. You haven't got that yet?"

"No, I haven't."

"What we got so far is that Berger's father's a big-time arms dealer out of France. A guy named Jean-Pierre Berger. J.-P., he's called."

"An arms dealer? You mean like a gun-runner?"

"Not exactly. He brokers deals with governments. Want an air force? An armored division? Maybe a ballistic missile sub? He's your man."

"You think he's behind it?"

"He could be, but most likely, it's some of his people, doing the daughter a favor. She's a piece of work herself, from what we gather. Spent the summers when she was a teenager blowing up coke refineries in Central America with a bunch of people her old man contracted out to somebody. Nobody knows who they were working for."

"He sounds like your competition," Montalba said.

"I wish. He's been in the game so long he's part of the establishment, him and his network. They're in a different league from me. I can't help you if you're going to tangle with him."

"We've already tangled with him, it seems," Montalba said. "What do you recommend?"

"We need a way out," Delaney said. "Lay a false trail, so you and me and O'Toole are out of the line of fire. There's no way to mix it up with Berger and his bunch without attracting attention we don't want."

"A false trail? Leading where?"

"We need a scapegoat. I can handle laying the false trail, but we need a plausible fall guy."

"I have an idea," Montalba said.

"Who?"

"Let me do a little homework. I'll call you back."

"Don't take too long," Delaney said.

16

"Did you just do what I think you did?" Dani asked, as Liz came back up into the cockpit.

"Most likely. I thought we needed to talk, and with them on the foredeck, this seemed like a good time. And the light was off, so the system's not active anyway. Just help me remember to turn it back on if she goes below."

"Sure," Dani said. "What's on your mind?"

"Do you think we dare call Luke?" Liz asked. "We'd have to use the sat phone this far offshore, but if they notice, we could just tell them we were checking in with the charter broker. If we're careful, they won't hear us, the way the wind's blowing."

"Why do you want to call him?" Dani asked.

"It's been two full days since we talked with him. I was thinking he might have some more information on Beverly."

"It's worth a try," Dani said.

Liz took the phone out of the locker in the steering pedestal and moved back behind the helm, sitting next to Dani and holding the phone between their heads.

"Pantene," Luke answered.

"It's Liz and Dani," Liz said.

"Good. I made a little progress; I've passed it on to Phillip, but he didn't think I should call you. Can you talk?"

"Not much," Liz said. "We still have guests aboard, but we wondered if you had anything new for us. They're just out of earshot."

"Okay," Luke said.

Liz had turned the volume down to where she and Dani had to lean their heads together so they could both hear. "Tell us," she said.

"She's a high-end escort, a rich man's companion for hire, we think. No record; she's clean as far as we can tell. Lives in a two-million-dollar-plus condo that's owned by a corporation. Company name leads to a dead end. She supposedly has a trust fund; no living relatives."

"Sounds interesting," Dani said. "Anybody else with her?"

"You mean besides the politician?" Luke asked.

"Yes," Dani said.

"No, not as best anybody knows. He's her one and only at the moment. The question is, how can he afford her?"

"No way to know, huh?" Dani asked.

"No, but whoever's paying the bills, it's not him. Someone's spending a lot of money to set him up. That's about it, unless you've got something for me."

"We'll have to get back to you," Liz said. "We don't have anything urgent. You said you'd talked to Phillip."

"Right. I'm current up through early this morning," Luke said.

"Then you know as much as we do. Thanks for the update. We'll be in touch," Dani said.

"G'bye, you two. Be careful," Luke said.

"We always are," Liz said, as she disconnected the call. She put the phone away.

"Phillip's notion of rattling SpecCorp has been fermenting in the back of my mind," Dani said.

"Uh-oh. Is something bubbling up to the surface?" Liz asked.

"Yes. Ever since we talked to him last night, I've been toying with the idea of confronting Beverly."

"I'm not surprised."

"You're not?"

"No," Liz said. "I think she's gotten into something she doesn't understand."

"Why do you think that?"

"I've been replaying everything that's happened. I believe she's following instructions: I don't think she's in control of this."

"Okay," Dani said, "but do you have anything concrete to support that?"

"I peeked at her phone when I went below just now. I happened to see it on the shelf beside their bed when I secured the door to their cabin; it wasn't latched shut or hooked open -- just swinging with the boat's motion. I went forward to hook it, and the phone was right there."

"It's not passcode protected?" Dani asked.

"It is, but you know how sometimes they show text messages on the lock screen if you don't clear them?"

"Yes."

"Well, I turned it on, and there were two messages."

"Don't keep me in suspense."

"Early this morning, she sent a text to 'Berto.' It said, 'Dinner last night uneventful. Further instructions?' Then, just before she came up here a few minutes ago, Berto replied. He said, 'Make the most of your time in the islands. No further instructions; just get good video.' That's it. I guess she cleared the notifications last night, or something. I couldn't go further because of the passcode."

"That's consistent with the idea that she's part of the blackmail scheme, but you're right. She's not the one in charge, based on those two messages. We need to find out who Berto is," Dani said.

"How are we going to get her to tell us?" Liz asked.

"I don't know. We can't beat it out of her. Not unless we can separate her from Harry." Dani cut her eyes to the side and gave Liz a long look. "We know he likes you."

"No, Dani," Liz said. "I don't like that idea."

"You're just being narrow-minded. He's not that bad."

"Yes, he is, but that's only one of the reasons. I don't think that approach will work."

"Why not?"

"Think about the Norris guy that Sharktooth questioned," Liz said.

"What about him?"

"He didn't know who was paying SpecCorp."

"So?"

"Whoever's behind this wouldn't go to the trouble of using an outfit like SpecCorp just to let some high-end escort know their identity. Berto has to be another dead end, whoever he is."

"Good point. If you're right, all we'd do by leaning on her is drive them farther underground."

"That's where I come out. Besides, I think Harry's more interested in you today. I've told you before to ditch that shirt. It's two sizes too small for you. Couldn't you feel his eyes crawling over your -- "

"Watch it, Chirac. I've got the urge to hurt somebody. Don't tempt me."

"Suck it up, Berger. Channel that energy into figuring out how we can con Beverly into coming over to our side."

"Do you think we can do that?" Dani asked.

"Maybe."

"How?"

"I'm still thinking about that. Why don't you mull it over? I need to go below for a minute or two. Do you want anything?"

"No, but what are you up to?"

"I'm going to email Sharktooth. I want him to send me those video clips. I'm thinking we can get Harry liquored up and leave him aboard while we take her snorkeling, once we get to the Cays. It'll give us a chance to get her by herself. The video might come in handy. We'll talk about it some more when I get back."

MONTALBA WAS DOODLING on a yellow legal pad. He'd drawn a circle in the middle of a page and written "Velasquez" in it. Lines radiated from it like the spokes of a wheel, each ending in another circle. He had entered every name that he could link to Velasquez, including key members of the congressman's staff, senior party officials, his wife Miranda, Beverly Lennox, and Velasquez's parents.

He'd searched the internet, pairing every name with Horatio

Velasquez to see if the two names together produced a hit. After reading the articles that surfaced for each search, he'd scratched through all the names except Miranda's. He turned back to the computer on his credenza and typed in her maiden name, Miranda Bridget McGuire.

In the online newspaper archives, he found an announcement of her engagement to Velasquez. He scanned the article, jotting down the names of her parents and her two siblings. She had a brother two years her senior and another who was three years younger.

He decided to start with her father, Michael Francis McGuire. The first hit was an obituary from the year after her wedding. Besides being active in his church, McGuire had been a prime mover in the state Republican Party, though he'd never run for office. He was survived by his wife, Mary Rose Ryan McGuire, and three children, Michael Francis McGuire, Jr., Miranda Bridget McGuire Velasquez, and Patrick Ryan McGuire.

Moving to the next article, Montalba learned that Michael Sr. had been indicted by a federal grand jury under the direction of a Democrat State's Attorney on multiple charges related to gambling, loan sharking, money laundering, and income tax evasion.

"Big Mike" McGuire, as he was known, had been arrested and promptly released on bail. Pretrial maneuvering had consumed several months, and eventually the charges had been dismissed on technicalities. Big Mike had been celebrating with his cronies at a Miami steak house that was a notorious mob hangout when he'd been stricken with a fatal heart attack.

Montalba moved on to Mike Jr., known in the community as "Little Mike." Little Mike was active in commercial real estate development and also owned a number of night clubs in South Florida. From the pictures of him at various ribbon cuttings and social events to benefit Catholic charities, Montalba could see that he was a big man, tall and physically imposing in spite of his nickname.

Searching for Patrick McGuire revealed that he was a partner in a prestigious law firm in Tallahassee, as well as a lobbyist for several national agricultural organizations. Montalba drew a line through Patrick's name.

He tapped his pen against the legal pad as he looked over his scribbles. After 30 seconds, he leaned forward and drew several heavy circles around Little Mike McGuire's name. He opened the center drawer of his desk and took out a cheap prepaid cellphone. Pressing one of the number keys, he heard the tones from the speed-dial buffer.

He raised the phone to his ear in time to hear the answer. Recognizing the man's voice, Montalba said, "Get me everything you can find on Little Mike McGuire. I'm in a hurry."

"No sweat. We got a lot on him already. Gimme a few hours to get some updates. That okay?"

"Perfect," Montalba said.

~

"WE'RE GOING SNORKELING HERE?" Beverly asked, looking around and frowning as Dani brought the dinghy to a stop. They were several hundred yards from where *Vengeance* lay at anchor in the Tobago Cays. The reef was visible under the clear water, a hundred yards farther to the east.

"Not quite," Liz said. "We wanted to chat with you in private. We'll pick up one of those moorings on the fringing reef in a minute." She pointed to where a couple of empty dinghies bobbed at a mooring buoy. "That's one of the prime snorkeling spots."

"Chat about what?" Beverly asked, her frown growing deeper.

"Just among us girls," Dani said.

Liz had been feeding Harry rum punch for the duration of their sail from Bequia. They had left him snoring in a hammock under the foredeck awning.

Beverly picked at a fingernail and looked around. The other boats in the anchorage were even farther away than *Vengeance*.

"You got Harry drunk on purpose." She glared at Liz.

"He could have said no any time he wanted," Liz said, an innocent smile on her face.

"No, he couldn't, and you know it. He's a sucker for string bikinis, and I know you saw how he was looking at you."

"He *was* a little obvious, wasn't he?" Liz asked. "Me, you, Dani, anybody with breasts."

"I don't think that's -- "

"Save it, Beverly," Liz said, cutting her off.

Beverly's eyes went round and her mouth dropped open.

"Why are you doing this?" Dani asked.

"Doing what? Take me back to the boat, now."

"We know who you are," Liz said.

"And who *Harry* is," Dani said.

"This isn't any of your business," Beverly said.

"Oh, I don't agree," Dani said. "Whoever put you up to this stole our boat and installed surveillance equipment without our consent. That violates a number of laws, for starters. I think our being your victims makes it our business."

"I don't know what you mean," Beverly said, chewing on her lower lip. "I told you I wanted to go back. I -- "

"And then there were the drugs," Liz said.

"Drugs?"

"Don't play innocent. You'll piss me off," Dani said. "So far, this is a friendly conversation. It would be better for you if it stayed that way."

"Are you threatening me?"

"Do you feel threatened?" Liz asked.

"Yes, I do,"

"Good," Dani said. "So do we. I like to keep things in balance."

"*You* feel threatened? I don't understand."

"One more time from the top," Dani said. "You stole our boat and bugged it. Then you planted drugs on it and set us up for a Coast Guard search."

"I don't know what you mean by any of that. There were no drugs, either," Beverly said. "And why do you say I set you up? I thought it was a random search."

"Look," Liz said, holding her smartphone so that Beverly could see a picture of the stash that Sandrine's people had found. "Recognize your stateroom?"

"But they didn't find any drugs," Beverly said, shaking her head. "And I didn't set you up."

"No, they didn't," Dani said. "We think you set us up because you had us hug the shore for no good reason."

"But I told you why. And why do you think it was a setup, anyway? The other day you said -- "

"Because," Dani said, "one of the Coast Guard boarding party had pictures on his cellphone. Pictures that showed them where the drugs were. One showed a stash in the same spot as the picture Liz just showed you."

"So why didn't they find them, then?" Beverly asked, sitting up straight and staring into Dani's eyes.

"Because when we got the boat back, we gave her a thorough going over. We had a friend in French Customs bring a drug-sniffing dog aboard. That's how we found them," Liz said. "Otherwise, we'd have been in trouble yesterday, thanks to you."

"What makes you think I had anything to do with any of this?"

"Who's Berto?" Dani asked.

Beverly took a deep breath and looked away. "Berto? I don't know any Berto."

"Shall I?" Liz asked.

"You may as well," Dani said.

"What?" Beverly asked, glaring at Dani.

"We have a little video for you to watch," Liz said. "I'll warn you, it's a bit ugly in places, so feel free to close your eyes for the rough parts if you're squeamish."

"Wait," Beverly said. "What is it?"

"Just watch and listen. You'll figure it out. And think about whose side you want to be on," Dani said.

"Whose side?"

"You can either be on our side, or theirs," Dani said.

"Theirs?"

"Whoever you and Berto and the guy in the video are working for. Play it, Liz."

Three minutes later, the video ended. Beverly's face was pale and drawn. Dani and Liz let the silence hang until Beverly said, "That was awful. Who did that to him?"

"It doesn't matter," Liz said. "You heard what he said."

"But he was all bloody," Beverly said. "What happened to him before he started talking?"

"He was in the wrong place at the wrong time," Dani said. "But now you know why we're sure you set us up. You heard what he said about our dinner last night."

"What is this company, SpecCorp?" Beverly asked. "He said he worked for them."

Dani and Liz traded looks.

"You sure you don't know?" Dani asked. "We think *you* work for them."

Beverly shook her head, her whole body beginning to tremble. "I don't know," she sobbed. "I've never heard of them. I'm scared," she said, her voice quavering.

"Not without reason," Dani said. "I'm losing patience with you. Who's Berto? Does he work for SpecCorp?"

"I ... I don't know," Beverly said. "He had me arrange this trip. All I know is he wants to blackmail Harry. Harry's real name is -- "

"I told you," Dani said. "We know who you both are. Who is Berto?"

"You know I'm a ... an -- "

"We know," Liz said. "We know about Velasquez, too. He deserves what he's getting, but we're angry about being caught up in this. We don't care about your background, or that you're helping blackmail Velasquez. That's your business. We do care about who's threatening us, though. We want Berto, and whoever hired him."

Beverly studied Liz through eyes like slits, not saying anything for almost a full minute. She finally broke the silence. "I think I believe you," she said. "When I got into this, I knew Velasquez was going to get hurt. Like you said, he deserves it. I wasn't expecting anybody else to get in trouble. I thought this was just about politics."

"And now?"

"I want out. I have a good life. Maybe most people wouldn't agree, but ... it's what I do. It's like a service industry, you know?"

Liz nodded.

"I know I have a sell-by date; I can't trade on my looks forever. I'm saving money, investing it. I want out of this game while I still have a chance at something like a normal life. I thought they were offering me an opportunity to bank enough for that."

"They?" Dani asked, frowning.

"Berto?" Liz asked.

"And this other guy, Manny LaRosa."

"Who's he?" Liz asked.

"Well, think of him as my booking agent, kind of."

Dani and Liz nodded.

"He set me up with Velasquez, and after that was all going smoothly, he sent me to Berto."

"In addition to Velasquez?" Liz asked.

"That's what I thought, too, but it didn't turn out like that. Manny said Berto was the boss, and I should do what he told me. Berto coached me on how to set this all up, and he said I could be his partner, because there would be others like Velasquez. We could teach them to be better people, or something like that, which I knew was bullshit, but hey. It was a better deal than I'd had before, and I saw it as a faster exit strategy. And Berto treated me well, with respect. Plus, he's really handsome and had elegant manners."

"Berto coached you on setting all of this up?" Dani asked. "What do you mean by 'this?'"

"The charter, and how to work the surveillance stuff. I have a thing that wakes up the system when it's time to, uh ... make a recording. But he didn't tell me how the stuff got on your boat. At first, I thought you two were part of it, part of his plan, you know?"

"And when did you decide we weren't?" Liz asked.

Beverly frowned for a few seconds, then shook her head. "I don't know, exactly. It wasn't any one thing, you know? In my line of work, you learn pretty fast how to size people up. It's a survival skill. You don't fit with Manny and Berto. You're different. They're ... I don't know ... you just know not to trust people like them. The way they act. Like I said, it's no one thing."

"Then what made you think we were part of their scheme to begin with?" Liz asked.

"Well, I didn't know you, and Berto was very specific about chartering *your* boat and not letting the agent substitute another one. And he told me about how the recording stuff was built in. So I thought you had to know about it."

"That makes sense," Dani said.

"Yeah," Beverly said, "but then after the Coast Guard thing, I got this text from him about getting you off the boat that evening, like for dinner. That was after you guys told me about the scams the drug peddlers pulled on tourists down here. It got me to thinking, you know?"

"Thinking?" Liz asked. "About?"

"About whether I was being stupid. See, I thought it was all pretty simple when Berto put me up to this. We were just going to make some videos of Horry and put the squeeze on him."

"I'm not getting your point," Liz said.

"Yeah. Sorry. I'm still trying to make sense out of it myself, but I got a bad feeling. Berto didn't tell me anything about the drugs, and it looks like you're right. He was using me to set you up for that, so he was kind of playing me. I'm wondering why."

"Why he would play you?"

"Yeah, exactly. I thought we were in this together, Berto and I. But he set this drug thing up and didn't tell me. Why didn't he tell me? Was he setting me up too, somehow? I mean, I heard the guy on that video just now. They tipped the cops, both times. What if we got busted?"

Dani shrugged. Liz started to say something, but Dani shook her head.

"I caught what the guy said in the video, about the cops hitting Horry up for a bribe, but what if they decided to arrest us?" Beverly asked. "Like Horry pissed them off somehow, or wouldn't pay them? Or couldn't? Horry doesn't have any money to speak of; it's all his wife's. We could have been in the shit, you know?"

"That's how we feel," Liz said. "Suppose the wrong cops decided to search us, for some reason?"

"I didn't even think of that," Beverly said. "Berto made a big deal out of my being partners with him, but now I'm sure he'd hang me out to dry in a second. If he had been serious about our being partners, he would've told me about the whole deal, don't you think?"

"That's how I see it," Liz said.

"Me too," Dani said. "To someone like him, everybody's expendable."

"I'm really sorry I got into this," Beverly said. "I walked into it with my eyes open, nobody to blame but myself. But you guys didn't even have a choice. That sucks."

"Yes," Liz said. "That's why we want to find out who's behind it. Then we've got a chance to stop it before we get hurt."

"I wish I knew a way out," Beverly said, "but Manny's vicious. One of Berto's selling points was that if I did this for him, I'd never have to see Manny again. You have no idea what Manny would do to me. I saw what happened when he got angry with another girl." She shuddered, her face going pale.

"Maybe we can help," Liz said, "if you can help us."

"How?" Beverly asked.

"I don't know yet," Liz said. "What do you think, Dani?"

"You have a phone number for Berto?" Dani asked, "and a last name?"

Beverly nodded. "A phone number, but that's all. I don't know his last name."

"And how about Manny LaRosa?" Dani asked. "How much do you know about him?"

"I've got his phone number, and he runs a club in South Beach. He practically lives there. But he's dangerous. You have no idea."

"If you'll give us whatever information you have on the two of them, we'll get our friend in Miami to see what he can find out."

Beverly's brow was furrowed as she studied Dani for several seconds. "The same friend that told you who we were?"

"Yes. That's right," Liz said. "Don't worry; he's discreet. There won't be any repercussions from his inquiry."

"Okay," Beverly said. "I have the phone numbers and the name of Manny's club. That's it, except for the names. I'll jot them down for you when we get back to *Vengeance*."

"Let's take a little break," Liz said. "This has been pretty intense. We could all stand to digest what we've talked about."

"Let's snorkel the reef and look at the fish for a while," Dani said. "It'll do you good. We'll talk more later."

17

"Good afternoon, Mr. Delaney," Montalba said. "I've had some time to consider what we talked about earlier."

"Okay, good," Delaney said. "But first, I gotta tell you. I pulled the team out of Bequia. After what happened with Norris, it's too risky to run eyeball surveillance on them. They're gonna be on high alert."

"Norris?" Montalba asked. "Was he the former Navy SEAL?"

"Correct. I had them put a satellite tracking device on the boat, so we can find them anytime we want. If we need to, we can have another team in place in a few hours, at most. I've got plenty of people, but since we've got the surveillance gear and a tracker on the boat, it's not worth the risk of having a team on them. Especially since we don't know how they spotted Norris."

"Very well," Montalba said. "The only problem I see with that is that we'll need to retrieve the recordings at some point."

"Yeah, I know. We'll need the people off the boat to do that, so we'll have to work something out. You have somebody on the inside -- a woman?"

"Yes, " Montalba said. "Wait a second. From a technical aspect, how complicated is it to retrieve the recordings?"

"Not too tough. There's a solid-state drive. You just unplug it and plug in a replacement. Why?"

"Can you send me detailed instructions?"

"Yeah, sure. I'll have to get somebody to put 'em together, but that's not a big deal. You thinking the woman could do it?"

"Yes. To me, it seems that would reduce our exposure," Montalba said.

"Yeah. She's already there. I like it. I'll get somebody on that as soon as we finish. Email work for you?"

"For me, yes. But put it in a format that I can send to her as a text message. We're communicating that way, and it's encrypted. Also, there's the problem of getting the replacement drive to her."

"Shouldn't be a problem," Delaney said. "I can have it dropped off wherever she wants -- bar, gift shop, anywhere. Just give me as much notice as you can."

"Hours? Days?" Montalba asked.

"A day would be great. We could work with a few hours if it's somewhere that's easy to get to, though. You said you'd been thinking about a fall guy. Got somebody in mind?"

"Yes. Velasquez's brother-in-law. His name's Michael Francis McGuire, Jr. He's a real estate developer, and he owns several night clubs around the state."

"Florida?" Delaney asked.

"Yes. He lives in Miami."

"I'm liking this," Delaney said. "He's got a built-in motive for spying on Velasquez."

"That's what I thought, too," Montalba said. "He'd want to take care of his little sister. And he's a shady enough character to make a good suspect."

"Is he mobbed up?" Delaney asked.

"Not obviously, no," Montalba said. "But there are rumors of connections to organized crime. Their father, Michael Sr., was indicted for gambling and loan sharking. Money laundering, too."

"No shit?" Delaney asked. "Is he doing time somewhere?"

"No. The charges were dismissed. I suspect there was some political pressure. The old man was a mover and shaker in the Republican Party."

"Would he make a better scapegoat?" Delaney asked.

"Except for being dead, maybe he would," Montalba said. "He had a heart attack while he was celebrating after he beat the charges. Michael Jr. inherited the business. There's also a younger brother. He's a lawyer, a lobbyist."

"That's great," Delaney said. "This younger brother, does he work in D.C.?"

"Yes. At least, he has an office there. He's a partner in a law firm in Tallahassee, but he spends most of his time in D.C. Why?"

"Access," Delaney said. "I got people who work the lobbyists in D.C. all the time. Send me whatever you have on both of them. I'll put some people to work on this, and once we have a plan, I'll run it by you, okay?"

"All right," Montalba said. "Anything else?"

"Not now. I'll get you the instructions on swapping out the disk drive. That'll probably be this evening, yet. The other will take a little longer."

"Good enough," Montalba said. "Have a good evening."

"Yeah. You do the same."

"Did you turn everything off but the anchor light?" Dani asked, as Liz joined her in the cockpit. Their guests had retired for the evening.

Liz chuckled. "Yes." She handed Dani a glass of wine and sat down beside her.

"What are you laughing about?"

"Your circumspection. I know I shouldn't; it's good to be careful."

"Was it inactive?" Dani asked. "She said she'd let us know if she was going to record something."

"It was. The light was off, but I decided to play it safe," Liz said. "I'm not sure how far I trust her."

"Me either," Dani said. "She came around to our side pretty easily, didn't she?"

"Yes. Do you think she's just humoring us?"

"I'm not sure. I think she was already suspicious of this Berto character, though."

"Yes. And she's scared of the other one," Liz said. "Who do you suppose they could be?"

"I don't know, but I'll bet Luke can find out something about Manny LaRosa. A scumbag running a nightclub in South Beach should be like an open book for him."

"We can call him tomorrow," Liz said, "while she shows Harry the reef."

"Right. Did you put something in that rum punch you were feeding him?"

"No. He just couldn't help himself." Liz smirked.

"Where'd you get that string bikini, anyway?" Dani asked. "I've never seen you wear that."

"I save it for special occasions."

"Well, it worked. I thought his eyes were going to pop right out of his head. Why did you decide to do that? You could have gotten him smashed without putting on such a show."

"I was curious about her reaction."

"*Her* reaction?" Dani paused for a moment. "You mean because of what he said about a threesome? Liz, I had no idea you -- OW! That hurt, damn it."

"Good. Don't pick on me. I wanted to see if she was at all jealous; it just occurred to me to test that. It could have been important to know if she had feelings for him. I was killing two birds with one stone."

"Oh. You had me wondering, for a minute there."

"Ha ha, Dani. Anyway, all I picked up from her was disgust at the way he was leering at me."

"It's obvious that her relationship with him is purely professional," Dani said.

"It is now that she's opened up with us, but I didn't want to assume that. You can't ever tell."

"How do you suppose she got into this whole escort thing?" Dani asked, after a moment of silence. "She's smart, she's attractive, and she carries herself with dignity. Why would she stoop to that?"

"I'm sure I don't know," Liz said. "You could ask her."

"I like her, Liz." Dani frowned.

"So do I. But what's that got to do with it?"

"I don't want to embarrass her," Dani said.

"I see. I don't know if it would bother her. She seemed matter-of-fact about it."

"Yes, but if I were her, I'd be embarrassed. I mean, she's a ... well, you know what I mean."

"As she said, she walked into this situation of her own accord. You'd be embarrassed, and so would I, but that doesn't mean she would. If you think it's important, though, we should ask her about it, embarrassing or not."

"What do you think?"

"I haven't thought about it -- not that way. What she told us so far hangs together; I'm feeling all right about her. How much harm can she do us now, really?"

"Good point," Dani said. "Okay. Maybe it's just prurient interest on my part. I'll put it aside. I just can't imagine doing what she does for a living."

"And she probably couldn't imagine doing some of the stuff you and I have done. You saw her reaction to that video Sharktooth sent us. She'd be horrified at some of the things we've done."

"We haven't done anything I'm ashamed of."

"We've done some things that most people would think should have sent us to prison. She'd agree with them, based on how she felt about that video."

"Yes, but we only did that stuff because we had to; it was us or them. We didn't have much choice. Kill or be killed, right?"

"Right, but she might feel the same way about her choices," Liz said. "Most people rationalize their decisions somehow; not many think of themselves as inherently evil."

"I never looked at it that way. Anyway, if you trust her, I'm satisfied."

"Well, as I said, I haven't thought about it. Maybe I'll change my mind after I sleep on all this."

"While you're sleeping on it, don't forget that she's still in communication with Berto."

"Yes," Liz said. "We can keep an eye on that, though. She doesn't carry her cellphone around with her all the time."

"She may start clearing the messages from the notification screen, though. She might suspect that's how we got Berto's name."

"You're right. I didn't think about that. Where are we going with all this, anyway? What's our goal?"

"I want to know why Berto or whoever he works for picked *Vengeance*. There has to be a reason beyond blackmailing a congressman," Dani said. "They could have done that on any charter boat, or in a resort, for that matter."

"I agree, but what about her?" Liz asked. "And Harry? What happens with them?"

"Well, that depends on what we learn. Right now, that looks like a separate problem to me. I don't really care about them. Let her blackmail him. So what?"

"But if we blow this whole thing open, whoever's behind it may take it out on her," Liz said. "I mean, she's changed sides, we think. Don't you feel like we owe her something?"

"Maybe. We'll have to see what happens, I guess. And see how she behaves from here on. Let's go to sleep. We can talk more tomorrow after we call Luke."

MONTALBA WAS LEANING BACK in his swivel chair, an untouched glass of wine on his credenza. He was pondering Delaney's earlier statement that Berger's father had a contract with somebody to disrupt drug processing laboratories in Central America years ago. Delaney, with a government contractor's bias, had assumed that Berger had been working for some government agency. Montalba had a different perspective.

The rumors about Connie Barrera coupled with her connection to Dani Berger took on new meaning for Montalba. Dani Berger's father could well be behind this mysterious cartel with which Barrera was connected. If Dani had been wrecking laboratories in her teens, J.-P. Berger had been in the narcotics trade for a long time.

The fact that Montalba had never heard of him spoke to Berger's skill at concealing his activities. It also made it likely that he was behind the large, mysterious cartel that no one could find.

Montalba was impressed by J.-P. Berger's use of his daughter and Barrera to run his operation in the Americas. The charter business was an obvious cover. The use of yachts to smuggle drugs was tried and proven, though it had fallen out of favor in recent years. It was an inefficient way to move large quantities of product. However, using small luxury yachts run by young women was ingenious as a cover.

The charter business provided a perfect excuse for the women to move around the Caribbean basin. In his daughter and Barrera, Berger had two well-concealed front-line managers. Dani Berger was blood kin, too. That didn't guarantee loyalty, but it helped. She was also in a position to keep an eye on Barrera, who was likely the person with connections to suppliers in Latin America.

Montalba was in a quandary. He needed solid intelligence on the Berger operation, including Barrera. He didn't trust Delaney; the man was a pure mercenary, and Delaney was in awe of J.-P. Berger. He could use Delaney to subvert O'Toole's political competitors, but he couldn't afford to let Delaney know why he was interested in the Bergers. He would have to revert to using his own people.

The security risk inherent in that was troublesome. Montalba's strategy for survival was to allow no one to know he existed. No one except his sister, Graciella, knew anything about him. He kept his contacts with others to a minimum, using secure text and encrypted telephones, or prepaid, "burner" cellphones. The few times he had to meet his people face to face, he stayed in the shadows and allowed them to see only the scarred side of his face.

Far less often, he would resort to theatrical makeup to cover the scars, as he had done when he met Beverly Lennox. He capitalized on the persona of the "scar-faced bastard" among his minions, occasionally dropping hints as to what had happened to his face.

His favorite legend was that he had burned his own face with acid to make himself unrecognizable and then killed everyone who knew what he had done. His ruined face distorted into what might have been a smile as he thought about that story.

Besides his sister, the only people left alive who had seen him were

Senator O'Toole and Beverly Lennox. O'Toole had met him in a dimly lit car, and Montalba had shown only the scarred side of his face. Lennox would recall him as a handsome man.

He took a sip of the wine and held it in his mouth, savoring it. After a few seconds, he swallowed and sat up straight. He needed to see Graciella; she could take his mind off this enigma for a little while, allowing him to approach it with a fresh outlook later.

18

"Good morning, Luke. It's Dani and Liz."

"Good morning, ladies. Can you talk?"

"Yes. Our guests are off the boat, and we've disabled the surveillance system just to be sure."

"Okay. I'm not sure I know any more than I did the last time we spoke. Nothing new on Beverly Lennox or Velasquez. Phillip's kept me up to date on the two guys that got arrested in St. Vincent, but you probably know about that. Oh, and he asked me to run a records-check on Norris. Did he share that with you?"

"We haven't had a chance to talk to him," Dani said. "Anything there we should know?"

"Not really. Norris was kicked out of the navy because he killed several civilians in Iraq, apparently just because he could. The other two were dishonorably discharged from the army for drug-related offenses. They're going to do some hard time in St. Vincent, from what Phillip said. What's new on your end?"

Dani and Liz spent a couple of minutes filling Luke in on what they had learned from Beverly Lennox. When they mentioned Manny LaRosa, Luke interrupted them.

"The name 'Berto' doesn't mean anything to me, but Manny LaRosa's a different story," he said. "He's bad news; one of those characters who manages to stay out of prison because the witnesses change their stories before his court dates."

"Beverly Lennox said a big part of why she liked Berto was that he told her if she worked with him on this, she'd never see LaRosa again," Liz said.

"That would do it for me," Luke said. "But Manny told her Berto was the boss?"

"That's what she said," Dani said.

"Could you tell whether that meant he was Manny's boss, or was it just a figure of speech?"

"When she said it, I took it as a figure of speech," Dani said. "Liz?"

"The same, but now that you ask, I wonder."

"Because of what she said about Berto telling her she'd never see Manny again?" Dani asked.

"Yes," Liz said, "exactly."

"That's interesting," Luke said. "Think you could pursue that with her?"

"Sure," Dani said. "I think so. How about it, Liz?"

"I agree. She'll talk with us about it. She's uncomfortable with the whole situation, since we showed her the video."

"What video?" Luke asked.

"Of Sharktooth questioning Norris," Liz said.

"Careful," Dani said. "She doesn't know who was doing the questioning."

"Oh, right," Liz said.

"Why did that make her uncomfortable?" Luke asked. "Something Norris said?"

"Partly," Liz said. "But also because Norris wasn't in very good shape."

"What happened to him?" Luke asked.

"Sharktooth happened to him," Dani said. "Norris put up a fight when Sharktooth caught him breaking into *Vengeance*." She winked at Liz.

"Where's this Norris now?" Luke asked.

"Sharktooth said he escaped," Liz said. "but we probably don't want to ask too many questions about that. You know Sharktooth. Anyway, the video upset Beverly enough so that she wants to change sides."

"She seems pretty rattled by this whole situation," Dani said.

"Can't say as I blame her," Luke said. "I interrupted you. Anything else that you picked up from her?"

"No, I think we've covered everything. We thought maybe you could check out LaRosa," Dani said.

"I'll definitely do that," Luke said, "and let me know what she says about Berto, okay?"

"Sure," Dani said.

"Wait," Liz said. "She gave us a phone number for Berto; that's all she knows about him." She gave Luke the telephone number.

"Okay," Luke said. "That's a start. See what else you can get from her, especially on the 'boss' question."

"Okay," Dani said. "Anything else?"

"No, I think that's it," Luke said. "Let's stick to you two calling when you can talk, rather than me calling you."

"Right," Dani said. "We'll be in touch after we talk with her again."

MONTALBA WAS ENJOYING the morning's first cup of coffee when the SpecCorp phone rang.

"Yes?" he said.

"It's Delaney. Did you get the instructions for swapping out the disk drive okay?"

"Yes, thank you. It looks straightforward."

"Yeah. She shouldn't have any trouble. Just let me know when and where to drop off the replacement drive."

"I'll do that. I haven't forwarded the instructions to her yet, but I will do it soon. I may just have her exchange it at the end of the charter. That will be in Rodney Bay, St. Lucia, in a few days."

"That'll be easy, then. No problem getting her a replacement there. That's not why I called, though. I wanted to run the plan for Mike McGuire by you."

"Very well," Montalba said. "Go ahead."

"One of our lobbyists knows the younger brother; sees him fairly often. She's having lunch with him today. I had her go ahead and set that up. If you don't like the plan, it's not a big deal. She's got other stuff she can talk to him about, but I figured we should move fast on this."

"Why would we bother with Pat?" Montalba asked. "Why not go directly to Mike?"

"Two reasons. One is access. Our lobbyist knows Pat McGuire well; this would be a natural thing for her to pass on to him. The second is the increased impact. Mike's going to be much more upset that this rumor is making the rounds in Washington than he would be about a local scandal. It'll seem harder to contain."

"I see," Montalba said. "What is she going to tell him, then?"

"She's already had conversations with him about his brother-in-law's possible run for the nomination, so it'll be natural enough for her to pass along this rumor she's picked up about him. She'll tell Pat McGuire that word is somebody's set a trap for Velasquez down in the islands, that he's on a yacht with his mistress right now."

"I suppose that will incense Mike McGuire, but how does it lead them away from us? I thought you wanted to lay a trail to Mike."

"She'll let Pat know that she discovered this because her client, Spec-Corp, has had a problem. Several of their people have bailed out and are freelancing; they stole some surveillance gear and cut a deal with somebody -- she doesn't know who, but there's speculation about some divorce lawyer. The ring leader's some ex-navy SEAL named Norris."

"Ah. That sounds plausible. It doesn't shift the blame to Mike McGuire, but I suppose that doesn't matter as much as leading them away from us."

"It may or may not shift the blame to him. We think Mike McGuire will probably take some kind of action. He and Pat aren't supposed to be close. Our lobbyist is gonna try to lead Pat to think maybe his brother's behind this. I mean, his sister's married to this asshole, right? Mike McGuire's the kind of guy that would want to kick his ass, from what we've been able to learn. So Pat may just buy that his brother's behind it. If not, then the wife or her lawyer will get blamed, if anybody's looking to blame somebody."

"I see," Montalba said. "Is your person going to do anything else to further these ideas?"

"She'll play it by ear. She's got the web address for the tracker we put on the boat. She may give that to Pat if it seems like the right thing at the time. It's part of the stuff Norris stole, supposedly. He wouldn't have known that the company kept a record of the web address and all that stuff."

"A web address for the tracker?" Montalba asked. "What does that mean?"

"It's a commercial tracking device. They're dirt cheap these days. It broadcasts a GPS position via satellite every hour to the manufacturer's computer, and they put it on the web. People use them for all kinds of things. Boaters do it so their family can keep up with them. Same for hikers, hunters, like that."

"So just anyone can track the boat, then?" Montalba asked.

"Not just anybody. You have to have the web address and login credentials."

"Interesting," Montalba said. "I could track them?"

"Yeah, sure. You want me to email you the details?"

"Yes, please. What do your people think Mike McGuire's likely to do?"

"Like I said, he's probably gonna kick Velasquez's ass. That's what I'd do. Maybe break up the marriage. Who the hell knows? I don't figure it makes any difference to us. If McGuire blows it sky high, that'll end Velasquez's candidacy, so we get what we want. If he hushes it up, we've got the recordings your gal's making of Velasquez doing the dirty with her. Either way, he's finished. What do you think?"

"It may work," Montalba said.

"Is that a 'go ahead?'"

"Yes," Montalba said. "Go ahead. When will it happen? Did you say they are having lunch today?"

"Yeah. Their lunch date's at one o'clock.'

"I want the details," Montalba said.

"Sure, no problem. She'll be recording their conversation."

"Is that normal?" Montalba asked.

"Well, not quite, but it's not that unusual, either. I want to be able to show that the McGuires knew SpecCorp wasn't behind it -- that keeps you and me both clean, right? Just in case?"

Montalba said, "Send me a copy of the recording, please."

"Yeah, okay. No sweat. I'll include the transcription, too. Sometimes it's tough to make out everything on the recording. But our gal on the scene will help clean it up. That's why we do transcripts right away."

"Good. Keep me posted on how this unfolds."

"No problem. I'll give you a call once I've emailed that stuff to you."

~

MIKE MCGUIRE HAD RETURNED from a late lunch to find an urgent voice mail from his younger brother. He dialed his brother's private line in Washington, surprised when Pat answered after one ring. "Hey, Mike?"

"Yeah. Pat?"

"Yeah, it's me."

Mike McGuire frowned. "I haven't heard from you in forever. Something wrong?"

"Yeah. I just picked up some gossip I thought you ought to know about."

"So tell me."

"Our shithead brother-in-law's running around on Miranda."

"So? That's news?"

"It is when somebody hires people to document it on video."

"You shitting me? Where'd you get that from?"

"Somebody I know. I gotta keep her name out of it."

"One of your floozies, little brother?"

"It doesn't matter," Patrick McGuire said. "Somebody's setting the dumbass up. We don't need that."

"Who's behind it? You know?"

"Uh-uh. Rumor is it's some divorce lawyer, but if there's video, or even photos, it's bound to leak once he starts getting more press coverage. Then we're screwed."

"Damn Miranda," Mike said.

"Damn Miranda? Why damn Miranda? She hasn't done anything."

"Yeah, exactly. If she was any kind of wife, he wouldn't do shit like this."

"Come on, Mike. That's horseshit, and you know it. That Cuban son of a bitch never could keep it in his pants. And that's beside the point, anyway. We both have a lot riding on him getting the nomination."

"And I guess you want me to fix things," Mike said. "Like always."

"You're the one with the contacts, Mike."

"Yeah, yeah, mister hot-shot Washington lawyer. Don't want to get your hands dirty, do you?"

"This isn't something I can handle, Mike. Don't give me a ration of shit, okay? I do my part; you do yours."

"What exactly do you think I should do?"

"Go get the dumb bastard and send him home with his tail between his legs, like usual, I guess."

"Where is he?"

"You're gonna love this. He's on a damn luxury charter yacht down in the Caribbean with his latest mistress and two other women."

"Three women? He's upped his game."

"Yeah," Pat said. "Maybe, maybe not. They're the crew."

"The two extra women? Crew?"

"They run the yacht, supposedly."

"My ass, they run the yacht," Mike said. "You don't believe that, do you?"

"It doesn't matter, Mike. The problem is, there's three women involved in this that could wreck our plans. You need to get him outta this mess and make sure they aren't gonna talk."

"You know where they are? Exactly?" Mike asked.

"Yeah. There's a tracker on the yacht. I'll email you the details, but you -- "

"A tracker? Who the hell put a tracker on the yacht?"

"That's a long story. Just trust me, we got lucky on this one. You gotta move quick. The charter's supposed to end in a few days. After that, it'll be tougher to deal with the women. And the longer we wait, the more likely it is there'll be a leak. Right now, it's kind of contained."

"Shit!" Mike said. "All right. Send me what you got. What do you think I should do about the women?"

"That's out of my realm of experience. I trust you to convince them not to come back to bite us. That's what you're good at."

"Uh-huh. You don't want to know. That it, baby brother?"

"Like I said before, I do my part; you do yours. The less we know about each other's business, the safer for everybody."

"Maybe I should just waste the piece of shit and be done with it," Mike said.

"Don't say things like that, Mike."

"Why? You gonna tell somebody?"

"No, but we've got too much invested in setting him up for this run at the White House. Christ, we've been working toward this since we first fixed him up with Miranda. We can't let the asshole ruin it now. All we need him to do is stay straight for a couple of years."

"He still has to beat O'Toole in the primary. That's no sure thing."

"Let me worry about that. O'Toole's too cocky for his own good. Shit's gonna happen. Trust me."

"What kind of shit?"

"You don't want to know, Mike. Believe me."

"Okay. Send me the info. I gotta round up my troops and get the plane warmed up. You gonna tell Miranda?"

"Yeah, I'll talk to her," Pat said. "Let me hear when it's done; I'll make sure she's ready to take him back, one more time."

"Yeah," Mike said, disconnecting the call.

19

"You wore him out, didn't you?" Dani asked, chuckling at the sound of Harry's snoring. He was sprawled in a hammock in the shade of the foredeck awning, exhausted from snorkeling. She and Liz and Beverly were in the cockpit, drinking fruit punch.

"He doesn't get much exercise," Beverly said. "Physical fitness isn't important to him, except for women. He wants them to be in peak condition." She shook her head, smiling. "Did you find out anything from your friend in Miami while we were gone?"

"We talked with him," Liz said. "He knows who Manny LaRosa is, and he confirmed what you said about him. LaRosa's a nasty piece of work, according to him."

"What about Berto?" Beverly asked.

"He was going to do a little work on that; the name didn't mean anything to him. He'll try putting it in context with LaRosa, I imagine," Dani said.

"But he did want us to ask you about Berto again," Liz said.

A vertical crease appeared between Beverly's eyebrows. "I don't know any more than what I told you."

"No, we understand," Liz said, "but he was curious about Manny's characterization of Berto as 'the boss.' Do you think he meant Berto was *his* boss, or just the boss in terms of Berto's dealings with you?"

"Now that's a good question," Beverly said, raising her right hand and stroking her cheek as she gazed out at the turquoise water around them. After several seconds, she said, "I've been with Horry for a couple of months. I mean, just with him. Exclusively. You can't imagine how nice that is for me."

She looked down at her hands, picking at an imaginary hangnail and chewing on her lower lip. After a brief silence, she looked up, first at Dani, then at Liz. She frowned for a second and shrugged. "You know what I am, what I've been doing. I pretend it's not, but it's a shitty way to live. Some girls don't know any better, but ... well, never mind." She shook her head.

"We all do what we have to do, sometimes," Liz said. "That doesn't change who you are unless you let it."

Beverly nodded. She took a deep breath and let it out in a sigh. "Okay. I'd been Horry's mistress for a couple of months, and I was comfortable with that. It was the best gig I've had since, well ... anyway, Manny called me up and told me he had a new client for me, that I should call this man named Berto. He gave me a phone number.

"I was upset. I hid that from Manny, but it shook me up pretty badly. I asked him if that meant I wasn't supposed to continue my relationship with Horry."

She paused, looking off into the distance for a few seconds, then continued. "He laughed at me. He has this evil laugh, sick, like. It makes the hair on the back of my neck stand up. He laughed that way once when he was ... hurting a girl. He made me watch him that time while he ... never mind."

She shuddered and went on. "He said, 'You do what Berto says. He is the boss. If he wants you, then you are his. You don't have a choice, you dumb whore. Do I have to teach you that again?' or something like that." She stifled a sob.

Liz nodded. "Now that some time has passed since that happened, how do you interpret his use of the word 'boss?'" she asked.

"I think he just meant that I had to do what Berto said," Beverly said. "I don't know if Manny works for somebody else, or if he's his own boss. I never heard him say anything that made me think he had a boss, you know?"

"Okay," Liz said. She saw Dani raise her eyebrows. Liz caught Dani's eye and nodded.

"Did he ever use the word 'boss' to refer to any of the other men he ... ah ... " Dani asked.

"Sent me to?" Beverly asked.

"I guess," Dani said.

"It's okay, Dani. It's what I did. Like Liz said, I'm not going to let it define who I am. And to answer your question, no. I don't remember him ever referring to another client that way. That could be telling, I suppose."

"Thanks, Beverly," Liz said. "I know that wasn't easy. We'll do our best to make sure it was worth it."

"I'm going to take a dinghy ride for a few minutes and call Luke," Dani said. "I don't want to risk Harry waking up and overhearing me." She stood and took the satellite phone from its locker in the steering pedestal.

"Luke?" Beverly asked.

"Our friend in Miami," Liz said.

"Tell him to be careful; Manny's dangerous. I've heard that he's killed people, and I believe it."

"I'll tell him," Dani said. "He's accustomed to dealing with people like that, though. Don't worry."

"Billy?" Mike McGuire asked, when his phone call was answered.

"Yeah?"

"It's Mike. I got a job for you and the boys."

"Okay, boss. When?"

"Right now. Who you got available on short notice?"

"Me and Seamus and Joey. I can probably come up with a couple more if -- "

"Nah. You three'll be perfect. Seamus and Joey ready to go?"

"Yeah, Mike. We're all three sittin' here in my den, watchin' the game. What's up?"

"My dumbass brother-in-law's got his ass in a crack and doesn't even know it. We gotta go bail him out and get him home where he belongs."

"Where's he at, then?"

"On a friggin' sailboat, down in the islands."

"Down in the islands *where*?"

"Right now in the Tobago Cays, but there's a tracker on the boat in case they move before we get there."

"You said short notice, Mike. When do you wanna leave?"

"Soon as we can put all the pieces together. If we haul ass, we can probably catch 'em early tomorrow morning."

"That's fast," Billy said. "We takin' the Lear?"

"Yeah. I figure the Lear to San Juan, then a big twin engine turbo-prop to Mustique. Can't land the Lear there. Here's what I want you to do, okay?"

"Yeah. Lay it on me."

"Get hold of our guy in St. Vincent. We'll need a go-fast boat waitin' for us in Mustique, and get him to make sure there's nobody from customs gonna mess with us at the airstrip in Mustique. Got it?"

"Yeah, no problem. What time you figure we'll touch down there?"

"Say we go wheels up at Opa Locka in an hour. It's two and a half, three hours to San Juan, and roughly an hour and a half from there to Mustique. That's if I can get that guy with the Super King Air we usually use. Give us an hour to change planes and get out of San Juan, so let's say we'll touch down in Mustique around midnight, just to be safe."

"Got it. Who we goin' up against? We gonna need extra firepower?"

"Nah. Just his girlfriend and the two women that run the boat. Should be a piece of cake."

"Just handguns, then?"

"Yeah, and that's probably overkill."

"All right, Mike. Sounds okay. So we're gonna snatch Velasquez and bring him back. What about the women?"

"They're all yours. You each get one. How's that for a nice evening's entertainment?"

"I take it they ain't walking away from this, then."

"That's correct. I need you to ask 'em a few questions. They're setting Velasquez up for blackmail. I need to know who they're working for.

Once we snatch Velasquez, one of you can run me and him back to Mustique while the others take the ladies for a boat ride out over the horizon to the west. Drop me and the shithead off, and take the go-fast back out to the yacht. Once you got what we want from the women, make them and the boat disappear. Okay?"

"Got it. Like you said, piece of cake."

"Good. After the job's done, you three return the go-fast boat to our pal in St. Vincent. I'll send the Lear back for you boys; it can pick you up in St. Vincent, no sweat."

"Cool, Mike. Like you said, a nice evening's work."

"Okay, Billy. Let's make it happen. I gotta line up the planes. You handle the speedboat and the arrangements for the authorities in Mustique to look the other way. See you and the boys at Opa Locka in an hour."

～

"I FEEL SORRY FOR HER, LIZ." Dani dropped the folding anchor over the side of the dinghy. She and Liz had let the RIB drift a hundred meters or so downwind from *Vengeance* after their guests had retired to their cabin. "I didn't like overhearing them. I can't help thinking about her having to put up with that slimeball -- "

"Stop it. She doesn't need your pity. Think about something else."

"Like what?"

"Tell me what Luke said when you called him about Berto a little while ago."

"He'd checked on the phone number she gave us for Berto. It's a prepaid cellphone. He managed to get warrants for phone records for Berto and Manny LaRosa on the strength of what she told us about Berto's connection to the blackmail."

"That was fast," Liz said.

"He said it helped that the victim was a congressman. But anyway, the only calls on Berto's number were to and from Beverly. Texts, too. The dates of the texts match the dates she's been aboard. That's it."

"What about LaRosa?"

"No calls to or from LaRosa on Berto's number. Luke's got some people working through the call records from LaRosa's phone for the period when he set her up with Berto. He said they're looking for calls to numbers that match up with the location of Berto's prepaid phone. All Berto's calls to and from Beverly were from the same location."

"Where is it?" Liz asked.

"It's a cluster of high rise office and condo buildings on the waterway in Miami. Luke says unless they can get some kind of cross reference with LaRosa's calls into the same geography, it's not of much use. There are too many cellphones in that small area, otherwise. If they match up LaRosa's calls, they'll be able to get a list of phone numbers in those buildings. That's only landlines, but it would narrow their search for Berto."

"Did he have any more to say about LaRosa?" Liz asked.

"Yes, but he doesn't know what it means. In the last few months, LaRosa's started hanging out at a club in South Beach. It's called the Pink Pussycat."

"Yuck," Liz said. "That name evokes a certain image, doesn't it?"

"Yes. From what Luke said, the club was home to a couple of suspected drug dealers in the recent past. Pinky Schultz was one, and the next one was Dick Kilgore," Dani said. "The names mean nothing to me, but Luke said Schultz had run the place for as long as anybody could remember, until several months ago. He disappeared, and Kilgore took it over for a few months. Now he's vanished, and LaRosa's there."

"What did he think of Beverly's comments about Berto being 'the boss?'"

"He didn't say much about it," Dani said. "Damn!"

"What?" Liz asked.

"It just hit me. I knew we were missing something about Berto."

"What about him?"

"She said he was handsome," Dani said, "'really handsome, and has elegant manners,' she said."

"Yes," Liz said, "I remember her saying that."

"She's met him, Liz!" Dani said. "She knows what he looks like."

"Damn! You're right," Liz said. "How did we miss that?"

"We didn't miss it. It just took a while for it to register, mixed in with everything else. Wonder where she met him?"

"Do you think she might know where he lives?" Liz said.

"Not much chance of that," Dani said, "not if he didn't give her his last name and only communicates with her using a burner cellphone. Besides, she would have told us that, don't you think?"

"Probably so," Liz said.

"But it's still something," Dani said. "If she met with him somewhere, maybe somebody else saw them together, or saw him arrive, or something. It's more than we had."

"We need to ask her about it and call Luke," Liz said. "But I guess we'll have to wait until tomorrow."

"Yes," Dani said. "Speaking of tomorrow, did she say anything about plans for going somewhere?"

"No, but their time's running out."

"Oh, you're right. I'm not used to one-week charters. What do they have? A couple of days?"

"Yes," Liz said. "We should be dropping them in Rodney Bay the day after tomorrow. It may be time to head back."

"I wonder about the recordings," Dani said.

"What about them?" Liz asked.

"Somebody will be wanting to retrieve them," Dani said. "That's something else we should ask her about. We need a diversion for Harry tomorrow. Do you have another string bikini?"

"Watch it, lady. You want to swim back to Rodney Bay?"

"No ma'am. Just teasing you," Dani said, grinning. "Can I borrow it?"

"It?"

"That string bikini," Dani said.

"Now I *know* you're teasing," Liz said. "Let's go back to *Vengeance*."

20

"That's them," Mike said, leaning over and cupping his hand around Billy's ear. "*Vengeance*. It's like daytime with this moon. Cut off our running lights and ease on in there, dead slow. Kill the extra engines. When we get close enough, shut everything down and we'll coast alongside them."

"Okay," Billy said. "Got it. I'll stop a little upwind and we can drift back."

"Good," Mike said. He turned to the other men, his right index finger across his lips. When they nodded, he pointed at *Vengeance* and gave a thumbs-up.

Billy worked his way to a position about 50 meters off *Vengeance's* starboard bow and killed the one engine that was still running. Mike stationed Seamus and Joey along the port side of the go-fast boat, whispering instructions to them to fend off *Vengeance*. He didn't want to announce their arrival by bumping the yacht.

Mike didn't expect much trouble from the three women and Velasquez, but he wanted the element of surprise on his side. It took them 30 seconds to drift back alongside *Vengeance*. All four men were holding the speedboat in place, leaving an arms' length gap between the two boats.

At Mike's gesture, Seamus and Joey crept over the yacht's gunwale, slithering under the lower lifelines.

They moved forward, out of the way, and Mike came aboard. Billy handed Mike the bow line from the speedboat and hoisted himself aboard, twisting as he rose so that he ended up sitting on *Vengeance's* toe rail, his feet holding the speedboat away from *Vengeance.* He looked over his shoulder, caught Mike's eye, and raised his eyebrows.

Mike nodded, and Billy shoved the speedboat away with his legs as Mike payed out extra line. The wind caught the speedboat and it began drifting aft, several feet off *Vengeance's* starboard side. Mike walked along, the line in his hand, watching to make sure the boat didn't drift back in and bump *Vengeance.* Fifteen seconds later, it was trailing behind *Vengeance.* Mike squatted and tied the bow line to a cleat on *Vengeance's* aft quarter.

Rising from his crouch, he made eye contact with each of the three men before he moved to the companionway. He lifted the soft nylon mesh bug screen, moving it aside and peering below for a few seconds. Staying low to avoid silhouetting himself in the moonlight, he crept down the ladder, facing forward.

He had studied the yacht's web page this afternoon, so he knew that the guest accommodations were in the forward cabin. He felt his way toward the bow, careful to make no sound. He sensed Billy following close behind him. They had agreed earlier that the two of them would get in position to subdue Velasquez, leaving Joey and Seamus in the aft part of the living quarters to deal with the two women if they came out of their aft cabin.

Mike stopped at the door to the forward stateroom and looked back at the companionway. His vision had adjusted to the dimly lit space well enough so that he could see the two men come down the ladder and disappear into the shadows of the galley area. He caught Billy's eye. Billy nodded, and Mike turned and put his hand on the knob of the paneled teak door that closed off the forward stateroom. Taking a deep breath, he turned the knob and pushed against the door.

It didn't swing freely. The wood was swollen from the damp evening air. He applied more pressure, and the door gave way with a soft creaking sound. He stepped into the forward stateroom and turned on the penlight that he held, shielding it with his other hand to avoid giving himself away. He crept through the short corridor between the head and the dressing area until he could see Velasquez and the woman, sprawled naked on a queen-sized berth in the silver moonlight that filtered through the overhead hatch.

He turned off the penlight and slipped it in his pocket, taking a moment to admire the woman. Velasquez might be a shithead, but he had good taste. The boys were going to have fun making her talk. Mike grinned and reached to put a hand on Velasquez's shoulder, pausing when he heard a muttered curse from the back of the boat, followed by the thud of a body striking some of the wooden cabinetry.

DANI WAS on her feet before she was wide awake. She put a hand on Liz's shoulder and leaned down to whisper in her ear. "Did you hear that?"

Liz nodded and rolled to a sitting position on the edge of her berth. Cupping a hand around Dani's ear, she whispered, "Door to the forward stateroom. It sticks, remember."

Dani turned and opened their door, stepping out into the small area between the galley and the chart table. Liz saw a blur of motion on Dani's left side and watched as Dani flew across the open space to crash into the shelves above the chart table. She registered that Dani collapsed on the seat at the chart table, dazed.

Liz grabbed the big three-cell flashlight from its bracket by the door, grasping it in both hands like a baseball bat. She put her left foot on the threshold and drove forward off her right leg, pivoting to the left and bringing the heavy flashlight around in a horizontal arc at head height. She heard a satisfying crunch and felt the jolt in her wrists from a solid contact. She saw the blood-covered face of the man called Joey as she cocked her arms for another blow.

Before she swung, Seamus landed a blow on the base of Liz's neck with his weight behind it, and she went down. Shoving her aside, he stepped forward to help Joey. Before he got to his friend, Dani drove the folded knuckles of her right hand into Seamus's right kidney. He gasped for air, paralyzed for a second.

She didn't waste her opportunity, making a claw of her left hand as she snaked it over his shoulder. She hooked her middle finger into the inner corner of his left eye socket, planted her right palm on the back of his head, and scooped his eye out.

She dropped her left hand to cup his chin, getting ready to break his neck. She'd begun to twist his head when the overhead lights in the main cabin came on and a pistol with a suppressor barked from up near the forward stateroom. Maintaining the pressure on his neck, she looked over her right shoulder to see Billy grinning at her as he pointed a Glock 19 at her face.

"Let him go, ya wild bitch," he said, with a chuckle. "Drag yer girlfriend back in yer cabin. Come out before I tell ya to and I'll kneecap ya both. Move!"

Dani released her grip on Seamus and stepped back as he slid to the cabin sole, moaning. She reached down and helped Liz to her feet, supporting her as they followed Billy's instructions.

"Everything under control back there?" Mike asked, from the forward cabin.

"Yeah," Billy said. "They're a couple a fuckin' wildcats. Joey knocked one of 'em on her ass, then the other one brained him with one of them big flashlights. Seamus put her down and the first one woke up and jumped him. Put his fuckin' eye out; was tryin' to break his worthless neck. That's why I popped a cap."

"You shoot her?" Mike asked.

"Hell no, Mike. Shot out the back door. I ain't about to waste her. Gal like that, we gonna have us some serious fun with her before this is over. Where's Velasquez?"

"Getting dressed and gathering up his shit," Mike said.

"How about his girlfriend?"

"I slapped the shit out of her and shoved her in the head. Tied the door shut and told her if she made a sound I'd let you skin her alive. See if you can wake up one of these losers. You need to run me and Velasquez back to the plane and get this boat out of here before daylight. We don't need witnesses seeing you leave here towing the speedboat."

"Okay," Billy said. "Lemme secure the women." He stepped around Seamus, who was beginning to breathe more evenly between his moans. Leading with his pistol, Billy reached for the door to the aft stateroom and pulled it closed.

"Can you grab a piece of rope from upstairs and tie that shut for me while I play nursemaid?" he asked.

"Yeah, sure," Mike said, scrambling up the companionway ladder.

By the time Mike got back, Billy had thrown several glasses of water in Joey's face. Joey was spluttering and wiping away the blood from the wound over his left ear. Mike tied the door shut while Billy turned his attention to Seamus.

"You awake, Joey?" Mike asked.

"Yeah." He shook his head. "Man, she nailed my ass. I'm gonna make -- "

"You'll get your chance to get even later. Right now, get this fucking boat moving," Mike said. "Just pull the anchor up and drive straight west, once you get out of these reefs. Billy will be back with you in a few minutes. Don't mess with the women until he gets back. You gotta find out who they're working for, remember?"

"Sure Mike," Joey said. "That's cool." He got to his feet, leaning against the bulkhead for a second.

"You okay?" Billy asked.

"Yeah, man. Fine as frog hair. What happened to Seamus? That his damn eyeball?"

"Yeah," Billy said, wrapping a makeshift bandage diagonally over Seamus's head, loosely holding the eyeball over its socket. "That first one you cold-cocked woke up and tore into him. She was about to break his damn neck. Knew what she was doin', too. Watch her ass, you hear me?"

"Yeah, man. I got it."

"Don't get any ideas about the women until I get back. You ready, Mike?"

"Yeah. Pull the boat in while I get Velasquez."

MONTALBA HAD SLEPT POORLY last night; he was frustrated by SpecCorp's ineptitude. He had hoped to use them for his future surveillance needs, but they had failed him twice now. He should know later today whether Delaney's attempt to salvage their plan to ruin Velasquez would be successful, but that still left his wish to spy on Berger and Chirac unfulfilled.

SpecCorp's use of military misfits was proving to be a liability when it came to dealing with Montalba's competitors in the drug trade. Delaney and his people consistently underestimated "civilians." They used the term in a disparaging way; they weren't accustomed to contending with people who were as skilled, tough, and well-equipped as they were.

Montalba had reviewed the instructions Delaney sent him for the retrieval of the recordings from *Vengeance*. He was impressed with the level of detail; there were even photographs of the installation, showing the disk drive and the plug-in connectors. Beverly Lennox should have no trouble collecting the fruits of her labor.

The notes described the technique for bypassing the proximity key to make the system record continuously. Montalba had sent the entire package to Beverly in a series of text messages a few minutes ago, including his order to set the system for continuous recording before she left the yacht in Rodney Bay. When he didn't get a delivery notification back after a few minutes, he began to wonder whether her phone was turned off, or if they were out of cellphone range.

He remembered the GPS tracking link that Delaney had sent him. Opening Delaney's email, he copied the link and pasted it into the web browser on his computer. He logged in with the user name and password Delaney had provided and watched as a map filled the screen. After a few seconds, the map updated with hourly position plots for *Vengeance*. The plots were marked with time and date and were connected in chronological order by a blue line.

He traced the yacht's route from Bequia to the Tobago Cays and discovered that if he hovered the cursor over a plot point, a text box would open with the latitude and longitude coordinates and the vessel's course and speed.

Montalba spent a couple of minutes studying the information. He frowned when he realized that the boat's most recent position was about thirty miles due west of the spot in the Tobago Cays where they had spent the last couple of days.

He scribbled notes on a yellow legal pad as he digested what the tracker was telling him. They had left the Tobago Cays a few minutes after four this morning. He glanced at the clock on his desk. It was eight a.m. in Miami; that would be nine a.m. Atlantic Standard time. They had left the Tobago Cays roughly five hours ago. He considered that the plots were only updated hourly, so his calculation wasn't precise.

There were two plot points between the Tobago Cays and their current position. Both of those points showed a course of 270 degrees magnetic, and a speed of eight knots. The point for their current, or most recent, position showed them moving to the west, still at eight knots. This made no sense to Montalba, given how far offshore they were.

They were out of sight of land, and there was no landfall on their course for hundreds of miles. He looked at the world map on the wall behind his credenza. Nicaragua was roughly 1,300 miles to their west. They wouldn't be going to Nicaragua, would they? He tried to imagine what they were doing out there and shook his head. Then he remembered that Berger had worked in Central America years ago, fighting in some kind of drug wars.

Reaching for the SpecCorp phone, he called Delaney.

21

Dani sighed with relief when Liz blinked. She stared at Dani for a second, frowned, and shook her head. Raising a hand to her mouth, she turned her face to the side and retched. She recovered without throwing up and looked back up at Dani.

"What happened," she asked. "Why am I -- "

Dani laid a hand over Liz's mouth, her touch gentle, and shook her head. "Shh," she said. "They're still here."

"Who?" Liz whispered. "Why's the engine running?"

Dani smiled, glad that Liz was asking questions that made sense. She leaned down, her lips close to Liz's ear. "I don't know who they are. There are three of them. Four of them came aboard. I walked out our door, thinking our guests were awake, and one of them knocked me for a loop. You came out fighting and cracked him with the flashlight. He went down, but another one hit you hard on the back of the neck and took you out. I think you've got a concussion. You've been in and out for over an hour. You following me so far?"

"Yes, but -- "

"Just listen; let me get you caught up. One of them, a guy they called Mike, took Harry and left. Mike seemed to be in charge. His second-in-command is named Billy. Billy took Mike and Harry to Mustique in a speed boat and left them there. They said something about a plane.

While they were gone, the one you brained -- he's Joey -- hauled in the anchor and got under way. Billy came back and tied their speedboat to the stern. We've been heading west at eight to nine knots for about an hour and a half. Got it?"

"Yes, but you said there were three, and Mike's gone. That leaves Billy and Joey. Is there another one aboard?"

"Very good! You're back with me. The other one is named Seamus. He's out of action, at least for a while."

"What happened to him?"

"I put out one of his eyes. I was about to break his neck, but Billy stuck a Glock in my face and told me to back off. So I let him live. For now."

"What about Beverly?"

"They shut her in the forward head and tied the door shut. Our door's tied shut too."

"Where are they taking us?"

"Mike told Billy to take us offshore far enough so nobody would see what happened. He and Joey are supposed to find out who we're working for and then do away with us and sink *Vengeance*."

"Great," Liz said. "So there are two of us and two, maybe three, of them?"

"And Beverly, but she's probably just going to be in the way. Maybe she'll be good for a distraction. But I'm not sure you're in fighting trim. Can you stand up?"

Liz swung her legs over the edge of the berth and pushed herself to a sitting position. Standing, she held on to Dani and swayed for a few seconds. "I'll do what I have to," she said.

"That's the right attitude, anyway. Save your strength and focus on getting your bearings, for now."

"How long do we have?" Liz asked.

"I'd say not very long. From the GPS in my phone, we're around 25 miles out. I'm surprised they haven't already started in on us."

"Damn it!" Liz hissed. "Maybe I can fight sitting down."

"We'll be okay. I've got a surprise for them," Dani said.

Her eyes went round as the engine was throttled back.

"What surprise?" Liz asked.

Dani put a finger over her lips and shook her head as the engine rumbled to a stop.

"Get the one that blinded Seamus," a man's voice said, from the other side of the cabin door. "We'll start with her. Mess her up real good and leave her for the others to look at while we question them."

"You want her now, Billy?"

"Yeah. Wait, you dumb fuck. Don't cut that rope. Untie it. I'll drag her ass out here and you tie the door shut again; keep that other one in there. She can listen, but we'll do one of 'em at a time, okay?"

"Okay, Billy. Flip you to see who gets her first?"

"In your dreams, Joey. You ain't man enough for that one, anyhow. She's a fuckin' wildcat, remember? Now, open the door and I'll get her out before they realize what's happening. You watch the other one and get the door closed fast. Here goes."

Dani looked back over her shoulder and smiled at Liz, giving her an exaggerated wink.

WHEN HE HEARD Delaney answer the phone, Montalba forced himself to remain calm. "Good morning, Mr. Delaney. I'm pleased that you're available so early this morning."

"Yes," Delaney said. "What can I do for you? I'm due in a meeting in the next few minutes. Is there something specific?"

"That's no way for you to greet your single largest investor, is it Mr. Delaney? After your recent, lackluster performance, I would expect you to be more deferential."

"I'm sorry to be short with you, but it's hard to be warm and friendly when I don't even know your name," Delaney said.

"It is better that you don't know my name," Montalba said. "If you knew my name, you might be facing death right now, instead of just an unhappy patron."

"You dare to threaten me?"

"Mr. Delaney, I shouldn't have to remind you that your defenses are, shall we say, less than perfect. How are your guards and their dogs? Have they recovered from their recent misfortune?"

"Look," Delaney said, "I'm struggling; I want to satisfy you. I apologize again. How may I help you?"

"That's better, thank you, Mr. Delaney. I want to know what's happening with the Velasquez problem."

"Fair enough. Here's what I know. We had surveillance on Mike McGuire starting yesterday afternoon. He and three of his men used his company's Learjet to fly to San Juan last night. They left Opa Locka around 7:30 and switched to a Beechcraft Super King Air in San Juan. They flew to Mustique and landed there shortly after midnight. McGuire came back to Opa Locka with Velasquez about an hour ago. They went to McGuire's house."

"And the three men?" Montalba asked.

"Not with him. We think he left them down island to deal with the women."

"Deal with the women? What do you mean?"

"McGuire's motivation is to hush this whole thing up; he and his brother have a big stake in Velasquez's candidacy."

"That doesn't answer my question," Montalba said. "I used the tracking information you sent me. The yacht is headed west at eight knots. They were over twenty miles from the islands for the last position fix. How is that 'dealing with the women?'"

"Let me have a look," Delaney said, tapping on a keyboard. "While it's coming up, you have to understand that we don't control what McGuire does. Having said that, it doesn't matter what he does, because we're going to put this whole thing in the spotlight."

"How will you do that?" Montalba asked.

"Okay," Delaney said. "Just a second ... there. There's a new position fix. The yacht's about 30 miles out and it's moving to the northwest at about three quarters of a knot. I'd say they're drifting. Now, back to your question, I'm guessing at this, based on what I'd do if I were in McGuire's shoes, okay?"

"Yes," Montalba said. "What would you do?"

"I wouldn't want to leave witnesses. Would you?"

"You're suggesting that his men will eliminate the three women. Is that it?"

"And the boat," Delaney said. "That's what I'd do. You see it differently?"

"That makes sense, but I didn't know McGuire did business that way."

"Maybe he doesn't. It won't make any difference to you and me if he lets the women live and they spill the story."

"That's so," Montalba said. "But suppose he does eliminate the women and sink the boat. Velasquez would still be a viable candidate, then, because losing the boat means we can't retrieve the recordings."

"We don't need to," Delaney said. "I've already taken care of that."

"You already have the recordings?"

"No. Remember the two men who were working with Norris?"

"The ones who are in jail in St. Vincent, you mean?" Montalba asked.

"Yes. They've been primed by the lawyer we hired. He's going to tell them to reveal the identity of their employer in exchange for a lighter sentence. He'll negotiate that with the prosecutor today."

Montalba swallowed hard. "But how does that help us?"

"Our story is that Norris and those two had been fired from SpecCorp. They stole the surveillance equipment from us, and they were freelancing. Told their client they worked for us, for the credibility that would buy them. They're going to say they were hired by Patrick and Michael McGuire to get the goods on their low-down, cheating brother-in-law. The McGuires were pissed off at Velasquez for the way he treated their sister."

Montalba relaxed. He laughed to himself, and said, "That's ingenious."

"That's not quite everything. There will be a controlled leak from SpecCorp to the press, disowning Norris and his team and denying our involvement in what was apparently a blackmail attempt directed at the congressman."

Montalba laughed aloud at that.

"Satisfied, now?" Delaney asked.

"I'm not happy that your people allowed us to get into such a situation, but your recovery is impressive."

"I'll keep you informed of developments, but I really need to run right now. I have a meeting at Lang ... ah, out in northern Virginia."

"Very well," Montalba said. "Go to your meeting."

BILLY OPENED the door into the aft cabin and grinned when he saw Dani backed against the opposite wall. "Come to Daddy, sugar," he said, stepping toward her.

She smiled sweetly and raised the Glock 21 she'd taken from Seamus when she blinded him. She shot Billy in his left thigh, marveling at the stopping power of the .45 ACP hollow point bullet. Before he hit the cabin sole, she raised the pistol, aiming it at Joey, who stood just outside the door with his hands in the air.

"Don't shoot," he said. "I'm cool."

She chuckled. "Well, I'm not, asshole," she said, lowering her aim and blowing away his left kneecap. He screamed and collapsed.

Turning her attention back to Billy, she saw him struggling to free the suppressor on his pistol; it was caught in the waistband of his jeans. "Uh-uh," she said. "Don't do it."

When he ignored her, she put a round in his right shoulder. She leaned over and took the pistol from him, tossing it to Liz, who sat on the edge of her berth. "If he moves, take his left kneecap. Think you can do it?"

"With my eyes closed," Liz said. "Where'd you get that cannon?"

"The one I blinded had it. I figured he didn't need it anymore."

"Let's talk about this," Billy said.

"Hold that thought, shithead," Dani said. "I'll get back to you directly."

She stepped through the doorway and aimed her pistol at Joey's face. He was moaning and clutching at his ruined knee, his attention focused on his wound.

"Joey," Dani said. "Look at me, sweetie, or I'll make the other one match."

"N-no, please," he said, looking up into the barrel of the big pistol.

"Where's your gun, Joey?"

"In the back of my jeans."

"Okay. You get one chance. Put your right hand on top of your head."

He did as she ordered, his face pale from shock.

"Now, reach back with your left hand and pull the gun out of your waistband with your thumb and forefinger. "Wait!" she said, as he started to move.

He froze.

"What did I say?" she asked.

"Pull the gun out with my thumb and forefinger."

"Good boy. Now keep listening. I want you to put the gun on the cabin sole and slide it to me when I tell you to. If you grip it with your whole hand when you pull it out, I'll blow your arm off. Understand?"

"Yeah. I'm cool. Don't shoot me again."

"No promise on that. I may shoot you again, but at least you get points for listening. Now, pick the gun out and slide it to me."

When she had his pistol, she stepped to the side. "Can you see this one, too, Liz?"

"Yes."

"Good. If either one of them moves, kneecap both of them. I need to check on Seamus." She went into the main cabin where she found Seamus sitting up on the starboard settee, a crude bandage covering most of his face.

"Thanks for the loan of the pistol," she said. "You saved my ass, but I don't think your friends are very happy. Can you speak?"

"Yeah," he said.

"Good. When I tell you to, I want you to lie down on your stomach on that settee, legs straight and feet together. No fast moves, okay?"

"Yeah."

"Do it now," she said.

He rolled to the side and stretched out, his hands under his shoulders as he adjusted his position.

"Good," she said. "Put both hands behind your back and cross your wrists."

He complied with her instructions.

"I'm going to tie you up, Seamus. Are you right-handed or left-handed?"

"Right-handed," he said.

"Okay. If you give me any trouble, I'm going to blow your right arm off with your .45. Understand?"

"Yeah. No trouble."

"Good boy." Moving quickly, she took a large cable tie from her pocket and slipped it under his crossed wrists. With a practiced motion, she fastened it using her left hand while she kept the pistol trained on him with her right. "Good," she said. "I'm going to do your ankles now. Move, and I'll blow your balls right through the top of your head. I love this .45. Thanks again for letting me borrow it."

Dani went back to the chart table and opened a drawer, rummaging in it for a few seconds. She picked out a rigging knife and closed the drawer. "Liz?" she called.

"Yes?"

"Everything under control back there?"

"Yes."

"Good. I'm going to let Beverly out, then I'll come back and secure the other two prisoners."

"Take your time. The one back here in our cabin's passed out."

"What a candy-ass," Dani said, opening the rigging knife as she went forward. When she reached the forward stateroom, she cut through the rope securing the head door with a few strokes of the razor-sharp knife.

"Beverly?" she said, opening the door.

"What happened?" Beverly asked. "I heard gunshots."

"We had a little excitement," Dani said. "Come on out and let's figure out how to entertain our guests."

22

D ani knelt beside Joey, who was face down on the cabin sole, his wrists and ankles bound with cable ties.

"It's your lucky day, Joey," she said. "Do you know why?"

When he didn't answer, she prodded him, poking his shoulder with the blade of her rigging knife. "If you answer, you'll live longer," she said. "And with a lot less pain, too." She pressed harder with the knife, drawing blood.

"Okay, okay!" he said. "Why is it my lucky day?"

"Because you get me first, just like you wanted. You don't even have to flip for it."

"Huh?" he asked.

"You wanted to flip a coin with Billy to see who got first crack at me."

"I was just kiddin' around," he said.

"Aw, I'm disappointed. Here I was, flattered, and now I find out you weren't even serious. Actually, I'm pissed off by that. It's not nice to tease a girl that way."

"Uh, I meant to say ... "

"Joey?" she interrupted.

"Yeah?"

"Don't dig yourself in any deeper. The damage is done. The best thing for you would be to answer a few questions. What do you say? Want to do that? Or should I cut you a little bit?"

"Don't cut me. I'll talk."

"Why are you here?" Dani asked.

"Um, we came to get Velasquez."

"Why?"

"Why did we come for him?" Joey asked.

"You're stalling," Dani said, drawing the knife across his upper arm, making a shallow cut about two inches long.

He screamed as a few drops of blood oozed out along the cut.

"I'm losing patience," Dani said. "Shallow cuts are painful, and you've got a lot of skin for me to work with."

"I'd talk if I were you," Liz added. "She's just getting started. You have no idea how much she's going to enjoy making you scream. It would be better if -- "

"Dani? Liz?" Beverly interrupted, her face pale as she watched Dani cut away Joey's shirt, exposing his back.

"Yes?" Dani asked, running a fingernail along Joey's exposed spine as he writhed on the cabin sole.

"Don't do this, please."

"What?" Dani rocked back on her heels and looked up at Beverly. "I want to know who was behind this. These pieces of garbage were going to kill us after they got through using us to amuse themselves."

"I already know who it was," Beverly said. "I'll tell you everything I know, but you have to promise me you won't torture them."

"Do you know these bastards?" Dani asked.

"No."

"Then why do you care? They were going to do worse to us, and they kidnapped your lover boy."

"You're a better person than this, Dani," Beverly said.

"You're in no position to tell me who's a better person." Dani stood, scowling as she stepped close to Beverly. "You don't exactly occupy the moral high ground."

Liz put a hand on Dani's arm. "Dani," she said.

"What?"

"Beverly might be able to save us some time and trouble."

"We've got plenty of time, and the trouble's not ours."

"No," Liz said, "but the aftermath will be."

"What are you saying? What aftermath?"

"We've already got enough of a mess to clean up. Why get more blood on the upholstery and the cabin sole if we don't have to?"

Dani, her eyes like slits, looked at Liz for a few seconds. Relaxing, she stepped back from Beverly and said, "Okay. I'll listen."

"First, this wasn't a kidnapping," Beverly said. "He left voluntarily."

"He didn't have much choice," Dani said.

"I was there, Dani, right in the stateroom with Horry and the guy he called McGuire. McGuire was angry with him, but he never threatened Horry, and Horry finally suggested he'd just go home with McGuire."

"McGuire?" Dani asked. "He's the one these guys called Mike?"

"Yes. Horry called him Mike, too, some of the time."

"Mike McGuire, then," Dani said. "So who was he working for?"

"I don't think he was working for anybody," Beverly said. "I had time to piece it all together while I was locked in the bathroom."

"Piece it all together?" Liz asked.

"Yes. What Horry and Mike said to one another, plus what I've picked up over the last couple of months."

"Tell us, then," Dani said.

"Horry's wife's maiden name was McGuire. Mike is his brother-in-law."

"Are you telling me this is some kind of family quarrel?" Dani asked.

"Yes. At least partly, I think."

"I'm missing something, though," Dani said. "I see that Mike might be angry about the jerk betraying his sister, but why kidnap him like this?"

"The McGuire family's funding Horry's campaign, for the most part. Mike was berating him for risking it all 'for a piece of ass,' as he referred to me." Beverly took a deep breath. "Mike said something about protecting his investment. He threatened to castrate Horry if he didn't stay straight until after the election."

"Did McGuire know about you?" Dani asked.

Beverly frowned. "I'm not sure what you're asking. He was standing there, looking at me."

"The blackmail scheme," Dani said.

Beverly shook her head and stepped close to Dani, leaning in to whisper in her ear, "We shouldn't let these guys overhear things they don't already know."

Dani grinned. "Don't worry about them. They won't get a chance to tell anybody."

"Even so," Liz said, "I agree with Beverly. Let's take this conversation up to the cockpit. I need fresh air, and these boys can't get into any trouble now."

"OKAY, NOW IT'S JUST US," Dani said, her voice low. She sat down in the cockpit, and Liz and Beverly followed suit.

"I don't think they had anything to do with Berto's plans," Beverly said. "Just the opposite, the way I see it. Berto wanted to ruin Horry's chances at the presidency, for whatever reason. Mike McGuire was angry that Horry was blowing his shot at the nomination by being here with me."

Dani sat, frowning, as she stared off into the distance. "I see what you mean."

After several seconds, Beverly said, "I have a question for you, if it's okay."

Dani shrugged. "Sure. Ask away."

"What did you mean when you said McGuire's men wouldn't get a chance to tell anybody?"

Dani's eyebrows shot up. She glanced at Liz and then stared at Beverly for a moment. "They're fish food, unless we think of something else to ask them."

"That's what I was afraid you meant. Don't kill them, Dani. Please?"

Dani's face flushed. "They were going to kill us. Why shouldn't I return the favor?"

"Because you're not like them," Beverly said. "I know you think I'm not in a position to judge you, and I understand why you feel that way."

"I'm sorry I said that, about the moral high ground," Dani said. "It was a cheap shot; you deserve better; you put your trust in us."

"You needn't apologize," Beverly said. "Certainly, it stung, but all the more because it's true. What I am doesn't mean you should lower yourself to the level of these men. I said it a few minutes ago; you're a better person than that. I may be a whore, but that means I know how to recognize the scum of the earth. They are, and you're not."

"But we're in the middle of nowhere; we have a right to defend ourselves," Dani said.

"And you have. You had every right to do what you did to them. If you had killed them in the process, that would be different, but you didn't. Don't you see? You won. They're no threat to us now. Killing them would be cold-blooded murder."

Dani looked at Liz. Liz held her gaze and said nothing.

"I see your point," Dani said. "What do you think we should do?"

"Call the police," Beverly said.

"We're in international waters," Liz said. "Which police?"

"Who would have jurisdiction over a ship in international waters? Dani, you're the captain. That's the kind of thing you must know."

"It's fuzzy," Dani said, "but we're U.S. flagged, so the U.S. Coast Guard's a good place to start. They have jurisdiction over U.S. flagged vessels anywhere in the world."

"Can you call them?"

"We can, but ... What's your take, Liz?"

"Where was Mike McGuire headed?" Liz asked. "Do you know where he lives?"

"Miami," Beverly said. "They were flying there, he said."

"We could call Luke, for a start, then," Dani said. "It wouldn't hurt to have him involved to help fight our corner. There will be miles of red tape."

"You've mentioned Luke before," Beverly said. "Who is he?"

"He's a captain in the Miami Police Department," Liz said. "He's in charge of homicide, among other things."

"Homicide?" Beverly asked.

"He's also responsible for liaison with a bunch of federal agencies, like the DEA and the Joint Terrorism Task Force," Dani said. "He's got the contacts to shepherd us through this."

"And he's a friend, right?" Beverly asked.

"Well, yes. The guy who used to be his partner on the police force is married to a good friend of ours," Liz said. "It's a long story, but he'll help us."

"Right," Dani said. "He'd be a good place to start. What do you think, Liz? Should we take the high road on this?"

"There's no going back if we do that," Liz said. She looked at Beverly. "We'll be tied up with questions for who knows how long, and you were planning to fly back to the States the day after tomorrow."

"I don't have any real need to, now," Beverly said. "I don't want to impose on you, but I could get a hotel room or something if I need to stay somewhere while we sort this out."

"You don't need to do that. We're not booked for the next couple of weeks," Liz said. "What do you want to do, Dani?"

"Now that I've cooled off, I think it's the right thing to do. Let's call Luke. But first, should we see about first aid for this sackful of assholes we've caught? It wouldn't do to let them bleed to death, now that we've decided not to kill them."

"I already did the best I could with Billy," Liz said. "I put a tourniquet on his leg and a pressure bandage on the shoulder. I thought I should keep him around so we could question him. Should I look at Joey?"

"He took a round to the kneecap. Lots of superficial damage, and he's probably not going to walk right from now on, but he's not bleeding much," Dani said.

Liz opened the small locker in the steering pedestal where they kept their satellite phone. "I'll call Luke. Can you get a position fix?"

"Sure," Dani said, punching buttons on the chart plotter mounted above the helm. "Those idiots didn't have it turned on; it'll be a minute getting a fix."

23

"That all happened much more quickly than I thought it would," Beverly said, "but what do I know about this kind of thing?"

"It surprised me, too," Dani said. She and Liz and Beverly were sitting in the cockpit, watching the two orange U.S. Coast Guard RIBs that were disappearing toward the western horizon. One of them was towing the speedboat that McGuire's men had tied to *Vengeance's* stern earlier.

"I'm surprised they didn't ask more questions, from what you said earlier," Beverly said.

"That will no doubt come later," Dani said. "It's thanks to Luke that we're not tied up in red tape right now."

"Yes. Luke said they'd be back in touch," Liz said. "They wanted to get those three to the sick bay aboard the cutter ASAP."

When they had spoken with Luke a couple of hours earlier, he had put them on hold to talk with his DEA liaison. A medium endurance cutter had been holding station some 30 miles to their northwest, involved in a mission to interdict drug smuggling. Luke had arranged for the Coast Guard to arrest McGuire's three henchmen and return them to Miami.

Given their relative positions, Dani had decided to sail to the north-northeast rather than drifting while they waited for the boats from the cutter. *Vengeance* was making a comfortable nine knots in the direction of St. Lucia. When the Coast Guard RIBs had intercepted them, Dani hove to for them to pick up the three wounded captives. The transfer had taken mere minutes, and they were once again under way.

"What time will we get to St. Lucia?" Beverly asked.

Dani fiddled with the chart plotter for a few seconds before she said, "Around nine this evening, if the wind holds."

"You should be able to make your flight tomorrow with no trouble," Liz said. "What time does it leave? Do you need to confirm?"

"I've been thinking about that," Beverly said. "I'm not sure I want to go back just yet."

"What did you have in mind?" Liz asked.

"I don't know. Based on what's happened, I'm not comfortable going back to Miami, though."

"What about your place there?" Dani asked.

"My place?"

"Where you live," Liz said. "is someone looking after it for you?"

A wistful look crossed Beverly's face. "I don't have a 'place,' like most people do. I don't have much of anything, actually, except a few clothes -- and some jewelry in a safe deposit box."

"I thought you had a condo or something," Dani said. "When we checked you and Velasquez out, we heard you were living in the high-rent district on the Intracoastal Waterway in Miami."

Beverly shook her head. "I was hanging out there; it was part of my gig as Velasquez's mistress. I don't even know who owns that place. There's nothing there for me to go back to; that's for sure."

"Could it have belonged to this Berto character?" Dani asked.

"Maybe. I don't really know. Manny LaRosa gave me the keys to it when he set me up with Velasquez."

"Does Velasquez know who owns it?" Liz asked.

"I led him to believe it was mine," Beverly said. "I told him my parents left me a trust fund when they were killed in an auto accident my senior year in college. I'm afraid to go back there, after all that's happened. Manny won't be too happy with me."

"I thought Berto told you you'd never see Manny again," Dani said.

Beverly laughed. "One thing I've learned in the last few years is not to trust anything a man tells me. Especially not one as handsome as Berto. He has his own game; I'm just a pawn."

"What will you do?" Liz asked. "How will you live?"

"I'll think of something. I have some money -- enough to keep me afloat for a good while, if I'm careful. If it looks like it's safe, maybe I'll finish grad school and get a real job. As boring as that sounds, I've had enough excitement for a while."

"What were you studying?" Dani asked.

"International finance."

"What was your undergraduate field?" Liz asked.

"I did a double major in accounting and French."

Dani and Liz began to laugh.

Beverly's face flushed and she said, "Well, the hell with you, then."

"Wait, Beverly!" Liz said. "I'm sorry. We're not laughing at you."

"Yeah, sure. A whore with a master's degree," Beverly said. "Pretty funny, isn't it?"

"We're laughing at the irony," Dani said. "Fate bringing us together is what's funny."

Beverly turned an angry stare on Dani and didn't say anything.

"We never told you about ourselves," Dani said.

Beverly shook her head, but her face still radiated anger. "You said you worked in a family business."

"Yes," Dani said. "Investment banking, in New York. I have a master's in international finance."

"Is that where you learned to mutilate people?"

"No. My time in finance was much more brutal and far less honest than what we did to those jerks."

"Were you in the military or something, then?"

"Something. I didn't have a normal adolescence, that's for sure. I did enough strange stuff to learn not to judge other people's choices. Can we leave it at that, for the moment?"

"Uh-huh." Beverly shifted her stare to Liz.

"I have a master's in finance, too," Liz said. "I worked for the E.U. in Brussels for a few years. That's why we were laughing, Beverly. Relax, please. We like you. What you've done is done. I'm certainly not in a position to criticize your past."

"I have a chip on my shoulder," Beverly said. "Whatever you say about my past, I'm not proud of it."

"You can't do anything about it," Dani said. "You can either wallow in it, or suck it up and move on."

"You sure you weren't in the military? I've heard combat veterans use almost that exact phrase."

"Me, too," Dani said. "I picked it up from a family friend who had a career in the U.S. Army. He was in business with my father when I was growing up. He's like an older brother."

"I see. You said your father was French, but from Martinique, originally?"

"That's right."

"What kind of business was he in?"

"International trade. He's still active; he deals in heavy equipment, mostly, and the training that goes along with it."

"Wow. You had an entrée into finance from both sides. How did you end up doing this?"

"I burned out on investment banking, and I broke up with an asshole that I was supposed to marry. I've sailed with my father since before I can remember; he taught me to love the sea. I bailed out of an unhappy period in my life and started crewing on big yachts. I was between boats when Liz and I bumped into one another in Antigua and decided to give this business a try. Liz?"

"I was on a sabbatical down here, running from some unhappiness of my own," Liz said. "I'd been in the islands for around six weeks, chilling out, trying to figure out what I wanted to do. I hitched a ride to Antigua on a classic boat. It turned out the guy who was sailing it was nuts, but that's another story. He wrecked it on the approach to Antigua, and he was lost at sea. I washed up on the beach, literally. A friend of mine from university has an art gallery there, and I was visiting her. I was in her gallery, working on a painting of the yacht that was wrecked. Dani happened along and looked over my shoulder."

"I recognized the yacht she was painting," Dani said. "I'd had an encounter of my own with the whack-job who was sailing her. Liz and I had a long lunch and hit it off with one another, so the next day, I took her sailing on a friend's boat. *Vengeance* was on the market in Antigua, and I'd been thinking about buying her and going in the charter business, but I needed a partner. Liz and I decided to give it a go, and here we are."

"That's so cool," Beverly said. "I'm at a low point, myself. It's good to hear that things work out, even just sometimes."

"You'll find something you like," Liz said.

"Thanks, both of you. Sorry I snapped; it was more about me than it was about you. You've been kind to me, especially considering that I got you into this mess of mine."

"Actually, you didn't," Dani said. "I've been thinking about that. Somebody picked *Vengeance* as the setting for springing the trap on Velasquez. It can't have been random."

"But why?" Beverly asked. "Are you connected to any of these people?"

"We must be," Liz said, "but we don't know who 'these people' are, even."

"I don't know either," Beverly said. "I'd never run across Mike McGuire before last night. I don't know much about him, except that he's Horry's brother-in-law."

"Do you remember any details of what the two of them said to each other?" Liz asked.

Beverly shook her head. "No. I was too rattled by the whole thing. But it should be on the recording. I forgot to turn -- "

"Wait!" Dani said. "You recorded it?"

"Yes. I forgot to turn it off before I fell asleep. Should I go switch it off now?"

"Please," Dani said. "But hurry back. I want to ask you something about Berto."

～

"SHE'S TOUCHY ABOUT HER PAST," Liz said.

"I'm not surprised. I feel bad that I said that to her about the moral high ground."

"She's seems to trust us. What did you want to ask her about Berto?" Liz asked.

"While we were talking just now, I remembered what hit me last night before we went to sleep."

"About Berto?"

"Yes. She's seen him, remember? Met him for dinner a couple of times. We talked about that in the dinghy last night."

"That's right," Liz said. "We were going to talk with Luke about it today. I forgot all about it in the excitement. Should we call him? We can tell him about the recordings, too."

"Not so fast," Dani said. "There's nothing that won't keep, and I'm nervous about the recordings."

"Why?"

"As I was drifting off to sleep, I thought about the recordings. We have no idea what's on them."

"We've been careful; we knew about the risk," Liz said.

"We tried, but we might have slipped up ... besides, think of Beverly," Dani said.

"She did that voluntarily," Liz said.

"And she's ashamed of that part of her life," Dani said. "She thought the recordings were going to be held over Velasquez's head by Berto. She never expected anybody to see them, other than maybe those two."

"What are you thinking, then? Do you want to hide them from Luke?"

"We need to take a look at them. Then we can decide what to do. But I'm thinking that at most, Luke could use the parts where McGuire and Velasquez were talking."

"So we'd edit them?"

"Yes," Dani said. "Just cut out the parts that don't relate to McGuire. Nobody needs to watch what she and that scumbag were doing. And then there's whatever we might have said without thinking. We don't need anybody second guessing how we dealt with those three pieces of slime, either."

"I see what you mean," Liz said. "How are you proposing to do that?"

"Marie could help us. Then we can send Luke the parts that are relevant to his case against McGuire. Or Berto."

"What about McGuire and Berto?" Beverly asked, climbing into the cockpit.

"We were talking about the recordings," Liz said, "and sharing them with Luke."

"Oh," Beverly said in a soft voice, her face turning red. She folded her hands in her lap and looked down at them, sighing. "I guess if we have to ... I don't -- "

"Beverly?" Dani said, interrupting her.

"Yes?"

"We were talking about cutting out everything except the parts between McGuire and Velasquez."

Beverly looked up at Dani, raising her eyebrows. "Could you do that? I mean, I don't -- "

"First," Dani said. "Nobody knows about it but the three of us."

"And Marie will, if she helps us," Liz added.

"Marie?" Beverly asked.

"She only knows the recording system exists right now," Dani said. "Marie is a friend in Martinique who works as ... well, she does a lot of undercover work for some government agencies. She found the system when we asked her to check over *Vengeance* after we got her back. She installed the cutoff switch we told you about, too."

"How could we cut out parts of the recordings?" Beverly asked.

"I don't know, but it's the kind of thing Marie does all the time. She'll help."

"Could I see what's going to be sent to the police? Before it ... "

"That's the point," Liz said. "Nobody needs to see what happened between you and Velasquez."

"That," Dani said, "and the recordings of my plotting 'cold-blooded murder,' as you put it, Beverly. I don't want those floating around out in the world."

"But I actually did the things that are in the recordings. You were just upset and talking out of your head. You weren't really going to kill them."

"Of course not," Dani said.

Beverly gave Dani a hard look. "Or were you? I saw you cut that one man, to make him talk."

"As you said, she was upset," Liz said. "Dani does have a temper."

"Will this Luke man be okay with us doing that? He's a cop."

"He's a friend," Dani said. "Besides, he's not here. We three decide what we're comfortable with sending him. That's what he gets. He wouldn't want or need the rest of it."

Beverly nodded. "Okay. I'm in, if that's what you two are asking me. What do we have to do?"

"I think we should head for Martinique," Dani said.

"I'm for that," Liz said. "How about it, Beverly?"

"I'd like that. I've always wanted to go there, ever since I was in college. How long will that take?"

"To get there?" Dani asked.

"Right," Beverly said.

"An extra hour and a half, two hours, at most. It's around 20 miles from Rodney Bay, but we'll shave off some time by setting a course straight there," Dani said, beginning to plug the course change into the chart plotter. "You can meet our friends there, too. The guy I told you about who's like an older brother?"

"He's there?"

"He and his wife live in a villa overlooking our favorite anchorage," Liz said. "You'll enjoy them, I think. Phillip and Sandrine."

"Sandrine sounds French."

"She is. She's a senior officer in the French customs service there. She's a real kick," Dani said. "You'll like her."

"I hope so," Beverly said.

"There's another thing I wanted to ask you about," Dani said.

"What's that?"

"You told us you had dinner with Berto a couple of times."

"Yes, I did. What do you want to know?"

"Would you be willing to sit down with a police artist and help to develop a sketch of him?" Dani asked.

"Sure. They really do that? I thought it was just a television thing, maybe."

"They really do. The other thing is, can you remember the restaurants he took you to?"

"They're in my calendar app. That's no problem. Will I have to go to Miami?"

Dani frowned.

"For the artist?" Beverly asked.

"Oh," Dani said. "No. Sandrine can arrange that, right in Ste. Anne."

"Ste. Anne's where we anchor when we go to see them," Liz said, seeing the puzzled look on Beverly's face.

"Thanks, Liz," Beverly said. "You're thinking the police will be able to track him down that way?"

"It's a start," Dani said. "I want to find out whose idea it was to steal *Vengeance*. There's more to this than blackmailing Velasquez. I want to know why they picked our boat."

24

"It's Luke," Dani said, looking at the LCD screen on their satellite phone. She pressed the green icon to accept the call.

"Hi, Luke," she said. "You're on the speaker. Both of us are here."

"Good afternoon, you two. Is your guest there, too?"

"No, she's below," Liz said, "taking a nap to recover from the excitement last night. Should I get her? Or did you want just the two of us?"

"It's okay either way. There's nothing sensitive coming. I just wondered. You can pass this along to her. I wanted to let you know we arrested Mike McGuire a little while ago. He's charged with grand larceny and kidnapping you three, for now. The state's attorney is reviewing other charges as well, based on what's coming from St. Vincent. Plus, we're still waiting to question his three minions; they're in pretty rough shape. I'm not sure how long it'll be before we get to them."

"Poor babies," Dani said. "They thought they were so tough."

"Hell hath no fury like an angry woman, or something like that," Luke said.

"What did McGuire have to say?" Liz asked.

"Nothing. He's lawyered up. But he left an easy trail to follow. He's going down. The only question is how far down and how long he stays."

"What about Velasquez?" Dani asked. "Where's he?"

"Home trying to make peace with his wife, I guess."

"You didn't arrest him?" Liz asked.

"There's no law against being a shithead," Luke said. "Just as well, too. We wouldn't have enough space in the prisons."

"That's a good reason to make it a capital offense," Dani said. "Eliminate overcrowding in the penal system."

"Careful, Dani. This is one of our fine, upstanding congressmen you're talking about. If being a shithead were a capital offense, we'd be hard-pressed to have a federal government. On a different subject, where are you headed? We may need to arrange a video deposition with you in the next few days."

"Ste. Anne," Dani said. "We were going to call you in the morning, anyway. In all the confusion, we forgot something."

"What's that?"

"We realized last night that Beverly has seen this Berto person, face-to-face."

"Whoa! How'd we miss that? I should have asked. Can she pick him out of a book of mugshots?"

"I don't know about that. We're headed in a different direction. We thought Sandrine could set her up with a police sketch artist. Beverly thinks she can give a good description of him."

"That'll work. Where did she meet him?"

"She met him twice, for dinner. Two different restaurants. She has the names in her calendar. We'll send them along with the sketch when it's done."

"Good. We're at a dead end on that one, unless he does something to reveal himself. Has she gotten any more texts from him?"

"Not that she's mentioned, but the cell service was iffy in the Tobago Cays, and we've been out of range since we left there."

"Some of the heat's off him," Luke said, "since we picked up McGuire. Once things settle down, I imagine McGuire's lawyer will let us talk to him. We may be able to find out a little more, then."

"Do you have some reason to think he's connected to Berto? Or was he just pissed off about Velasquez running around on his sister?" Dani asked.

"Too early to tell," Luke said. "I think the McGuire family was backing Velasquez in the primary, though. Mike's at least smart enough to see this as a scandal that could derail his campaign, even if Velasquez is oblivious to that."

"What I want to know is whether or not you can connect McGuire to the theft of *Vengeance* from Miami," Dani said. "I assume what he's charged with is taking her from the Tobago Cays, for right now. I can't make sense out of the other yet."

"We don't have anything either way on the theft from Miami. Maybe it'll come clear when we know more. I agree; right now, it doesn't add up. I need to get moving, unless you have something else," Luke said. "We can talk in the morning."

"I have a quick question," Liz said.

"Ask away, Liz."

"You mentioned the state's attorney was waiting to see what else came out of St. Vincent. What's going on there?"

"Thanks for reminding me. I meant to mention it before. The two guys who're locked up down there are offering to talk in exchange for reduced charges. Their lawyer is hinting that they might know who hired them."

"That's probably bullshit," Dani said. "SpecCorp doesn't let the peons know who's paying the bills, according to Phillip."

"Yeah, you're right. But that's the other thing I meant to tell you about them. SpecCorp has disowned that operation."

"Disowned it, how?" Dani asked.

"They've put out the word to the law enforcement community that Norris and those two guys were no longer associated with SpecCorp when they stole *Vengeance*. SpecCorp says they quit and ran off with a bunch of their equipment and were freelancing for an unknown party."

"That's a little too convenient for SpecCorp, isn't it?" Dani asked. "I can hardly wait to hear whom they say they were working for."

"Yeah. Well, that's the news from this end. I gotta run; the state's attorney's got a meeting set for us with McGuire and his lawyer. Talk with you tomorrow."

∾

MONTALBA STARED AT THE COMPUTER. The glass of wine he had poured an hour ago stood beside it, forgotten. He had been tracking the yacht throughout the day. It had been stationary for an hour this morning after he talked to Delaney, but then it had begun moving on a course to St. Lucia.

He needed to know what was happening aboard. He understood Delaney's lack of curiosity about the yacht. Still, he found it frustrating. The only remaining goal he shared with Delaney was seeing O'Toole in the White House.

Montalba could insist that Delaney undertake further investigations for him. He wouldn't, though, because he wasn't impressed with Spec-Corp. In his view, Delaney's operation was overmatched by the Bergers and Barrera.

He could use his own people, but there was risk in that. His minions had narrow, well-defined responsibilities. He was reluctant to task them with anything beyond the day-to-day movement of product.

Having them spy on Barrera and the Bergers would make him vulnerable. He knew a great deal about his people and their organizations. In contrast, they knew nothing about him.

LaRosa was the one exception. LaRosa knew too much about Lennox and Velasquez. Once this was over, he would eliminate LaRosa. Meanwhile, he could use LaRosa's contacts in the Caribbean.

First, he would call Delaney. He wanted to know if Delaney's men in St. Vincent had pointed the finger at McGuire. The McGuire scandal would take Velasquez out of the presidential race. That left only the issue of the yacht unresolved.

The two SpecCorp men in jail in St. Vincent claiming McGuire had hired them to plant the drugs would be the coup de grâce. Montalba picked up the SpecCorp encrypted phone and made the call. On the third ring, Delaney answered.

"Good evening, Mr. Delaney. I was hoping for an update on the situation in St. Vincent."

"It's happening. The lawyer has cut the deal. The two men will be deposed tomorrow morning. Then the real shit-storm will start for McGuire. No worries; he's finished, and so's Velasquez."

"That's what I wanted to hear."

"I told you we would take care of it," Delaney said.

"The only loose end is the yacht," Montalba said.

"What about it?"

"I've been tracking it; it's under way."

"Under way? Where?" Delaney asked.

"It appears to be headed to St. Lucia. It has covered about two thirds of the distance from where it was drifting when we spoke this morning. My estimate is that they'll arrive tonight."

"Those are McGuire's people. I have no idea what he told them to do, but I'm sure they're not going to let the three women live to tell what happened. They're probably already dead. Or wish they were." Delaney laughed, an ugly sound.

"Then why are his men sailing the yacht? I thought they were going to sink it," Montalba said.

"Who the hell knows?" Delaney asked. "It's not our problem anymore. Velasquez is ruined. O'Toole's got a lock on the nomination. We just need to focus on whoever the frontrunner is from the other party, right?"

"I see," Montalba said. "Enjoy the rest of your evening."

Montalba leaned back in his chair. He saw the forgotten glass of wine from the corner of his eye and picked it up, taking a sip. He took out the prepaid cellphone he used to communicate with Beverly Lennox. She still had not responded to his message about retrieving the recordings.

Montalba wondered if he should destroy the phone. It was the only link to Beverly Lennox. If McGuire's men had killed her, the phone was of no consequence. If she were still alive, she might respond to the last text message when she next got cellphone service. Then he would know; he could decide what to do.

"WHAT DID I MISS?" Beverly asked, joining Liz and Dani in the cockpit.

"You made it up here just in time for what promises to be a glorious sunset," Liz said. "Be glad you didn't miss that."

"Feeling more rested?" Dani asked.

"Yes. I really crashed; I don't remember when I've slept so well. I'm feeling good about life, for a change."

"Good for you," Liz said. "We called Phillip and Sandrine while you were asleep. We're going to have breakfast with them tomorrow morning, if that's okay with you."

"Sure. I'd like that."

"Sandrine will arrange for the police artist to meet you at her office," Dani said. "It's in the marina complex. We're going to meet her and Phillip at one of the restaurants there, and she'll walk you to her office after we eat."

"I'm excited to see how that works, this sketch business. Could you do that, Liz?"

"I don't think so; not without some training, anyway. I think there's more art in drawing out the person making the description than there is in rendering the sketch. I'm not sure about in Martinique, but I know in some places, they use software that has a lot of different features: hundreds of different eyes, ears, noses, lips. It's fascinating to me, but I wouldn't know where to start. I'll be interested to hear how it goes."

"Why can't you come with us? Maybe you could watch over my shoulder."

Liz smiled. "Dani and I are going to take Marie LaCroix back to *Vengeance* while you do that. She's going to retrieve the disk drive that has the recordings on it, and we'll sit with her while she extracts the parts we want to send to Luke."

Beverly frowned, looking off into the distance and chewing on her lip.

"Don't worry," Dani said. "You'll get your chance to go over the final product."

Beverly looked at her and smiled. "Thanks. I appreciate that, but what's going to happen to the original recordings?"

"We haven't talked about that," Liz said. "Do you want to erase them?"

"That's certainly my first reaction," Beverly said.

"Do I sense that you have some reservations about that?" Dani asked.

"Yes, I guess I do. What if we miss something? Like something Horry might have told me. I may be way off track, but what if there's something that turns out to be important, later? That we wouldn't pick up on right now?"

"I had that same thought," Dani said, "for slightly different reasons, maybe. I think we should hang on to the original disk drive, at least for a while."

"What do you mean, different reasons?" Liz said. "I thought you were worried that what you and I were threatening to do to those men might be a problem for us. I was sure you'd want to destroy the recordings, once we pulled out what we want to send to Luke."

"I do want to destroy them, eventually," Dani said. "But there are bits of conversation on there between McGuire and his minions. There could be something there that we'd overlook now. Once we've gotten deeper into this, we might wish we could revisit some of what they said."

"I've got an idea," Beverly said.

"Well, let's hear it," Dani said.

"Can we get a safety deposit box in Martinique?"

"Yes. I have one," Dani said.

"So do I," Liz said.

"My idea is that we get one that's in all our names, that requires all three of us to be there to open it. I know that's a little odd, but I'll bet it could be done. That keeps anybody from forcing one of us to turn it over."

"That's a good idea," Liz said. "If we can't do it directly, we can most likely do it through a lawyer. We can talk to Phillip and Sandrine about it. I'm sure they know somebody who can help us."

25

"Y ou'll like Beverly," Dani said.

She and Liz were in their dinghy with Marie LaCroix. They were taking her back to the marina, where they were going to wait for Sandrine and Beverly to join them for midmorning coffee. Sandrine had called to let them know that the sketch artist was finishing her work just as they were wrapping up the editing of the recordings.

"I already like her," Marie said. "Anybody working to take down a politician is my kind of woman." They were rounding *Vengeance's* bow when Marie cried, "Stop!"

Dani throttled back and shifted the outboard to neutral. "What's the matter?" she asked.

"Take us back under your bowsprit," Marie asked. "There is something irregular."

"Irregular?" Liz said, as Dani stopped the dinghy and grabbed the bobstay, pulling them under the bowsprit. "Irregular how?"

"Something that does not belong. You have cable-tied something here?"

Marie was standing now, holding on to the starboard whisker stay with her left hand and pointing with her right. A black nylon cable tie encircled the bowsprit about halfway between the bow of *Vengeance* and the end of the bowsprit.

"I don't know why that's there," Dani said, "But I'll find out. Hold the dinghy, you two."

She stood on the side of the inflatable and grasped the whisker stay with both hands, raising herself to a chin-up position. She swung her legs to her left, hooking her left foot over *Vengeance's* gunwale. Scissoring her legs together, she got her right foot on the gunwale as well and rolled herself under the lifelines, taking up a prone position on the anchor platform.

Dani pulled herself forward with her left hand, feeling along the underside of the platform with her right hand. The anchor platform was made of teak grating with holes that were about three centimeters square. It was mounted on spacers above the bowsprit, leaving a couple of inches between the platform's underside and the bowsprit. When her right hand touched the cable tie, she looked down through one of the square holes in the grate and spotted the satellite tracker in the space between the platform and the bowsprit.

"That's how that bastard found us after Joey got us underway," Dani said.

"What do you have?" Marie asked.

"One of those cheap satellite trackers," Dani said.

"They must have put that on after you left here," Marie said. "We would have found it, otherwise."

"I'm sure they put it on in Bequia, or maybe even the Tobago Cays," Liz said. "Dani's right. I wondered how that guy, Billy, found us after he took McGuire and Velasquez back to Mustique. That explains it."

"The problem is, they may still be tracking us, and since we let those assholes live, they'll eventually find out we're still alive," Dani said. "I should've killed them instead of listening to Beverly."

"I've got an idea," Liz said. "Let's send them on a wild goose chase."

"With the tracker?" Dani asked.

"Yes," Liz said. "We'll put it on another boat. That'll keep them busy for a while."

"But it might get innocent people hurt," Dani said.

"This Beverly, she has changed the way you think, Dani," Marie said. "Since when do you worry about people getting hurt?"

"She talked me into a mistake, is what she did. But those guys were asking for it. If we're going to do what Liz suggested, we need to put it on a boat that will match our speed, or whoever's watching will figure it out."

"A small steamer," Marie said. "That would work."

"But that could still get somebody hurt. We don't know how they might decide to deal with it. They were going to kill us and sink *Vengeance*," Liz said.

"I have a steamer in mind, an interisland freighter headed for Venezuela. They are smuggling drugs and people north and food south. Cut the cable tie. I will have someone meet us at the marina and take this device around to Fort-de-France. We will make sure it moves at no more than 9 knots and follows the coast around to where the freighter is anchored. Okay?"

"Okay." Dani took out her multi-tool and clipped the cable tie, handing the tracker to Marie. "Call your person and let's go get some espresso and *pain au chocolat*."

SANDRINE AND BEVERLY were sitting at a table, heads together, reading a newspaper as Dani and Liz entered the restaurant. Sandrine waved them over and asked where Marie was.

"She stopped to give one of her people instructions," Dani said.

"Instructions?" Sandrine asked.

Dani and Liz told them about finding the satellite tracker on *Vengeance*.

"They know where we are?" Beverly asked, frowning. She marked her place in the article she was reading with her finger and turned her attention to Dani and Liz.

"They know *Vengeance* stopped here for the night, but that's about it. And they probably think those three jerks are still running loose," Dani said. "Liz had the idea of putting the tracker on another boat to lead them away from us, in case somebody's still following the tracker. That's what Marie's doing."

Beverly said, "But they might -- "

"It's okay," Liz said. "Marie's arranging for someone to put it on a freighter that's smuggling drugs. They deserve whatever happens to them."

"What are you reading, anyway?" Dani asked, pointing at the newspaper.

"Look," Sandrine said, flipping a page back to reveal a copy of the police artist's sketch of Berto.

"I see," Dani said, "But -- "

"Now look at this." Beverly shifted the sketch to the left and aligned it with a portrait of a pretty, dark haired woman in the newspaper. "Imagine her with her hair pulled back."

"There is a strong resemblance, isn't there," Dani said.

"They could almost be twins," Liz said. "Do you know her?"

"No," Beverly said. "I've never seen her before."

"Are you sure?" Liz asked. "Because if you know her it could have influenced -- "

"No. I see what you're getting at, but that's not what happened. I never saw her or her picture until after the sketch was done. Somebody left yesterday's Miami Herald on the table. It was open to the society page. When Sandrine and I sat down I saw this article about her engagement to Senator William O'Toole."

"Is he somebody we should know?" Liz asked.

"He's the one Horry Velasquez was trying to beat out for the presidential nomination," Beverly said.

"Hmm," Dani said, pulling out a chair and dropping into it. "Who is she?"

"Graciella Montalba is her name," Beverly said. "The article says she's an Argentine socialite who's lived in Miami for quite a while. She's a jet setter -- lots of money."

"Does the article mention a brother?" Liz asked.

"No. The article says she's the only child of wealthy parents who died when she was in her late teens. She has no close relatives, according to this, and no remaining connection to Argentina. She's a naturalized U.S. citizen."

"Did you already send this to Luke?" Dani asked, looking at Sandrine.

"The sketch?" Sandrine asked. "Yes, we emailed it from my computer a few minutes ago. I called him to let him know, but he's out of the office for a couple of hours."

"Let's have our coffee, then," Dani said. "Then we can go back to *Vengeance.*"

"It is done," Marie said, interrupting. She pulled out a chair and joined them. "Am I too late for coffee?"

"No," Liz said. "We were about to order. Sit down and say hello to Beverly Lennox."

"I am called Marie LaCroix." Marie extended her hand across the table.

"I'm pleased to meet you," Beverly said, shaking her hand. "Dani and Liz have told me about you. Thank you for helping; I'm indebted to all of you."

"It is only a small matter among friends," Marie said. "I am happy to do what I can."

"Tell us about this freighter," Sandrine said. "Should I be looking into their cargo?"

"I think you already know this one," Marie said. "We have been in touch with some of your colleagues. We wish to let this ship go to Venezuela; the plan is to discover with whom they trade there. Then, we will stop their supply at its source, and you will arrest them when they return here. Now we have a tracker aboard, for what that is worth. My people have cracked the login for it. I will give it to you later, if you wish."

"Yes, please," Sandrine said.

"*Bonjour, mesdames,*" the waitress said. "*Qu'est-ce que vous voulez?*"

"WHAT DO you think of the video?" Liz asked. She and Beverly sat in front of a laptop computer at *Vengeance's* chart table.

"It's okay with me," Beverly said. "There's nothing there to worry any of us. Just Mike McGuire and Horry arguing. Can we get away with sending that little to Luke?"

"We won't offer anything more," Dani said. "Since he's not expecting any recordings, it'll most likely be okay. If he asks about more, we'll play it by ear. Let me do the talking, though, okay?"

"Sure. Speaking of talking, I should turn on my phone. The battery was stone dead when we got in last night. We should see if I have any texts from Berto before you call Luke, right?"

"Yes," Dani said.

Beverly went into the forward stateroom and returned with her iPhone. Once it booted up, she entered the unlock code.

"I have two texts from him. Let's see," she said, tapping the screen. "Okay, the first one is from yesterday. It's a long set of instructions with a couple of pictures. He's telling me how to remove the disk drive from the recording system and replace it with a new one."

"Do you have a new one?" Liz asked. "Marie already put another one in, and she set it to be active all the time, without the proximity thing you have. She showed us how to do that."

"No. He says I should let him know where we'll be when I make the switch, and he'll arrange for me to pick one up. But he wanted me to set it like you just described, to eliminate the need for the key. That seems odd, since he thinks I'm leaving you today."

"Yes," Dani said. "There's more to this than blackmailing Velasquez. He wants to spy on Liz and me for some reason."

"But why?" Beverly asked.

"I wish I knew," Dani said, "but I have no idea. That's worrisome."

"I can see that," Beverly said.

"You said there was a second text," Liz said.

"Yes. From earlier this morning. He's asking if I got the first one, and whether I can switch the disk drives. What should I tell him?"

"Don't answer him," Dani said. "It could be a trick."

"A trick?" Beverly asked. "How?"

"If he knows about McGuire, he could be checking to make sure you're not still alive."

Beverly's face went pale. "But how would he know about McGuire?"

"We have no way of knowing what Berto's motive is in this whole thing," Liz said.

"But if that really is his sister who's engaged to Senator O'Toole, wouldn't he want Horry Velasquez out of the race?" Beverly asked. "That would seem to put him on the opposite side from McGuire, wouldn't it?"

"There are a lot of *ifs* strung together," Dani said. "There are too many things we don't know. I think not answering him is the safe course."

"Okay, I'm fine with that," Beverly said, "but could you explain your reasoning?"

"I'll try. He probably knows cellphone service doesn't extend very far offshore, for a start."

"Yes, he does. He told me that once."

"Then if you don't answer, he could assume that we're at sea, on our way to St. Lucia."

"But my flight was supposed to be today."

"Yes. He would guess that something's wrong. He may have even heard the news that McGuire was arrested and that Velasquez is back in Miami. That may be on local television in Miami."

"I never thought of that," Beverly said.

"If he's picked that up, then he would guess that we've had some kind of problem, but until McGuire or one of his three thugs talks, he can't know what our status is."

"I see that. But if I answer his text, he'll know more, and maybe ask me what's going on."

"Yes. Unless he knew about McGuire when he sent the text. If that's the case, he may also have access to the tracker, which will give him a whole different picture in the next few hours."

"Wow. You have a devious mind, Dani."

"I work at it. But in any case, I don't see a benefit to sending him an answer, at least not until we talk to Luke."

"We should be able to reach him by now," Liz said. "Should I email the video clip to him before we call?"

"That's my vote," Dani said. "How about it, Beverly?"

"I agree. Send it, and let's talk with him."

26

L uke Pantene was pondering his recent telephone conversation with the women aboard *Vengeance*. He'd spent a few minutes reviewing the video clip they had sent him. There was no new information there, but it confirmed what he already knew. The video would make things more difficult for Mike McGuire and his lawyer if it survived the inevitable challenges to its admissibility in court. That was assuming McGuire chose to go to trial. Luke was betting the lawyers would strike a deal of some sort.

He was more interested in the sketch of the man that they were calling Berto. He had to agree that it seemed likely that Berto was behind the theft of *Vengeance* from Miami a few weeks ago. The question was what motive he could have had for taking her. As Dani said, any yacht would have served his purpose of providing a backdrop for the blackmail of Horatio Velasquez.

That led Luke to the next question, which was why Berto wanted to compromise the congressman. Taking Velasquez out of the running for the presidential nomination was an obvious motive, but Berto's motive might not be related to the presidential campaign. There were any number of reasons why someone would want leverage over a congressman.

If Luke had a link between Berto and *Vengeance*, it could narrow the scope of the search for Berto. Luke agreed with Dani and Liz and Beverly. The sketch of Berto did bear a strong resemblance to Graciella Montalba, but Luke was wary of that, based on years of experience with eyewitnesses.

Beverly Lennox could be mistaken, or she could have seen pictures of Graciella before and forgotten it, or she could have her own less innocent reasons for making the sketch point to the Montalba woman. Dani and Liz seemed to trust her, but Luke was skeptical.

He had people updating the background information on Lennox, and he'd sent two detectives to Manny LaRosa's club with sketches of Berto. If LaRosa or anyone else at the Pink Pussycat recognized him from the sketch, Luke would be less doubtful about Lennox's description.

He also had people following up with the two restaurants where Lennox claimed to have met Berto. That was a long shot, in Luke's opinion. Unless the man was a regular customer or had somehow called attention to himself, the restaurant employees wouldn't remember a customer from a couple of weeks ago.

So far, they only had Lennox's word that Berto existed. Dani and Liz had a good track record with Luke; he usually trusted their judgment of people, but Lennox was still a suspicious character in his view.

Dani, in her typical way, had wanted Luke to confront Graciella Montalba. Luke chuckled to himself. Dani was the proverbial bull in the china shop. There would be adverse political ramifications to approaching the Montalba woman. She was the fiancée of one of the most powerful men in the country as well as being prominent in her own right. Luke didn't let politics interfere with his pursuit of his duties, but in this case, the risks far exceeded the rewards.

Politics aside, confronting Graciella Montalba might alert Berto, if he was indeed linked to her. Luke had not told Dani and her friends that Graciella Montalba's Miami residence was in the same cluster of buildings as Berto's cellphone. He knew what Dani's reaction to that would be.

If he could establish that there was such a person as Berto, and if he could put that person in the building that housed Graciella Montalba's condo, then he'd have a basis to canvass the building's staff and the neighbors, Graciella among them. Absent that, he would stick to basic, boring police work.

~

JORGE SALINAS SAT in a dark corner of the Pink Pussycat nursing a beer. When the two detectives came in and showed the bartender and the bouncer a sketch and started asking them questions, Jorge made a discreet departure. Walking down the street, he found a spot where he could watch the door to the club. He leaned against a lamp post and settled in to wait.

When the two detectives emerged from the bar, Jorge followed them to their car.

"Excuse me," he said, as one of them unlocked the driver's door.

"Yeah," the detective said, giving Jorge a quick once over. He wrinkled his nose and asked, "Whaddaya want?"

Jorge didn't have to work at staying in character; he was type-cast. He looked and smelled like a street person. Even in a place like the Pink Pussycat, he would have been unwelcome during the busy periods. "I seen you askin' questions in the Pussycat."

The other detective had moved into a position off Jorge's right side, watching him. Jorge ignored him, focusing on the one in front of him.

"So?" the first one asked.

"I saw him sneak out," the man to Jorge's right said.

"I didn't want no trouble with them people," Jorge said. "They let me come in and get a drink and food sometimes when they ain't busy, see. I hang out around here."

"Yeah? So what? You got something to tell us?"

"Maybe. I seen the bartender and the bouncer lookin' at one another when you was showin' them that picture. They looked to me like they was lyin' when they said they didn't recognize whoever it was."

"How do you know?" the second detective asked.

"I ain't messin' with you," Jorge said. "You know what I am. I ain't tryin' to blow no smoke or nothin'. You live like I do, you gotta be able to tell when people like them are bullshittin', see."

"You say you hang around here a lot?" the first one asked.

"Uh-huh. All the time. Ain't got nowhere else to be."

"Maybe you've seen this guy, then," the second one said. "Show him the sketch."

The first one shrugged and opened a manila folder. As he pulled out the sketch, several sheets of paper fell to the sidewalk. Jorge bent and picked them up, handing them to the detective as he took the sketch from him.

"Thanks," the detective said. He watched as Jorge studied the sketch. "You seen him before?"

"Maybe," Jorge said. "What's it worth?"

"Look, asshole, you seen him or not? Don't push it; I'll bust your smelly ass for vagrancy if you screw us around."

"Okay, okay" Jorge said, cowering. "I think I mighta seen him around the neighborhood, but I ain't sure. How 'bout I hang onto this, and if I see him again, I call you?"

"When do you think you saw him?"

Jorge blinked hard with both eyes, staring at the sketch. He scratched at his belly and shook his head. "A week or two ago, maybe?"

"Was he going in the club?"

"Uh-huh, goin' in the club," Jorge said. "I'll call you, okay?"

"Yeah, sure. Thanks a lot." He reached into his pocket and pulled out a crumpled $10 bill, handing it to Jorge. "Get yourself some food, man."

"Thanks, officer. God bless you." As he watched them leave in the unmarked car, Jorge was wondering how much he should tell them.

MONTALBA HAD JUST TAKEN the first sip of his midafternoon coffee when one of his prepaid cellphones chimed, signaling the receipt of a text message. Opening the middle drawer of his desk, he saw that it was the phone he used to communicate with Manny LaRosa. He frowned; LaRosa didn't normally send text messages.

Entering the phone's unlock code, he navigated to the message app and opened the only text there. He stared at the screen in disbelief, taking in the sketch that was unmistakably him in his theatrical makeup.

Oddly, he realized how much he and Graciella resembled one another. He'd never noticed that, but then he never saw pictures of himself, either. Manny had entered a two-word message below the image. "Call me," it said. Montalba placed the call, willing himself to relax.

"Yeah?" LaRosa said, when he answered. "You got the picture I sent?"

"Yes," Montalba said. "Who is it? Where did it come from?"

"Cops," LaRosa said. "Two detectives are flashing it around asking if anybody has seen that guy. They came in the Pussycat, talked to the guys. The bartender called me, and I came down."

Montalba was worried by the fact that LaRosa had sent him the sketch. He'd never let LaRosa or the others see him. "Did they say who he was?" Montalba asked, again.

"Yeah," LaRosa said. "The only name they got for him is Berto. That's why I sent it to you. That's the name you gave me to use with the Lennox broad. I thought maybe she'd ratted you out or something. None of us recognized the picture, but that's all I could figure, that maybe she'd seen you and given 'em a description."

Montalba forced a laugh. "I wish I were that handsome. I wouldn't be spending time with the likes of her."

"So that ain't you, then?"

"No. Any reason besides the name that made you think he might be connected with me?"

"No. I just figured better safe than sorry, you know?"

"Yes, I understand," Montalba said. "Thanks. And did they say why they're looking for him at your club?"

"Nah, it was kinda weird. He's wanted for questioning about stealing some million-dollar yacht from a marina down near Government Cut. They had pictures of the boat. Man, it's a beauty. Lots of class. And the two babes that run it? Knockouts, both of 'em. I'd rent that sucker for my next vacation if he hadn't stole the damn thing, you know?"

"Were there a lot of people in the club when they came in?"

"Nah. By the time I got downstairs, it was just my two guys. After the cops left, the boys told me there was a rummy in there when the cops came in, but he hauled ass."

"A rummy? Somebody they knew?" Montalba asked.

"Yeah. He lives on the street. They let him come in sometimes if there's no customers. He knows to leave if anybody comes in, like payin' customers, you know. The bartender buys him a beer and feeds him sometimes. Cut a deal with him to do that so he don't hassle the customers for spare change outside."

"All right." Montalba said. "Thanks, but I don't know the man in the sketch either. Call me if you find out any more about him, though."

Montalba disconnected the call. He scooped the phones from his desk drawer into a briefcase, folding up his laptop and putting it in as well. He snapped the briefcase closed and looked around the bedroom that doubled as his office.

It was an interior space of 150 square feet, hidden within Graciella's penthouse condo; there were no windows and little in the way of furniture. Access was via a door that was concealed behind a massive entertainment center in her living room. Her housekeeper had cleaned the rest of the condo today, so the only traces of his presence were in this room.

He slugged down the cup of coffee, annoyed that it had cooled to lukewarm while he was on the phone. He needed the caffeine, though. He took the cup into the tiny bathroom. Opening the cabinet under the sink, he took out a pair of latex gloves and put them on. He washed and dried the cup, leaving it on the back of the counter.

He opened the medicine cabinet and took out a dust cloth and an aerosol can of furniture polish. He began wiping down the surfaces that might have collected fingerprints, working methodically.

He had not used the shower in here during this stay, nor the bed. He'd spent most of his time with Graciella in the main living areas. In ten minutes, he was satisfied that he was leaving no prints behind. He took his personal cellphone out of his pocket and called his sister.

"Guillermo?" she answered.

"Yes. I'm in a bind; it's an emergency."

"Where are you?" she asked.

"Your place. I need to get to the safe house, fast."

"I'm on my way home from the spa. I'll pick you up at the elevator in the garage in five minutes, okay?"

"Yes. Call me when you're pulling into the garage. I'll get on the elevator then. Wait for me."

"The private elevator?" she asked. "The main one's faster."

"The private one. I can't risk being seen -- no time for makeup."

"I just turned the corner," she said. "I'm pressing the garage door opener button now."

"I'll be right down," he said, disconnecting the call.

27

"I don't think Luke's being aggressive enough," Dani said, choosing a piece of mango from the fruit plate Liz had prepared for the three of them. They sat in the shade of the big cockpit awning, watching the yachts coming and going in the anchorage off Ste. Anne.

"What do you think he should do differently?" Beverly asked. "He was going to send people to ask Manny about the sketch."

"He should rattle that Montalba woman and see what happens," Dani said. "That's what I'd do."

"But he's right to be cautious about that, Dani," Liz said. "All he has is that rough sketch that shows a superficial resemblance. There are all kinds of reasons not to rush into that."

"He's bound to have some doubts about me, too," Beverly said. "I'm not the best kind of witness; I know that."

"Your explanation is solid," Dani said. "He's just scared of her political connections."

"For good reason," Liz said. "Imagine what would happen if he confronted her and found nothing."

"I don't think that's likely," Dani said.

"Politics aside," Liz said, "If she is mixed up in this somehow, confronting her could tip off Berto. If he goes farther underground, then where would we be?"

"That's a thought," Dani said.

"What?" Beverly asked.

"Scare Berto into doing something; make him show himself," Dani said.

"I've seen that look before, Dani," Liz said. "You're making me nervous. What kind of scheme are you hatching?"

"I see Luke's problem," Dani said. "He's got a couple, actually. The political angle is one, but there's also the thin evidence connecting Berto to the theft. And no offense to you," she said, looking at Beverly, "but the whole case against Berto hinges on your credibility."

"I agree," Beverly said, "and I know I'm not a credible witness. I already said that."

"But we've got some other options," Dani said. "We don't have the constraints that Luke has."

"Uh-oh," Liz said. "Are you thinking about going to Miami?"

"It crossed my mind," Dani said, "but I've got a better idea. You mentioned driving Berto underground, and that made me realize something."

"What?" Beverly asked.

"He's already underground," Dani said. "There's only one person we know of who can identify him." She looked at Beverly. "And his plans aren't working out. I'd bet he's not a happy man. Velasquez didn't escape unscathed, but Berto doesn't have the recordings to hold over his head. If he wanted leverage for some reason other than the political campaign, he didn't get it. And he went to a lot of trouble and expense to install the surveillance gear on *Vengeance*. As far as he knows, McGuire's people have sunk her."

"Unless he has access to the tracker," Liz said.

"Right," Dani said. "But then he'd see his prize on her way to parts unknown, so he still wouldn't have what he wanted. What more could go wrong, from his perspective?"

"He gets arrested?" Beverly asked.

"Or exposed," Liz said. "He's got a lot invested in being invisible."

"Yes," Dani said. "How do you think he'd react if we threatened to drag him out into the light of day?"

"He'd attack us," Beverly said.

"That's one choice," Liz said. "Or he could run. That's more likely than attacking us, I think. He wouldn't know where to start if he wanted to come after us. He's got reason to think we're dead, remember. Or on our way to Venezuela."

"Either option suits me better than the status quo," Dani said. "He'll have to come out of hiding to do either one. Then we get a shot at him -- or Luke does."

"But I don't see how we could set that up," Liz said.

"Beverly could send him a text. She could threaten him with exposure unless he paid her off," Dani said.

"He'd have me killed," Beverly said.

"He's likely to do that anyway," Dani said. "Or try, like McGuire did. Look where it got *him*."

Beverly looked away for a few seconds and then looked back at Dani and nodded. "You're right. But nobody's going to believe me. Not the police, and not Berto, either. Why would he believe I could expose him?"

"You do have some credibility on that score, at least with Berto," Dani said. "That sketch is out there. If he hasn't seen it yet, he will, and he'll guess that it had to originate with you."

"But we've already let that genie out of the bottle," Liz said. "We can't do him any more damage unless we know where he is."

"Remember what Phillip did to the SpecCorp guy?" Dani asked.

"Yes, but I'm not following you," Liz said.

"Neither am I," Beverly said. "What SpecCorp guy?"

Liz gave her a quick summary of what Phillip's friends had done to Delaney.

When Liz finished, Dani said, "For the sake of argument, let's say that Graciella Montalba is related to Berto."

"Okay," Beverly said. "I believe that, based on their looks. She has to be his sister."

Liz nodded.

"And let's assume that he wanted Velasquez out of the race for the presidency so Senator O'Toole would have a lock on the nomination. If Graciella is Berto's sister, O'Toole's going to be his brother-in-law. Both of them are easy to find. If we go after them, we might provoke Berto to show himself."

"There's a flaw in your logic," Liz said.

"What's that?" Dani asked.

"You're assuming O'Toole knows about Berto," Liz said.

"O'Toole's about to marry her," Dani said. "If Berto's her brother, O'Toole's bound to know."

"That doesn't follow," Liz said. "The article in the newspaper said she's an only child. No living relatives, remember?"

"You're right," Dani said. "You think we should focus on her?"

"Yes," Liz said. "Confronting her is much cleaner. If Berto's her brother and it's their secret, she'll go to him straight away. If you lean on her and she calls O'Toole, then we can reconsider."

"You're right," Dani said. "Good thinking. Thanks."

"What if we're wrong, though," Beverly said, "and they aren't related."

"Then we've wasted a little time and brought a little excitement into the life of somebody who probably deserves worse," Dani said. "If she's not mixed up in this, she's mixed up in something else ugly. People like her always are. If she's innocent, she'll get over it. But I don't think she is, and neither do you."

"How are you thinking we can do this?" Liz asked.

"Sharktooth's cousins," Dani said.

"Sharktooth's cousins?" Beverly asked, frowning and shaking her head.

"Sharktooth's a friend of ours," Liz said.

"Another of my father's partners," Dani said. "Like Phillip."

"He lives in Miami?" Beverly asked.

"No, he lives in Dominica, but he has two cousins who spend a lot of time in Miami."

"But this could get them in trouble, couldn't it?" Beverly asked.

"It's the kind of thing they do for amusement," Dani said. "They have some kind of natural immunity to trouble; Sharktooth says they're carriers, like Typhoid Mary."

"What about Luke?" Liz asked. "If we do this, would we tell him? Otherwise, he'd feel betrayed, wouldn't he?"

"Let's think about that," Dani said. "We need to figure out exactly what we'd want Sharktooth's cousins to do, too. Is it too late in the afternoon for some coffee?"

"No. This may be a late night," Liz said. "I'll make some. I think Beverly has some questions for you while I'm doing that."

"What kind of name is Sharktooth?" Beverly asked, as Liz went below.

"NOBODY at the Pink Pussycat admitted knowing Berto?" Luke Pantene asked.

The two detectives who had taken the sketch to the club sat across the desk from him.

"No, but we got a 'maybe' from a bum that hangs around the neighborhood."

"How strong a maybe?"

"I think he was pretty sure he'd seen the guy. He made a kind of half-assed try to hustle us."

"Hustle you?" Luke asked. "How?"

"He asked what it was worth if he'd seen the guy, and I threatened to bring him in for vagrancy. That loosened his tongue a little."

"I don't know," the second detective said. "I think he was feedin' us a line to keep from getting busted. I keep thinking about what he said about them letting him come in there for a drink and food when they weren't busy."

"What about it?" Luke said. "You think he's going to try to play you off against the people running the club?"

"Maybe, maybe not. You know street people, captain. Always looking for an angle."

"Think he might talk if you brought him in?" Luke asked. "I don't mean hassle him. I mean give him a break. Put him up overnight, buy him a decent meal. Treat him like a witness."

"Might work," the first detective said.

"How did you leave it with him?" Luke asked.

"He's got a copy of the sketch. Said he'd call us if he saw the guy."

"I'm wondering if we could use him for leverage to squeeze LaRosa and his people," Luke said. "Tell them we have an eyewitness who can put Berto in the club."

"I don't like it, captain. They'd guess who it was. He was in the club when we got there. He snuck out when we started asking questions. We might get the poor bastard hurt. Or killed, with LaRosa."

They were interrupted by a knock on the door.

"Come in," Luke said.

A young woman in uniform entered the office, an iPad in her hand. "Sorry, Captain Pantene, but we thought you'd want this. It's from the trap on Manny LaRosa's cellphone. He sent a text about an hour ago. I have it here. There's also a recording of a return call from the number he sent the text to."

"That's about when we left the club," one of the detectives said. "An hour ago, give or take."

Luke took the iPad and looked at the screen for a couple of seconds. He passed it across the desk to the two detectives. "The text wasn't encrypted?" he asked.

"No, sir. It was sent between two cheap prepaid phones. We recognized the sketch and thought it might be important."

"Good job. Can you play the recording for us?"

She nodded and took the iPad, poking at the screen. The four of them listened to the conversation between LaRosa and the unknown man.

When it was finished, Luke asked, "Did you get a location for the other phone?"

"Yes, sir. It's that same cluster of buildings. Still no way to narrow it down."

"Okay, thanks. Good work," Luke said, handing the iPad to the woman.

She smiled and took the iPad, closing the door as she left the office.

"You still want us to pick up the bum?" the first detective asked.

"No, I think it's pretty clear that LaRosa's involved in this, whatever it is. But from the conversation, he doesn't know who the hell that guy on the other end of the phone is. I don't think we're going to get anything out of him."

"Him? The bum?" the detective asked.

"Any of them," Luke said. "All the bum would be good for is to squeeze LaRosa, but there's nothing there. The way that sounded to me, LaRosa's never seen the guy on the phone. I don't think it's even for sure that the guy was Berto."

"You don't think the guy he called is Berto?" the second detective asked, his eyebrows raised.

"If he's not, he sure as hell knows Berto," Luke said. "But I didn't get that LaRosa was sure he was Berto. How did you come out on the restaurants?"

"Nothing there. No reservations for anybody named Berto or even close at either place. Nobody recognized the sketch. The managers at both places said if we called them with a last name they'd check again."

"If, if, if," Luke said.

"I wish we could drag the Lennox broad in and grill her," the first detective said.

"What would you ask her? Anything specific?" Luke asked.

"We know she's seen this Berto character. Had dinner with him twice, she told you."

"Yes," Luke said. "Go on."

"We could play the recording for her and see if she recognizes his voice," the detective said.

"Good idea. I want you two to go downstairs and listen to that recording over and over until you're sick of it and you're reciting it in your sleep. Maybe there's something there we missed. But before you start, email me a copy of it. I'll get Lennox on the horn and play it for her. I need to talk to those women anyway."

28

"I think Luke's scared of causing a political flap," Dani said. She and Beverly sat with Phillip on his veranda, looking out over the anchorage where *Vengeance* rolled in the gentle swell that came around Pointe Dunkerque. Liz and Sandrine were preparing *hors d'oeuvres* in the kitchen.

"He has more constraints than just politics, Dani," Phillip said. "He has to worry about the admissibility of evidence if this goes to court. Plus, if she *is* connected to Berto somehow, the Montalba woman could tip him off that the police are getting close."

"But I don't have those constraints," Dani said.

"What are you suggesting?" Phillip asked.

"What you did to that guy who runs SpecCorp."

"That was a different situation."

"How?" Dani asked.

"For one thing, he wasn't being investigated by the police."

"Luke's not investigating her," Dani said.

"You can't be sure. If he were, he'd keep it quiet," Phillip said. "For all the reasons we just talked about."

"I don't think he is, but what would it hurt if we shook her up a little?" Dani asked.

"She's not going to open her door and invite you in when you ring the bell, Dani. If she's as rich as you say, she probably has protection of some kind."

"So did the SpecCorp guy. What's his name, again?"

"Delaney," Phillip said. "That was only possible because there were several people in his neck of the woods who had the skills and the inclination to teach him a lesson. The stars were in alignment on that one. You can't just go to Miami and do that kind of thing; they'll lock you up."

"I disagree. You taught me well. But I didn't have in mind a do-it-yourself exercise, anyway."

"No?" Phillip said. "What, then?"

"Lucilius and Tiberius. They're in Miami. I saw them at the airport."

Phillip laughed. "The Jones brothers. Have you talked to Sharktooth?"

"Not about this. Why?"

"I just wondered. What are they doing there?"

"They're on holiday. I thought they'd enjoy this."

"No doubt," Phillip said. "But let's look at it from Luke's perspective."

"Look at what from Luke's perspective?" Liz asked, coming out of the house with a tray of snacks. "He must have your house bugged."

"Why?" Phillip asked.

"He just called. He emailed us a recording he wants you to hear, Beverly. He wants you to listen to it and then we'll call him back. Sandrine's downloading it now."

"Should we go into my office?" Phillip asked.

"No," Sandrine said, joining them, an iPad in her hand. "It is here."

She put the device on the table and touched the screen as Beverly leaned forward. She listened to the exchange, her eyes closed. When it was finished, she looked up and said, "No question. That's Manny LaRosa and Berto, all right. Where did he get that?"

"He didn't want to say, until he had you listen to it," Liz said. "He was worried about biasing your observation, or something like that. He wouldn't even tell us who he thought they were."

"Well, I'm not in any doubt. I know both of those voices all too well. Let's call him."

"Can we hold off a couple of minutes?" Phillip asked. "As long as we're going to call him, I'd like to work through your idea first, Dani. Why don't you tell us what you have in mind?"

"I don't have much detail; they'd be winging it, for the most part."

"Back up to the beginning for Sandrine and Liz, then, and tell us as much as you can articulate. I'd like Sandrine's reaction; she's worked under similar constraints to the ones Luke's dealing with. Let's see if she thinks we could get Luke on board, instead of blindsiding him."

"Okay," Dani said. "Here's my idea."

"HE CALLED while we were listening to the recording," the lead detective said. He'd left his partner in the lab to keep listening to the recording, as Luke had ordered.

"The bum?" Luke asked, looking up from the papers on his desk.

"Yeah. He said he'd seen the guy in the sketch in a limo with Dick Kilgore."

"Dick Kilgore?" Luke asked.

"Pinkie Schultz's muscle," the detective said. "He took over the club after Pinkie disappeared. We figured maybe he did Pinkie in, but we didn't have any evidence.

"Oh, yeah," Luke said. "I remember, now. But I thought Kilgore was missing, too."

"Yeah, he is, ever since LaRosa took over."

"When was it?" Luke asked.

"That LaRosa took over?"

"No. That your witness saw Kilgore in the limo with Berto."

"Right before Pinkie disappeared," the detective said.

"I wonder where they were going," Luke said.

"Going?" The detective frowned.

"In the limo," Luke said.

"Oh. Nowhere. The limo pulled up in the alley and Kilgore came out the back door of the Pussycat and got in the back seat with Berto. They sat there and talked for a few minutes, then Kilgore went back inside and the limo left."

"So whoever Berto is, he was connected with the club before LaRosa came on the scene," Luke said.

"Yeah, sounds like it."

"The bum have anything else?"

"Yeah," the detective said. "Once he started talking, I couldn't shut him up. He said sometime after the meeting in the limo, he saw Kilgore load something that might have been a body into the trunk of Pinkie Schultz's car and drive away."

"Interesting," Luke said, "but what's that got to do with anything?"

"It might explain Schultz's disappearance," the detective said. "And maybe Kilgore killed him."

"Yes, and yes," Luke said. "But nobody's complaining about Schultz being gone, and nobody's seen Kilgore in a couple of months. He seems to be among the missing, himself."

"Yeah, that's true," the detective said. "It does kind of add up, though. So maybe this bum's not a total flake, you know?"

"Yeah, okay," Luke said. "I'll grant you that. He's telling us that Berto was hanging around the club before LaRosa took over from Kilgore. Is that about it?"

"Yeah, I guess so."

"Can he put Berto at the club *after* LaRosa got there? That's what we're looking for -- a connection between LaRosa and Berto. Can you get hold of the bum and press him on that?"

"Yeah, sure. I'll have to go looking for him, though. No way to call him."

"Okay," Luke said. "Do it."

"Mind if I ask what you're thinking, captain? So I'll know where to take the questions?"

"Fair enough," Luke said. "Right now, we have LaRosa telling the guy on the phone that we're looking for the man in the sketch and that we think his name's Berto. The guy on the phone says he's never seen the one in the sketch. LaRosa sounded like he thought maybe the guy on the phone *was* the guy in the sketch, because when he put Beverly Lennox in touch with the guy on the phone, LaRosa said she was to see Berto. You with me so far?"

"Yeah, so far."

"Good. Somebody's lying. Could be the bum's confused, or it could be the guy on the phone with LaRosa really is the one in the sketch. If that's so, though, LaRosa's never seen him. Right?"

"Yeah. I see that."

"Okay, then," Luke said. "If he's Berto and LaRosa has never seen him, then your bum hasn't seen him around the club since LaRosa's been running it. Right?"

"Right."

"In that case, we can't trust the bum if he tells you he saw Berto since LaRosa took over," Luke said. "On the other hand, if the guy on the phone is not Berto, he put the Lennox woman in touch with Berto, so he must at least know who Berto is. We need to know who the hell that guy on the phone is. If you can clear this up, we might be able to get a warrant for that phone LaRosa sent the text to."

"Okay. That makes my head hurt, but I see where you're going, now. Thanks for explaining. I'm off to find the bum."

"No problem," Luke said. "Would you close the door, please?"

BEFORE LUKE WAS able to recall what he'd been doing when the detective interrupted him with the news of the bum's call, his cellphone rang. He recognized Phillip Davis's number.

"Hey, Phillip. What's new?"

"We got the audio clip. The whole gang's here. We'll let Beverly talk."

"Good. Did you recognize either of the voices in that recording, Beverly?"

"Yes. Manny LaRosa and Berto – there's no question in my mind."

"Okay, thanks," Luke said. "Can I put you on hold for a second?" He tapped the screen of his phone, muting his side of the connection, and picked up the phone on his desk, calling the detective who had just left his office. When the call when to voicemail, he sighed and left a message asking for him to call before he interviewed the bum. Luke took the cellphone off mute.

"Sorry," he said. "I wanted to get that information to one of my people before he left. Thanks again, Beverly. Did you pick up anything else from the recording?"

"Well, obviously Manny's never seen Berto, and Berto was lying about that not being him in the sketch."

"Yes. The number LaRosa used to reach Berto was different from the number you gave us. Do you have any other numbers for him?"

"No, just the one I gave you."

"No email, or any other way to reach him?" Luke asked.

"No, only the number I gave you."

"Thanks. That's all helpful. I appreciate your cooperation. Wish I could be sitting there with all of you, but I've gotta get back to work."

"Luke?"

"Yeah, Phillip?"

"If you've got a minute, Dani had an idea we'd like to discuss about moving this case along."

"Okay. We're stuck; I'm open to ideas. Let's hear it. Dani?"

"Well, Phillip says it's kind of like reconnaissance by fire -- shoot into the bushes and see if anybody screams or runs."

"That got my attention. Who're we shooting at?"

Dani told him what she wanted to do.

Listening without comment, Luke weighed the possibilities as she went into more detail. When she was finished, he said, "You understand that in my official capacity, I can't condone what you're proposing. There are -- "

"But Luke," Dani interrupted. "It's the -- "

"Dani!"

"Yes?"

"Let me finish, please."

"Okay."

"I didn't catch the names of the two men you mentioned. Don't tell me; I don't want to know. They're running the risk of getting arrested, harassing important people. They shouldn't do that. But since I don't know who they are, I can't stop them. You understand?"

"Yes. I read you loud and clear."

"Good. There's one other problem you should know about."

"What's that?"

"In one hour, I'll have a team watching the woman's place. I can't move faster than that."

"Got it. You need one hour to cover the suspects. No problem. It may take me longer than that to find the right people."

"Okay," Luke said. "Thanks again, Beverly. I gotta run. Call me if you think of anything else."

29

G raciella Montalba was surprised when she came home from dinner. The front door of her condo was unlocked, but the alarm wasn't sounding. Thankful that she lived in a secure building, she wasn't worried, but she was annoyed with herself. She must have forgotten to lock the door and set the alarm.

She pushed the door open and looked across the foyer, her eyes drawn to a sketch taped to the mirror on the wall. The blood-smeared sketch was a good likeness of her brother as he looked when he was made up to hide the acid scars.

Stifling a scream, she stepped into the foyer, closing the door behind her and locking it with the deadbolt. She saw that there was a message scrawled in the lower corner of the sketch, but she couldn't read it from where she stood.

She stepped closer, tripping over the mutilated carcass of a goat. At that, she did scream. Sprawled across the goat, she gagged on the stench of blood and entrails. She swallowed hard and scrambled to her feet, moving to where she could read the crude script in the corner of the sketch.

"This is a warning for your brother. Tell him if he keeps it up, we'll be back to make you tell us where he is hiding. If he makes us return, the two of you will join the goat in the hereafter."

She reached for the phone in her purse, but her hand was shaking so that she couldn't grip it. She needed a drink before she called Guillermo. She crossed the foyer and reached for the light switch in the living room.

When the lights came up, she screamed again. The living room was a wreck; furniture was overturned, and everything that was breakable had been broken.

But the biggest shock was the giant Rasta man who sat on the upside down couch, cleaning his fingernails with a big, gleaming knife and grinning at her.

"Good evenin', mama." He laughed. "Welcome home. I trus' you gi' the message to yo brudder, yah?"

"Do you know who I am?" Graciella asked, forcing herself to speak in a calm voice.

"You a beautiful woman," the man said, still grinning, "an' yo brudder, he gon' get you both killed, I t'ink. He messin' wit' some people he don' know nothin' 'bout. Better he stop now. You tell him that, okay?"

She glared at him, and he laughed again. She staggered back as he got to his feet, and came toward her.

He cupped a big hand behind her head and pulled her toward him, leaning forward. Still holding her, he stared into her eyes.

"I be goin' now," he said, "but if yo brudder don' stop, I be back, an' we get to know one another bettah, you an' me, yah? You don' want that to happen, I promise. You make him stop."

He grinned and shoved her away. Falling over a piece of furniture, she lay still, listening to his chilling laugh as he went out the front door and closed it. She heard the deadbolt shoot home as he locked it from the outside. The bastard had a key to her front door.

She got up and found an unbroken bottle of rum, taking a swig. She waited a few seconds, her eyes watering from the raw liquor, and then took out her phone.

She pressed the home button and said, "Call Guillermo."

As she took another swig of rum, the phone said, "Calling Guillermo."

"Graciella? You're not supposed to -- "

"They've wrecked my place," she said, "and they know."

"Who, Graciella?"

"I don't know. The one that was waiting here was very tall and lean, with an island accent. And dreadlocks. A Rasta. But they *know*! Did you hear me? They know."

"What do they know?"

"About you," she said. "They know you're my brother, and they said if you don't stop, you'll get us both killed."

"Stop what?"

"I don't know. He said you were messing with some people that you didn't know anything about, and if you don't stop, he'll come back and kill us both. That's all he said. And he left a copy of that police sketch with blood all over it, and a dead goat in my foyer. Guillermo, I -- "

"Get a grip, Graciella. It's me they want. They aren't going to bother you; I've got a plan. I'll have to disappear for a while, but this will pass. I'll be in touch when I can. I love you."

And then he broke the connection.

"How much of that did you get?" Lucilius asked. He and his brother were in a white van parked across the street from the building that housed Graciella Montalba's condo.

"All of it," Tiberius said, pulling off his headphones, "but they weren't connected long enough for me to get a fix on his location."

"Damn," Lucilius said. "I should have questioned her."

"Uh-uh, my brother. Sharktooth said not to hurt anybody. Besides, she probably doesn't know. He was in a vehicle of some kind. I could hear road noise. That's why I had trouble getting a fix; he was moving while they were talking."

"You think he's already on the run?" Lucilius asked.

"Yeah."

"We didn't get much for all the work," Lucilius said.

"Yeah, we did. We know his name's Guillermo, and we confirmed he's her brother. Guillermo Montalba. That's progress," Tiberius said.

"Not much."

"Hey, look at that." Tiberius pointed at a computer monitor hanging on the side wall of the van. The screen was divided into six sections showing video feeds from security cameras in Graciella's building. "Top left is the elevator from the garage. That's our boy. He's in the building. He must have been on his way here when she called him. I caught a glimpse of his face as he stepped through the door."

"Where's he going?"

"Let's watch and find out."

"Should we call Dani so she can tell the cops?"

"Nah. She said they were going to stake out this place. They're probably watching the video feeds too."

"THAT'S HIM," the detective said. He was sitting in the security office in the basement of the condo building where Graciella Montalba lived. "Switch to the feed from the woman's apartment."

"That's not where he's going," the guard said. "Wrong elevator." He moved the mouse and clicked several times, pausing a few seconds between clicks. Each click brought up a view of elevator doors as he worked his way up, one floor at a time. "Okay. He's getting off at the seventh floor, walking down the hall. Looks like he's headed for the end unit."

"What's the unit number, and who owns it?" the detective asked.

"Unit 7E. That's an ocean view." The guard turned to a computer monitor and tapped on the keyboard.

"Why do I give a shit about the view?" the detective asked.

"Because you can't see it from the street. You said you had people out there, watching with binoculars. They can't see that unit's windows. The ocean-view units look out over the pool area. That's between the building and the Intracoastal. Here we go. It's owned by a Manfred LaRosa, leased to William M. Roberts."

"You know him? Roberts, I mean?" the detective asked. "Is that him that just went in there?"

"I don't know, but hang on." The guard clicked the mouse again. "Okay. Here's the resident's i.d. photo for Roberts. Looks like him to me. Like your sketch, too."

The detective looked at the computer screen. "Yeah, good enough. Not a perfect match, but close. Is that front door the only way in and out of the unit?"

"Yeah, unless he can fly. Well, I mean there's the kitchen door, but that's the one you see on the screen right next to the door he went in. It's a fire code thing; gotta have two entrances."

"Okay, good," the detective said. "Watch those doors while I call this in. I got people lined up to get a warrant for his arrest and a search of the premises. Shouldn't be more than ten minutes, but let's don't lose him."

"No way, man. I got this under control," the guard said.

MONTALBA TOOK a last look around the tableau he had arranged in unit 7E. LaRosa's position in the chair was consistent with a self-inflicted gunshot wound, and LaRosa's prints were the only ones on the pistol. The corpse of the gigolo would pass for Berto's; he was the right size and build. The draft memo on the PC would provoke a reaction from the Berger cartel, giving him a new trail to follow.

He put the chain on the front door and opened the sliding door onto the balcony, pausing to tie a piece of fishing line to the fold-down security bar. Stepping out onto the balcony, he pulled the sliding door closed, careful to leave enough of a gap to accommodate the fishing line. He tugged on the line, and the bar dropped, resting at a slight angle to the horizontal. He jerked the fishing line, releasing the slip knot that held it to the security bar. He pulled the fishing line out and put it in his pocket. Pushing the sliding door closed all the way, he saw the bar drop into place.

Montalba took a moment to look over the railing of the balcony, studying the swimming pool area seven floors below. This time of night, the pool wasn't lighted and the area around it was in shadow.

He checked that the rope he'd rigged earlier was as he had left it, looped around the railing on the side of the balcony. The rest of the rope was stuffed into a canvas bag, and on top of the coils was a climbing harness. Stepping into the harness, he fastened it around his waist and cinched up the leg straps.

He grasped the doubled rope near the railing and snapped it into the carabiner that was clipped to his harness. Reaching into the canvas bag again, he took out a pair of rappelling gloves and tugged them onto his hands. He began paying out the rope, keeping it as close to the building as he could. The bag was tied to the two ends of the rope. Once he saw that the bag was resting on the pool deck, he tossed the remaining length of rope over the railing.

He climbed over the railing and took the rope in his right hand, pulling it around his right side and holding it behind his back. He leaned back, easing out rope, letting it take his weight until his body was horizontal, the soles of his feet against the edge of the balcony. Grasping the tight part of the line with his left hand, he bent his knees and pushed himself away from the balcony, rappelling from balcony to balcony.

When Montalba reached the pool deck, he untied one end of the rope from the canvas bag and began pulling the other end, feeding the rope he retrieved into the bag. After he'd taken in a few yards, the weight of the remaining rope pulled the loose end up to where it was looped around the railing. The rest of the rope fell at his feet and he gathered it into the bag.

He picked up the bag and slipped through the dense hedge that separated the pool deck from the sea wall along the Intracoastal Waterway. He found the kayak he'd secured to the sea wall and climbed down into it, paddling away in the darkness.

ONE OF THE uniformed officers accompanying Luke Pantene and the two detectives banged on the door of unit 7E. When there was no response, he knocked again. "Police," he bellowed. "Open up. We have a warrant for your arrest."

There was still no response.

Luke turned to the security guard, who held a ring of keys. "Unlock it, please."

The security guard unlocked the door and stepped back. Luke turned the knob and pushed the door until it was stopped by a security chain. He took a step back and raised his leg, kicking the door and ripping out the screws holding the chain. The door swung open and he and the two detectives entered the unit, guns drawn.

"Jesus," one of the detectives said stopping at the sight of a man sprawled face up on the floor. "What the hell did that to his face?"

"Looks like raw hamburger," his partner said. "And they blew the back of his skull away, too."

"Call the M.E.," Luke said. He had stepped around them and was standing in the living room. "We've got another one in here. Looks like he ate his gun. Let's get out of here and wait for the crime scene techs and the M.E. There's nobody else in here."

They went back into the hall, and one of the detectives made the call. "Ten or fifteen minutes," he said, putting his phone away.

"Okay. While you wait, get on the horn and order up as many uniforms as you can find. I'll authorize overtime. Give them copies of the sketch and have them start canvassing the neighbors. Maybe somebody saw or heard something."

"Did you get a look at the weapon, captain?"

"Yes. Forty-five semi-automatic, with a suppressor. Why?"

"I was wondering about gunshots and thinking somebody had to hear them."

"All we can do is ask. Until forensics gets the pistol in the lab, we won't know how loud it was with the suppressor. Or how many shots were fired, either, until they get through with the scene."

"Right."

"Okay," Luke said. "I'm going back to the office and get things moving. Call if you get anything exciting."

30

"I t had to be LaRosa," the detective said.

Luke Pantene took a sip of his sour, lukewarm coffee. His eyes felt gritty from having been up all night. "Yeah, it looks that way to me. The only prints on the pistol were his; the door was chained from the inside. The sliding door to the balcony was locked, and anyway that's 100 feet from the ground. The big question is why he did it."

"No telling why he ate his gun," the detective said. "There's never a clear answer to that. But destroying that poor bastard's face like that, that's some kind of crazy. That's love-gone-wrong kinda shit. I never figured LaRosa was gay, so they musta been crossways about a woman."

"Well, they knew one another," Luke said. "Roberts was renting that place from LaRosa. But Roberts is a puzzle. You said none of the neighbors knew him?"

"That's what we got from the canvassing. Nobody ever even saw him. But they all said that's not unusual, either. Living in a high-rise condo is like that. It ain't the same as living in a house in a neighborhood. None of the neighbors see one another except at social gatherings and condo association meetings, and several of them said most renters don't go to those things. They're kinda second-class citizens, the renters are. He just about had to be Berto, though. Roberts, Berto? Don't you think?"

"We don't even know for sure that the second corpse is Roberts,"

Luke said. "All we've got is the driver's license and credit cards from his wallet."

"Yeah, and the driver's license is a fake," the detective said.

"No shit?" Luke asked. "You didn't tell me that."

"Yeah. Sorry; guess I'm punchy. We ran it after you left the scene. Completely bogus."

"It was a good one, then. It fooled me."

"Yeah, me too. The photo on it's a pretty close match for that sketch you got from the Lennox broad. Not perfect, but it's the same guy. Gotta be."

"Besides a crime of passion, the other reason LaRosa might have destroyed his face is to slow down the identification," Luke said.

"But why do that if you're gonna leave his i.d. in his wallet?"

"Good question," Luke said. "Maybe LaRosa wanted us to think the corpse was Roberts instead of somebody else."

"Why would LaRosa give a shit what we thought if he was gonna blow his own brains out?"

Luke shook his head. "Who knows? LaRosa probably wasn't thinking too clearly. Be interesting to see what the M.E. finds in his blood stream. Maybe he was high on something."

"Maybe, but everything we know about him points to him being a dealer, not a user."

"Yeah," Luke said. "We got prints from Roberts yet?"

"Yeah. We put a rush on that, like you asked. He's not in the system."

"Shit," Luke said. "So all the i.d. we've got for him is a fake driver's license. Anything from records under his name?"

"Nope."

"What about the contents of the condo?" Luke asked. "What did they find there?"

"Laptop computer, a locked iPhone, personal effects. He wasn't living there. No clothes in the closet, nothing in the kitchen but a few dishes, and a coffee maker. No groceries except coffee stuff and some soft drinks in the fridge. It looked like one of those temporary corporate apartment places."

"No luggage?"

"Nothing but the computer case, and it was empty except for the laptop."

"What about the laptop?"

"The techs were going over it downstairs when I came in. Want me to call them?"

"I got it," Luke said, picking up the phone and speaking in a soft tone. "They're almost done; not much there, but they'll bring it up in a few minutes," he said.

"While we're waiting, did you get any more from that confidential source of yours? The one that tipped us to watch the building for Berto?"

"Yeah," Luke said. "But it's not usable. Not that it matters. It doesn't tell us anything worth knowing. They had an illegal tap on somebody's cellphone. They're pretty sure that Berto was really Guillermo Montalba, but that doesn't help, either."

"No?" the detective asked. "You run him? This Montalba?"

"Yeah," Luke said. "They had enough more for me to narrow the search a little, but it went nowhere. There's no such person as this Guillermo Montalba; he never existed. Another enigma, like Roberts. Or maybe the same as Roberts."

"Excuse me, Captain," a small man with thick spectacles said, pausing at the door to Luke's office. "You wanted to know about the laptop from the LaRosa scene?"

"Yes, come in."

The man put the laptop on the edge of Luke's desk and opened it. While they waited for it to boot, he said, "There's not much on here, not even any software, except the stuff that came on it. Looks like it was used for browsing the web, and checking web-based email accounts, but there are no passwords, so we can't tell much about that. There's one text file that looks like a memo, and that's it."

"Show us the memo, please," Luke said.

The man clicked on a file that was labeled "draft report - *Vengeance*." A couple of paragraphs filled the screen. Luke and the detective read the file.

"Could you print that out for me?" Luke asked.

"Sure thing." The man tapped on the touch pad. "Let me just step out to the printer and pick that up for you."

"Did that mean anything to you?" Luke asked, while they were waiting.

"Wasn't that the yacht that Berto supposedly had stolen? *Vengeance?*" the detective asked.

"Yeah," Luke said shaking his head.

"Cheer up, boss. At least we got an easy solve on this one."

"How's that?" Luke asked. "We've got more questions than answers."

"Yeah, that's true, but none of 'em matter, when you think about it. LaRosa killed Roberts, or Montalba, or whoever the hell he was, and then blew his brains out. We got a dead scumbag that we never managed to pin anything on, and a dead man who never existed to begin with. On top of that, they're in a room locked from the inside. It don't get much more obvious than that. Case closed. The rest of it's just bullshit, right?"

"Yeah, but we should still learn what we can about the rest of it," Luke said. "You never know. The 'why' part might matter later on. But you're right from the standpoint of closing the case. There's not much there. Why don't you grab that printout from the tech and go drop it in the file? I need to make a phone call or two."

"IT'S LUKE," Dani said, slipping her cellphone from her pocket. She and Liz and Beverly sat on Phillip and Sandrine's veranda. They were lingering over the remains of a big breakfast that Liz and Sandrine had prepared.

"Good morning, Luke. You have the whole crowd," Dani said, answering the call. "Is that all right?"

"Sure," Luke said, yawning audibly. "Excuse me; I'm coming down off an all-nighter."

"Did you get the email?" Dani asked. "The one we sent about Guillermo Montalba being Graciella's brother?"

"Yes. Thanks for that. Things spun out of control about the time I saw it. I haven't gotten a look at it yet; I just skimmed it. Let me bring you up to speed."

"Okay, please do. We've all been wondering what was going on."

"Well, I'm not sure I can help you with that, but here's what I know." Luke summarized what had happened to LaRosa and the other man. "We're guessing he was Berto, or Montalba, assuming they were the same person," he said, wrapping up his explanation.

"No positive identification on the other man, then?" Phillip asked.

"No, I'm afraid that's a dead end. As the lead detective said, at least it's an easy close. One scumbag killed a guy who didn't exist and then blew his own brains out. And he was thoughtful enough to do it in a place that was locked from the inside, to keep us from thinking someone else might have been involved."

"That is too simple," Sandrine said. "This never happens. Always, there must be something left to investigate, yes?"

"Yes," Dani said. "And there is something that's unexplained, here."

"You mean about why it had to be *Vengeance*?" Luke asked.

"Exactly," Dani said. "That's a loose end."

"One of them left a laptop," Luke said, "we think it was Berto, but it could have been LaRosa."

"Aha!" Sandrine said. "And what was on it, this laptop?"

"A draft report about the installation of the surveillance gear on *Vengeance*," Luke said. "It mentions that *Vengeance* is a sister ship of *Diamantista II*, and that you know Connie and Paul. Also that you use the same charter broker and both focus on charters in the eastern Caribbean. That's about it, except for the particulars of the surveillance system, and where *Vengeance* was stolen from and where she was left."

Dani choked on a piece of melon, grabbing a napkin and coughing as Liz pounded her on the back. She sat up, red-faced, and waved Liz away. Taking a swallow of orange juice, she said, "I'm okay, thanks. Sorry about that."

"Is there any way to identify the body that might be Berto?" Phillip asked.

"It's not looking good," Luke said. "His prints aren't in the system. The M.E. says the face was destroyed by several .45 hollow points at close range. The bones are all shattered so badly they can't even do a forensic reconstruction. All we've got is a fake driver's license."

"Is there some way I could help?" Beverly asked. "I did meet Berto, twice. I could look at a picture, or something."

"Thanks, Beverly, but there's no way looking at the corpse will help," Luke said. "Unless ... "

"Unless what?" Beverly asked.

"Was there anything distinctive about him that you noticed?" Luke asked. "Tattoos, scars, missing fingers? Anything at all?"

"Yes, now that you mention it," Beverly said. "His right hand – the inside of it was all scar tissue. It was hard and slick. I noticed it when he took my hand, and then I saw that he couldn't quite straighten his fingers. When we were eating, they all kind of moved like they were stuck together, like claws. But the back of his hand seemed normal."

"Okay," Luke said. "That's great. I'll pass that along to the M.E. Anything else?"

"The recording," Beverly said. "That was his voice."

"Right," Luke said. "You identified his voice and Manny's."

"Not that one," she said. "The one we sent you last night."

"What? I missed something," Luke said. "You sent me a recording?"

"It was attached to the email," Dani said. "The one you said you didn't get a good look at yet. It's Gabriella Montalba and Guillermo Montalba, and she acknowledges that he's her brother."

"Oh, shit," Luke said. "How's the quality?"

"It's great," Beverly said. "I had no problem recognizing his voice."

"Berto's voice?" Luke asked.

"Right. But she called him Guillermo."

"Damn," Luke said. "We can run voice prints on that and the other one. And maybe I can get a public sample of Graciella's voice to match against it, too. But I'm still screwed."

"Why?" Dani asked.

"There's no way that recording you sent me will be admissible anywhere," Luke said. "But I'll still run it by the state's attorney. Who knows? Do you have anything else that I don't know about?"

"No, I don't think so," Dani said. "What's next?"

"I'll get the info on Berto's hand to the M.E. and listen to the recording you sent. Then I'm going to crash for a few hours. I'll call you late this afternoon."

EVERYONE WAS SITTING on Phillip and Sandrine's veranda, watching the sunset and sipping wine.

"Why would anyone ever live anywhere but here?" Beverly asked, as the sky turned crimson.

"Because they don't know how wonderful it is here," Dani said. "Don't tell; there are too many people in the islands already."

"What's next for you, Beverly?" Liz asked. "Are you still thinking about going back and finishing that master's degree?"

"Someday, but I need to chill for a little while. And Sandrine and I have some shopping to do. She's found this shop that has a slinky dress she wants to show me. It's for her, though. I'm done with slinky clothes. I'm going conservative from here on out. Fresh and clean; that's the new me."

"And the shoes," Sandrine said. "You must not forget the shoes. And we must look for the clothes for work, too."

"Work?" Phillip asked. "But you already have plenty of clothes for the office."

"Not for me," Sandrine said. "For Beverly. She will be teaching the American English for my people and the police. I have already the permission; we are looking for someone since one month, and now we have Beverly. She will start as soon as we are scheduling people."

"That's great," Liz said. "You said you've wanted to see Martinique ever since you were in college. You got your wish."

"Thanks to all of you," Beverly said. "I'm still not sure this is real."

"It is real," Sandrine said. "You have the contract already signed, and we have arranged the apartment for you in two days. It is the done deal, no?"

"Sounds done to me," Dani said. "Congratulations, Beverly."

"Thanks so much, all of you. I – "

The ringing of Dani's cellphone interrupted Beverly.

"Hello, Luke," Dani said. "Did you get some sleep?"

"A little, yes, thanks. Is everyone there?"

"Yes," Dani said. "What's new?"

"Well, let's see. The body that we found with LaRosa has no scars inside either hand, so he's not Berto. That's one thing. The voice prints match up; the man Beverly identified as Berto is the same one Graciella Montalba called Guillermo on the recording you sent me. And we matched her voice on the recording to a snippet from a speech she gave at a charity function a few months ago."

"That's great news, then," Liz said. "What happens next?"

"We're looking for Guillermo Montalba, but he's nowhere to be found."

"But his sister must know where he is, or at least how to get in touch with him," Dani said.

"Maybe," Luke said. "But we don't have any way to leverage that yet. The state's attorney wants no part of that recording, so we can't touch Graciella."

"You mean it's going nowhere?" Beverly asked.

"I wouldn't say that," Luke said. "We know she has a brother, and we know he was involved in the plot to blackmail Velasquez, and that he had *Vengeance* stolen. We're going to be watching her from now on. Guillermo did say he'd be in touch with her. When he shows himself, we'll nail him. This isn't over yet."

"How frustrating," Beverly said.

"Never mind," Dani said. "You're on your way to a better life, and Liz and I have *Vengeance*."

"But why did Guillermo Montalba have her stolen?" Liz asked.

"That's a real enigma, isn't it?" Dani said, an evil grin on her face. "I'm going to have the pleasure of making him tell us one day."

THE END

JOIN MY MAILING LIST

Join my mailing list at http://eepurl.combKujyv for notice of new releases and special sales or giveaways. I'll email a link to you for a free download of my short story, *The Lost Tourist Franchise*, when you sign up. I promise not to use the list for anything else; I dislike spam as much as you do.

A NOTE TO THE READER

Thank you for reading *Bluewater Enigma,* the thirteenth book in the **Bluewater Thriller** series. I hope you enjoyed it. If so, please leave a brief review on Amazon. Reviews are of great benefit to independent authors like me; they help me more than you can imagine. They are a primary means to help new readers find my work. A few sentences can help others find the pleasure that I hope you found in this book, as well as keeping my spirits up as I work on the next one. If you would like to be notified by email when I release a new book or have a sale or giveaway, please join my mailing list at http://eepurl.com/bKujyv. I promise not to use the list for anything else; I dislike spam as much as you do.

If you haven't read the other **Bluewater Thrillers**, please take a look at them. If you enjoyed this book, you'll enjoy them as well. I write another series of sailing thrillers — the **Connie Barrera Thrillers**. Connie had a key role in *Deception in Savannah*, my first book. I enjoyed writing about her so much that I wrote her into the **Bluewater Thrillers**. She plays prominent parts in both *Bluewater Ice* and *Bluewater Betrayal*. The **Connie Barrera Thrillers** are a spin-off from the **Bluewater Thrillers**, and feature some of the same characters. Dani and Liz taught Connie to sail, and they introduced her to Paul Russo, her first mate and soon-to-be husband.

In June of 2017, I released *Bluewater Enigma*, the thirteenth novel in that series. Now I've turned my attention back to Connie and Paul for their eighth adventure. You'll find progress reports and more information on my web page at www.clrdougherty.com. Be sure to click on the link to my blog posts; it's in the column on the right side of the web page. Dani has begun to blog about what's on her mind, and Liz and Connie are demanding equal time, so you can see what they're up to while I'm writing.

A list of my other books is on the last page; just click on a title or go to my website for more information. If you'd like to know when my next book is released, visit my author's page on Amazon and click the "Stay Up to Date" link near the upper left-hand corner. I welcome email correspondence about books, boats and sailing. My address is clrd@clr-dougherty.com. If you'd like personal updates, drop me a line at that address and let me know. Thanks again for your support.

ABOUT THE AUTHOR

Welcome aboard!

Charles Dougherty is a lifelong sailor; he's lived what he writes. He and his wife have spent over 30 years sailing together. For 15 years, they lived aboard their boat full-time, cruising the East Coast and the islands. They spent most of that time exploring the Eastern Caribbean. Dougherty is well acquainted with the islands and their people. The characters and locations in his novels reflect his experience.

A storyteller before all else, Dougherty lets his characters speak for themselves. Pick up one of his thrillers and listen to the sound of adventure as you smell the salt air. Enjoy the views of distant horizons and meet some people you won't forget.

Dougherty has written over 25 books. His **Bluewater Thrillers** are set in the yachting world of the Caribbean and chronicle the adventures of two young women running a luxury charter yacht in a rough-and-tumble environment. The **Connie Barrera Thrillers** are also set in the Caribbean and feature some of the same characters from a slightly more romantic perspective. Besides the **Bluewater Thrillers** and the **Connie Barrera Thrillers**, he wrote *The Redemption of Becky Jones*, a psycho-thriller, and *The Lost Tourist Franchise*, a short story about one of the characters from *Deception in Savannah*.

He has also written two non-fiction books. *Life's a Ditch* is the story of how he and his wife moved aboard their sailboat, *Play Actor*, and their adventures along the east coast of the U.S. *Dungda de Islan'* relates their experiences while cruising the Caribbean.

Join my mailing list for notice of upcoming releases and special offers.

www.clrdougherty.com
clrd@clrdougherty.com

OTHER BOOKS BY C.L.R. DOUGHERTY

Bluewater Thrillers

Bluewater Killer

Bluewater Vengeance

Bluewater Voodoo

Bluewater Ice

Bluewater Betrayal

Bluewater Stalker

Bluewater Bullion

Bluewater Rendezvous

Bluewater Ganja

Bluewater Jailbird

Bluewater Drone

Bluewater Revolution

Bluewater Enigma

Bluewater Thrillers Boxed Set: Books 1-3

Connie Barrera Thrillers

From Deception to Betrayal - An Introduction to Connie Barrera

Love for Sail - A Connie Barrera Thriller

Sailor's Delight - A Connie Barrera Thriller

A Blast to Sail - A Connie Barrera Thriller

Storm Sail - A Connie Barrera Thriller

Running Under Sail - A Connie Barrera Thriller

Sails Job - A Connie Barrera Thriller

Under Full Sail - A Connie Barrera Thriller

Other Fiction

Deception in Savannah

The Redemption of Becky Jones

The Lost Tourist Franchise

Books for Sailors and Dreamers

Life's a Ditch

Dungda de Islan'

For more information please visit my web site http://www.clrdougherty.com/

Or visit my Amazon Author's Page

Made in the USA
Coppell, TX
23 May 2022

78074669R00138